BLOOD BOND
Deadly Road
to Yuma

D0036370

BLOOD BOND
Deadly Road to Yuma

William W. Johnstone
with J. A. Johnstone

PINNACLE BOOKS
Kensington Publishing Corp
www.kensingtonbooks.com

PINNACLE BOOKS are published by

Kensington Publishing Corp.
850 Third Avenue
New York, NY 10022

PUBLISHER'S NOTE

Following the death of William W. Johnstone, the Johnstone family is working with a carefully selected writer to organize and complete Mr. Johnstone's outlines and many unfinished manuscripts to create additional novels in all of his series like The Last Gunfighter, Mountain Man, and Eagles, among others. This novel was inspired by Mr. Johnstone's superb storytelling.

All Kensington titles, imprints, and distributed lines are available at special quantity discounts for bulk purchases for sales promotions, premiums, fund-raising, educational, or institutional use. Special book excerpts or customized printings can also be created to fit specific needs. For details, write or phone the office of the Kensington special sales manager: Kensington Publishing Corp., 850 Third Avenue, New York, NY 10022, attn: Special Sales Department; phone 1-800-221-2647.

PINNACLE BOOKS and the Pinnacle logo are Reg. U.S. Pat. & TM Off.

ISBN-13: 978-0-7860-2001-0
ISBN-10: 0-7860-2001-6

First printing: April 2009

10 9 8 7 6 5 4 3 2 1

Printed in the United States of America

Chapter 1

"I'm thirsty," Matt Bodine said.

"When are you not?" Sam Two Wolves said.

"No, really, Sam, my whistle could sure use wettin'."

"I repeat—"

"We're stoppin' up there in that town," Matt said, interrupting his blood brother.

"Of course we are," Sam said. He waited a moment, then added, "Do you think we could try to stay out of trouble this time?"

"We always try to stay out of trouble. At least *I* do."

Sam just rolled his eyes, shook his head, and hitched his horse forward, starting down the long, gentle slope toward the flat where the settlement was located.

They had crossed the border between New Mexico Territory and Arizona Territory not long before, following the San Francisco River as it twisted through this bleak, rugged country. The Gila Mountains loomed to their right, the Peloncillos to the left. The settlement they were approaching was the first one Matt and Sam had come to in several days.

It had been a long, relatively uneventful ride from

Sweet Apple, Texas. The blood brothers were in no hurry to get anywhere, because they didn't have anywhere to be. They were just drifting, seeing what was on the other side of every hill they came to . . . the same way they had spent most of the past several years.

One of these days, they would settle down and return to the ranches they owned in Montana . . . one of these days. But until then, they had good crews running those spreads, so Matt and Sam were free to roam. It suited their restless nature to do so.

Best friends and blood brothers since childhood, Matt Bodine and Sam August Webster Two Wolves could have almost passed for real brothers. Both young men were tall and muscular and had ruggedly handsome faces.

Sam's longish hair was midnight black, a legacy from his Cheyenne father Medicine Horse along with the faint reddish tint to his tanned skin. Matt's close-cropped hair was a little lighter, dark brown rather than black.

The Cheyenne ritual that had bonded them together made them *onihomihan*—brothers of the wolf. They were brothers of the gun as well, because despite what Matt had said about trying to avoid trouble, it seemed determined to follow them wherever they went.

Luckily for their continued survival, both young men were plenty tough and plenty fast with a gun. In fact, Matt Bodine was known to be as slick on the draw as just about anybody west of the Mississippi, in the same league as famous pistoleros such as Smoke Jensen and Falcon MacCallister. He wore two irons in holsters supported by crossed cartridge belts and was deadly accurate with either hand.

Sam carried only one Colt and was a little slower than Matt . . . which still made him faster than nine of

ten men he ran into. A razor-sharp bowie knife rode
in a fringed sheath on his left hip.

There was fringe on his buckskin shirt as well, while
Matt wore a faded blue bib-front. A battered old brown
Stetson was thumbed back on Matt's head. Squared up
on Sam's head was a black hat with a flat brim, a slightly
rounded crown, and a band studded with conchos.

"What do you reckon this place is called?" Matt
asked as they reached the bottom of the slope.

Sam shook his head. "I have no idea. I don't think
we've ever been through here before."

"I couldn't remember. We've been so many places."

"That's certainly true. And in most of them, they
were glad to see us leave."

"Hey, that's not our fault."

"Didn't say it was."

This was ranching country—it wasn't good for
much of anything else—and the settlement appeared
to be a typical cow town with a wide, dusty main street
that stretched for several blocks. Most of the resi-
dences, a mixture of adobe and frame houses, were
on the cross streets.

A small, whitewashed church with a steeple sat at
the far end of the main street, just beyond a wooden
bridge that crossed the San Francisco where it looped
around the settlement. At the nearer end was a building that was probably a school. That put this place
ahead of some frontier towns that had neither of
those harbingers of civilization.

In between were businesses, including a livery stable
and blacksmith shop, barbershop and bathhouse, a
couple of mercantiles, and half a dozen saloons, another sure sign that this was a cow town. Cowboys had

to have plenty of places to blow off steam when they collected their forty-a-month-and-found.

A few wagons were parked in front of the general stores, and a couple of men on horseback moseyed along the street. Pedestrians made their way here and there, including several women in long dresses and sunbonnets. A big yellow dog dozed in the middle of the street.

"Peaceful-looking town," Sam commented.

"Mighty peaceful," Matt agreed.

Sam looked over at him. "How long do you reckon it'll stay that way?"

"Now, Sam, why do you have to be such a pessimist? Maybe nothin' bad'll happen while we're here. Maybe it'll be plumb dull the whole time."

"I went to college, you know."

Matt grinned. "Yeah, I seem to remember hearin' somethin' about that . . . like every time you try to convince me that I'm wrong and you're right."

"It's just that I study history. And there's an old saying about how those who fail to learn from history are doomed to repeat it."

"And what do you mean by that? I'm just a poor, uneducated cowboy, Sam. You're gonna have to explain things to me."

"I'm saying that just because someone annoys you, that's no reason to start a brawl . . . or a gunfight."

"You're sayin' that I'm touchy. That I lose my temper too easy."

"If the Stetson fits . . ."

"What's this got to do with my hat?"

Sam held up a hand. "Never mind. Let's just have a drink or two, stock up on supplies, and sleep in real beds for a change."

"For a redskin, you sure do like what you call your

creature comforts. You must've got spoiled back there at that university in the East."

"Yes, well . . . I'd say something insulting about you being a white man . . . but I can't think of anything right now."

Matt threw back his head and laughed. "Sam Two Wolves struck speechless! Lordy, I never thought I'd live to see the day."

"Just remember what I said about trouble," Sam grumbled.

He turned his head to nod politely to several ladies who were going into one of the mercantiles, but they didn't smile or return his nod. In fact, they hustled on into the store as if trying to avoid looking at him.

A man driving a wagon that they met refused to meet their eyes, too, Sam noted. The fellow whipped his team up into a trot instead as he rolled on past them.

A frown creased Sam's forehead under the broad brim of his hat, but he didn't mention the odd behavior of the townspeople to Matt, who seemed not to have noticed it.

They reined their horses to a stop in front of a false-fronted building with a gilt-lettered sign on its awning proclaiming it to be the Ten Grand Saloon. More fancy lettering on the big front windows promised cold beer and friendly hostesses.

A stocky, bearded old-timer in bib overalls and a plug hat was sitting in a chair on the saloon porch to the right of the batwings, whittling. He looked up at the newcomers and grunted, "Howdy, boys," as Matt and Sam swung down from their saddles and looped the reins around the hitch rail. "New in town?"

"That's right," Sam said. "What's this settlement called, if you don't mind my asking?"

"Don't mind in the least. This here is Arrowhead, territory o' Arizona."

"Friendly place, is it?" Matt asked.

"Oh, shoot, yeah. We're friendly as can be around here."

Sam said, "I noticed that the folks we rode past didn't seem to want to look at us, like maybe they didn't like strangers."

"No, I wouldn't say that. We get strangers passin' through here pretty often. Like to think we make 'em welcome."

Matt gestured toward the windows and said, "If there's really cold beer and friendly hostesses inside, I reckon I'll feel welcome, all right."

"Go on in," the old-timer urged with a wave of the piece of wood he'd been whittling on.

"What are you carving there?" Sam asked out of idle curiosity as he and Matt started toward the saloon's entrance.

The old man frowned as he studied the stick in his hand. "I dunno. A snake maybe?"

Matt chuckled as he pushed the batwings aside and stepped into the saloon. Sam was right behind him.

Both of them froze as the batwings flapped closed behind them. Men with shotguns had been concealed on both sides of the entrance, and now those Greeners were pointed at the blood brothers.

"Don't move, you sons o' bitches," one of the men warned. A dozen other men scattered around the room raised revolvers and pointed them at Matt and Sam. The one who had spoken before went on. "You try anything funny and we'll blow your damn heads off."

Matt took a deep breath and said, "Oh, yeah. Real friendly town, all right."

Chapter 2

Being careful not to move, Sam said, "I believe that you gentlemen are making a mistake."

"Shut your mouth, breed, and get your hands up," one of the men pointing pistols at them said. "We know exactly what we're doin' here."

"Pointin' guns at two men who don't want any trouble?" Matt said as he and Sam slowly raised their hands to shoulder level.

"We just stopped in your town to pick up some supplies," Sam added.

A disgusted snort came from one of the men wielding the shotguns. "You don't expect us to believe that, do you?" he asked. "We know damn good an' well that you're scouts for that bastard Shade."

"Shade?" Matt repeated. "Mister, the only shade I know is the shade under a tree . . . which would feel pretty good right now, come to think of it."

"They want a tree," one of the other men said, "let's give 'em a tree. Let's take 'em out and string 'em up!"

Enthusiastic cries of "Yeah!" and "Damn right!" and

"String up the dirty owlhoots!" came from the crowd in the saloon. Matt and Sam exchanged worried glances.

If they slapped leather, they might be able to shoot their way out of this. On the other hand, chances are they'd get their heads blown off by those Greeners, and no doubt some of the men in the saloon would be killed, too. Those hombres might not be what anybody would call innocent, but they seemed to be laboring under an honest misapprehension and probably didn't deserve to die for that mistake.

"Listen to me," Sam said. "We don't know anybody named Shade, we're not scouting for anyone, and we're not looking for trouble."

"We're peaceable men," Matt added.

"Oh, yeah?" one of the men said with a sneer. "Prove you ain't part of Shade's gang!"

"It's very difficult to prove a negative assumption—" Sam began, stopping when Matt shook his head.

"You've got my word on it, and that's proof enough," Matt said.

"Why should we believe you ain't lyin'?"

"Because I'm Matt Bodine . . . and I don't take kindly to bein' called a liar."

Murmurs of "Bodine!" came from several of the men. The name of Matt Bodine was well known across the frontier, from the Mississippi to the Pacific, from the Rio Grande to the Milk River.

"They say that Bodine travels with a Injun," one of the men said. "This fella looks part redskin anyway."

"My name is Sam August Webster Two Wolves," Sam said, introducing himself. He was proud of his Cheyenne heritage and never denied it.

"Yeah, Two Wolves, that was it!" the man said excitedly. "That's the name o' Bodine's sidekick!"

Sam grimaced, and Matt couldn't help but chuckle at that description of his blood brother.

"Can we put our hands down now?" he asked. "You'll take my word for it that we're not workin' for that hombre Shade, whoever he is?"

"Joshua Shade is a pure-dee hydrophobia skunk," growled the old-timer who had been sitting on the saloon porch. He pushed aside the batwings and sauntered into the saloon. He had put away his whittling knife. "Put them guns down, boys. Now that I've heard these young fellas' names, I recollect seein' pictures of 'em in the rotogravures. They're Bodine and Two Wolves, all right."

Matt lowered his hands. "Well, I'm glad somebody around here has sense enough to believe us."

"I got more sense than you'd think to look at me," the old-timer drawled. He lifted one corner of the bib front on his overalls that had come unbuttoned and fallen down.

Pinned underneath it was a sheriff's badge.

"I've also got a responsibility to protect this town," he went on. "I'm the law hereabouts. Name of Cyrus Flagg."

Sam lowered his hands as well and said, "We're pleased to meet you, Sheriff Flagg."

The lawman motioned to the other men in the saloon. "Go on about your drinkin' and gamblin' and whorin'," he instructed them. "I'm gonna buy these two boys a drink."

"We'd be much obliged for that," Matt said.

"As well as for interceding on our behalf," Sam added.

"Figured it was the least I could do, seein' as how it

was me who put these fellas up to throwin' down on you in the first place."

"And why was it exactly you did that, Sheriff?" Matt asked.

"Let's have a sit-down, and I'll tell you all about it," Flagg suggested.

He gestured toward an empty table in the corner and called to the bartender to send over three beers. Matt, Sam, and Flagg took chairs at the table, and a moment later a pretty blonde in a low-cut, spangled dress came over carrying a tray with three foaming mugs on it.

The young woman smiled and bent over as she placed the tray in the center of the table, providing a good view of her creamy breasts in the provocative outfit.

"Yeah, they're pretty as a couple o' speckled pups, Amelia," Flagg said. "Maybe later one o' these boys'd like to take a closer look at 'em. Right now, though, the beer's all we need."

"You're a spoilsport, Sheriff," the blonde said with a pout.

"Yeah, that's what folks tell me all the time. Now shoo."

Amelia flounced off. Flagg sighed and picked up one of the mugs of beer.

"Gals just don't understand that there's a time an' place for ever'thing," he said. "A fella ain't all that interested in romance when he's just had a pair o' Greeners and half a dozen six-guns pointed at him."

"Oh, I wouldn't say that—" Matt began with an appreciative glance toward Amelia as she walked off.

"You were going to tell us about Joshua Shade," Sam said, breaking in. "And about why you set that trap for us."

"I wouldn't exactly call it a trap," Flagg said. "I just believe in takin' precautions, 'specially when a lobo like Shade's roamin' around the countryside with a whole band o' gun-wolves taggin' after him."

Sam took a healthy sip of his beer and found that while it wasn't really cold, it was pleasantly cool. As he set the mug back on the table, he said, "I take it that Joshua Shade is an outlaw."

"You've heard of him then," Flagg said.

"Not before we rode in here today."

"But we've been over in Texas for a spell," Matt added. "They have their own badmen over there."

"An abundance of them," Sam said.

Flagg pushed his plug hat back on his thinning, red-dish-gray hair. "None as bad as Shade, I reckon, and I'd bet my last dollar on that. Shade's a plumb devil, and he's been raisin' hell all up and down the eastern half o' the territory for months now."

"Have you had trouble with him here?"

Flagg shook his head and said, "Not so far, and I'd just as soon keep it that way. But we heard that him and his gang were spotted between here and Springerville a few days ago, so we know he's in these parts. When I spotted you fellas ridin' down the hill, I thought you might be scouts for the gang, so I passed the word for ever'body to get off the street without bein' too obvious about it, and told the fellas in here to be ready and get the drop on you."

"Well, it worked," Matt said. "We weren't expectin' trouble, so we walked right into it."

Sam didn't say anything about noticing some odd behavior on the part of the townspeople as they rode in. He had noticed, but it hadn't done any good. He and Matt had still found themselves staring down the barrels of those shotguns.

"Is that the way Shade operates?" he asked Sheriff Flagg. "Sending men ahead to scout out the towns he raids, I mean."

Flagg nodded. "Yep. A couple o' strangers ride in, take a look around town, have a drink maybe, then ride back out and tell Shade where the sheriff's office is, and the bank, and anything else he needs to know. Then, a day later, Shade and his bunch come roarin' in with all guns a-blazin' and take over the town. They kill the local star packer and anybody else who tries to stand up to 'em, mistreat the womenfolk, load up all the loot they can get their filthy hands on, and ride out. Sometimes they leave the town burnin' behind 'em."

"Sounds like a bad bunch, all right," Matt said.

"Bad don't even begin to describe 'em." Flagg shook his head. "And maybe the worst part of it is, Shade used to be a man o' God."

"A preacher?" Matt asked, his eyebrows lifting in surprise.

"That's right. He had the callin' and preached for a while before he turned bad. In fact, I hear tell that when his gang is terrorizin' a town, he still claims to be doin' the Lord's work. Says he has to smite folks and take ever'thing they own so they'll stop worryin' about the things o' this world and start worryin' about the next."

"And while he's saying that he's allowing his men to rape and kill and loot?" Sam asked in amazement.

"Yep. Hell of a note, ain't it?"

Matt downed some of his beer. "I can see why you say the hombre's loco. But you can take my word for it when I tell you that Sam and I don't have anything to do with him."

"Oh, I know that now," Flagg said with a wave of his hand. "I've heard plenty about you two young fellas, but I never heard anybody say that Bodine and Two Wolves are owlhoots." He emptied his mug down his bearded throat and thumped it back on the table. "These beers are on me, boys. Enjoy your stay in Arrowhead."

"We're obliged," Sam said.

Flagg scraped his chair back and stood up. "My office is down the street. Stop by and visit for a spell any time you're of a mind to."

"We'll do that," Matt promised.

When the sheriff was gone, the blood brothers looked at each other across the table.

"I was afraid he was going to ask us to sign on as deputies," Sam said.

Matt nodded. "So was I. And I've had enough of wearin' a badge for a while. That stint as unofficial deputies in Sweet Apple was plenty to suit me."

"I agree." Sam smiled faintly. "Don't look now, but Amelia is coming back."

The blonde was headed toward their table. Matt smiled and said, "I always enjoy the company of an attractive young woman."

Amelia moved right past him, though, to stand next to Sam and rest a hand on his buckskin-clad shoulder. "Can I get you anything else, Mr. Two Wolves?" she asked as she leaned toward him.

Sam looked a little flustered, and Matt didn't know whether to be annoyed or bust out laughing. He'd thought that Amelia was interested in him, but here she was, making a play for Sam instead.

"How about it, Sam?" he asked with a grin. "See anything you like?"

Chapter 3

The narrow, twisting canyon in the Gila Mountains was choked with brush for much of its length, brush that could claw a man bloody if he wasn't careful. Nobody would ride up here unless they had a good reason to.

Ed Callahan had believed that he had a good reason, the best reason of all—gold. He had a nose for the stuff, or so he had always told himself even though he'd never found very much of it in the twenty years he'd spent as a prospector and desert rat.

The hardships of those years had honed him down to little more than skin and bones. His cheeks were hollow, and his eyes were sunk deep in pits of gristle.

One of those eyes didn't see too good anymore. Everything he saw through it looked filmy, like it had one of those thin scarves over it like the dancin' gals in the big cities used to hide and reveal their fleshy charms at the same time.

But Ed could still see well enough to know that he was in a whole heap of trouble. He swallowed hard as he stared down the barrel of the gun that was no more than four inches from the tip of his nose.

"What are you doin' up here, old man?" asked the rough-looking hombre who'd stepped out of the brush and pointed the gun at Ed. "You some sort o' damn spy?"

Ed's mouth had gone too dry for him to talk. He tried to work up some spit. After a couple of seconds, he managed to say, "N-no, sir. I ain't no spy. I'm just doin' a little prospectin'." He jerked a thumb over his shoulder at the supplies on the pack mule he'd been leading. "You can see for yourself. Just take a look at my outfit."

The man squinted past him at the mule. "Yeah, that looks like the sort o' shit a prospector'd have, all right. I never heard o' anybody findin' gold in these mountains, though."

"I . . . I'm gonna be the first," Ed declared. "Got me a hunch there's a fine vein up here just waitin' for me to find it."

"Yeah, well, that's too damn bad. You found more'n you bargained for, old man." The hardcase stepped back and motioned with the Colt in his hand. "Come on. You're goin' with me."

"Wh-where are we goin'?" Ed asked as he tightened his grip on the mule's reins and started walking along the canyon.

"Never you mind. You'll see in a minute."

And so he did as they rounded a bend and Ed saw that the canyon widened out a little. There was a spring flowing out of the rocks on one side, and near it a crude corral made of ropes and poles cut from saplings. Tents were pitched here and there, and bedrolls were also spread out in the open.

A fire burned near the spring. Ed had thought he smelled wood smoke a few minutes earlier as he'd worked his way up the canyon, but then the smell had faded and he'd decided not to worry about it. Hadn't been any 'Pache trouble around here for a while.

The men camping here weren't Apaches, Ed saw as he looked around, although a couple of them appeared to be Mexicans. The rest were white, and every bit as ugly and rough-looking as the gent who'd brought him here at gunpoint.

Oh, shit, Ed thought. They were outlaws. He had stumbled right into the hideout of a bunch of owlhoots.

The man who pushed aside the entrance flap of one of the tents and came out into the fading, late afternoon light didn't look like an outlaw, though. He wore a long black coat and a white shirt and a string tie. He was clean-shaven, with long, thick brown hair and a slightly lantern-jawed face. He smiled as he strode toward Ed.

"Welcome, brother," he said. "What brings you here to our humble but temporary home?"

The gunman behind Ed prodded him in the back with the Colt. "Answer the rev'rend.'

Reverend? The fella *did* look a mite like a preacher, Ed thought.

"I'm, uh, prospectin' for gold," he said. "Didn't mean to intrude—"

"Nonsense," the preacher said. "One of my fellow strugglers in this world could never intrude. We're glad to have you."

Ed wanted to relax. The fella had a way of putting a man at ease. But it was hard to relax too much while he was still surrounded by gun-hung hombres who looked like they'd as soon fill him with lead as spit.

"Obliged for the hospitality," Ed managed to say. "Name's Ed Callahan."

"It's a pleasure to meet you, Brother Ed. I'm Joshua Shade."

Oh shit oh shit oh shit. The words roared through Ed's brain, and it was all he could do not to yell them out loud.

He had heard of Joshua Shade. Everybody in this part of the territory had heard of the crazy owlhoot leader. Hell, probably everybody in the whole territory had heard of him. He and his men had been on a killing spree for months.

Shade was still smiling. He said, "I see you've heard of me, Brother Ed."

Ed's tongue felt as big and floppy and dry as a saddle blanket in his mouth. He struggled to say, "N-no, sorry, Mr. Shade, I n-never heard nothin' about you."

"Reverend Shade," the man corrected gently.

"Sorry. I mean Rev'rend Shade. But I still d-don't know who you are."

Shade came closer, reached out, and put a big hand on Ed's shoulder. "Are you a God-fearing man, Brother Ed?"

"Y-yeah," Ed husked. "I like to think I am."

"Then you know that by lying you're breaking one of the Lord's commandments."

"I ain't lyin'. I—"

Shade's hand tightened painfully on the old prospector's shoulder. "Don't make your sin worse by denying it, brother."

Ed choked back a sob and said, "I'm sorry."

"Don't worry. The Lord will forgive you and welcome you into His house. He has many mansions in heaven for us all, you know."

"Y-yeah, I . . . I heard a p-preacher say that once."

"And today you'll know the truth of it for yourself."

Ed's eyes widened in horror. "Today?" he croaked.

"Unless you're lying again, in which case I'm sure the Devil will have a . . . warm . . . welcome for you."

Shade looked at the man standing behind Ed and nodded.

Ed just had time to think that he'd already met the Devil before he yelled, "Wait! Oh, God, wait!"

Shade raised a hand, and the man behind Ed paused in whatever he'd been about to do.

"Why should we wait in carrying out the Lord's judgment, Brother Ed?" Shade asked.

Ed thought fast, remembering everything he had heard about Joshua Shade. He said, "If you l-let me live, I . . . I can help you."

"What can you possibly do for us, brother?"

"I remember . . . I remember hearin' how you like to send a man into a town before you . . ."

Ed couldn't bring himself to say it. He was too scared.

Shade smiled. "Before we deliver the word of the Lord unto them?" he asked.

"Y-yeah. That's what I mean. But folks know that about you now. They've figured it out. There's a settlement not far from here, but if you send some of your men there, folks'll be suspicious of 'em. Folks watch ever' stranger now mighty close."

Shade was beginning to look interested. "Go on," he urged.

"I can do it for you," Ed said. "They know me there. They think I'm just a harmless old coot." He let out a hollow cackle. "And up to now that's all I been, I reckon. But now I can help you, Rev'rend. I can help you do the Lord's work."

What he was doing was dooming a lot of innocent folks, Ed thought . . . but he was also saving his own life. A fella had to do what he could to save his own life, didn't he, even if it meant that other folks got hurt?

A smile spread across Shade's face. "I've always said that the Lord provides a solution to every problem, if only we open our hearts and our eyes and are prepared to see it." He rested his hand on Ed's shoulder again. "And now He has sent you to us, Brother Ed. Praise the Lord."

"Praise the Lord," Ed agreed in a weak, croaking voice.

Shade gestured to his men with his other hand. "Go on about your business, brothers. I'll talk to our new friend here." He steered Ed toward the tent from which he had emerged a few minutes earlier. "What's the name of this settlement you mentioned, Brother Ed?"

"It . . . it's called Arrowhead."

"Arrowhead," Shade repeated, rolling the name on his tongue. "Named after a weapon of the heathen redskins. It sounds to me as if the people there really need a visit from the messengers of the Lord . . ."

Ed hoped that Shade couldn't feel the tiny shudder that went through him at the sound of the evil in the man's voice.

Yeah, he had already met the Devil . . .

And the Devil's name was Joshua Shade.

Chapter 4

Amelia was persistent, and Sam Two Wolves was as human as the next fella. By evening, she had worn down his resistance and talked him into taking her back to one of the little rooms behind the Ten Grand.

That left Matt to take care of putting their horses up at the livery stable and renting a couple of rooms for them at the local hotel, which was one of only two two-story buildings in town, the other being the bank, which was built solidly out of red brick.

Matt didn't mind tending to those chores. Sam would have done the same if the situation had been reversed. In fact, he *had* done the same many times when it *was* reversed, which it usually was.

When he was finished with that, he wandered back to the Ten Grand. No sign of Sam and Amelia in the barroom, so he figured they were still occupied out back. Matt went over to the bar and nodded to the portly bartender, Archie Cochran, whose acquaintance he and Sam had made during the afternoon.

"Give me a beer, Archie," Matt told him. He dropped a coin on the hardwood to pay for it. He and

Sam weren't short of money, only supplies, and if they needed to, they could have more *dinero* wired to them the next time they came to a settlement that had a telegraph office.

"There you go, Mr. Bodine," Archie said as he placed the mug in front of Matt.

"I see Sam's not back yet."

Archie smiled. "Amelia's a mighty inventive gal when she wants to be. She can come up with all sorts of pleasant ways for a gent to pass some time."

"I'll bet." Matt took a drink of the cool beer. "What's the best place around here to get something to eat?"

"Got a jar of pickled eggs down at the end of the bar," Archie suggested.

Matt frowned and shook his head. "I was thinkin' of something a little more substantial, like a steak maybe."

"Try Hernando's, right down the street."

"Mexican place?"

"Hernando's a Mex, but he cooks American. Good, too. You got to watch him, though, 'cause every now and then he'll slip in some chili peppers." Archie rubbed a palm over his aproned chest. "Can't take 'em myself. They make me feel like I'm on fire inside."

"I like spicy food myself. We'll give it a try when Sam gets back."

Archie chuckled. "He'll probably have worked up an appetite by then, that's for sure."

Matt just smiled, shook his head, and sipped his beer. From the corner of his eye, he saw a man push the batwings aside and enter the saloon.

It was a matter of habit for Matt to watch everything that went on around him. A matter of survival, too, because there were varmints in the world who held grudges against him and Sam, as well as ambitious hombres who might want to make a name for themselves as the man who killed Matt Bodine . . . even if it took shooting him in the back.

Didn't take him but a second, though, to size up this newcomer to the Ten Grand and realize that the old-timer was no threat.

He was a scarecrow of a man, scrawny and dressed in ragged, dirty clothes and a shapeless old felt hat. When he came up to the bar, Matt got a look at his face and saw that one eye had some sort of film over it. He felt a twinge of pity for the old man.

Archie Cochran didn't look all that sympathetic as he went over to the newcomer and asked curtly, "What'll it be, Ed?"

"Can I . . . can I have a beer?"

"You got any money?"

"I do." The man reached into the pocket of his stained, torn corduroy trousers and pulled out a coin. "I got enough, see?"

Archie took the coin and said, "All right. That'll buy you a beer. One beer."

He drew it and set the mug in front of the old-timer called Ed, who licked his lips in anticipation.

Archie's mood seemed to grow a bit more friendly as he said, "Haven't seen you around for a while."

"I been busy. Lookin' for gold, you know."

"Yeah, I know. Doesn't look like you've hit a bonanza yet."

"Oh, you never know, you never know," Ed said. He picked up the mug and drained half of the beer, his Adam's apple bobbing up and down in his turkey neck as he swallowed.

When he lowered the mug, foam covered his upper

lip. He set the mug on the bar and gave a long sigh of satisfaction.

Then he glanced over at Matt, nodded, and said, "Howdy."

"Howdy yourself, old-timer," Matt replied. He didn't introduce himself.

Ed turned back to the bartender. "Anythin' interestin' goin' on here in town, Archie?"

"Not much. We had a little excitement earlier this afternoon when Matt there and his partner rode into town. Cyrus Flagg saw 'em coming and got worried they might be part of Joshua Shade's gang, scouting the town for that bunch of owlhoots. Turned out they weren't, though."

Ed glanced at Matt. "Is that so? The sheriff's worried about Shade, is he?"

"Wouldn't you be?" Archie asked with a snort. "After all the hell those varmints have raised, anybody with any sense *would* be worried. That's why Cyrus says we got to take precautions."

"What sort o' precautions?"

"Oh, you know, like watching out for strangers and posting lookouts."

"Lookouts?" Ed repeated.

This was the first Matt had heard of that, too.

"Yeah, he just decided on that a little while ago, after Matt and Sam rode in. Figured it might be a good idea to post some fellas on the roof of the hotel and the bank so they can keep a watch around the town all the time. That way, we'll spot anybody who's headed this direction."

"Yeah, that sounds like a good idea, all right," Ed said as he nodded. "Already got guards up there, does he?"

"You bet. One man on top of the bank, one on the hotel. Nobody's gonna sneak up on us now."

"Well, knowin' that'll make me sleep better at night while I'm in town."

"Yeah, me, too." Archie frowned. "You'd better be careful, roaming around the countryside like you do, Ed. You might run right into that bad bunch."

"I sure wouldn't want to do that. I figure if I ever saw that Joshua Shade, I'd plumb die o' fright right then and there."

As if just talking about the infamous outlaw leader made him nervous, Ed's hand shook as he raised the mug to his lips and drank down the rest of the beer.

Matt had paid just enough attention to follow the conversation between the bartender and the old prospector, although he had been somewhat interested in the talk about posting lookouts on the bank and the hotel. That sounded like a good idea to him, too, although it didn't matter all that much to him since he and Sam would probably only be in Arrowhead for one night.

At that moment, Sam and Amelia came in through a door in the rear of the barroom. Sam looked vaguely embarrassed but happy, and Amelia had a big smile on her face. Matt grinned and lifted his mug of beer in a salute to them.

Sam said something to Amelia, who came up on her toes to give him a peck on the cheek. Then he walked over to join Matt at the bar.

"Ready to go get something to eat?" Matt asked.

"Yeah, I am. Fact of the matter is, I'm pretty hungry."

On the other side of the bar, Archie chuckled and said, "What'd I tell you?"

Sam frowned. "What's he talking about?"

"Never mind," Matt said. "We're goin' to Hernando's."

"What's that?"

"Place with the best steaks in town."

"Sounds good," Sam said. "Lead me to it."

Hernando's turned out to be a narrow, hole-in-the-wall sort of place, but the smells that filled the air had the blood brothers licking their lips as soon as they went in. Hernando was a little fella with a lush, luxuriant mustache that curled up on the ends, and he greeted them with a big smile.

There were only three tables in the café and two of them were occupied, so Matt and Sam grabbed the empty one while they had a chance and ordered steaks with all the trimmings. When Hernando brought the food, they found that it was as good as Archie had said it would be.

Matt saw what the bartender meant about the spices, though. The steaks had a definite kick to them.

Once they were finished with the meal, they paid Hernando and promised that they would be back before they left Arrowhead. "Come back in the morning for my *huevos rancheros, señores*," he told them with a big smile. "The best you ever had!"

"We'll just have to see about that," Matt said with a grin of his own.

As they strolled back toward the hotel, Matt asked, "You want to stop at the saloon again for another drink?"

Sam stifled a yawn. "Actually, I think I'd rather turn in. We rode quite a ways today."

"Yeah, I reckon you'd be tired, all right, after that long . . . ride."

"Damn it, Matt—"

Matt dug an elbow into his blood brother's ribs. "Take it easy. I'm just joshin' you."

"Yeah, I know."

"And it could be that I'm just jealous. Amelia's a mighty pretty girl after all, especially for a soiled dove."

"She's just doing that for now, until she makes enough money to go to San Francisco."

"Oh. I see."

"You don't believe her?"

"I didn't say that."

A rueful smile crept over Sam's face. "Yeah, she was probably just telling me the same thing she tells everybody who goes with her. But maybe it was true. You never know."

"You sure don't," Matt agreed. "Anything can happen." He pointed with his thumb. "Here's the hotel."

They went inside, claimed their keys from the desk clerk, and headed up to the second floor. On the way, Matt told Sam about how Sheriff Flagg had posted sentries on the roof, as well as on top of the bank.

"Good idea," Sam agreed. "I hope Joshua Shade stays far away from this town, though."

"At least while we're here," Matt said. "You know how we love to avoid trouble."

Chapter 5

The man on top of the hotel was named Charlie Cornwell, and he was having one hell of a time staying awake. It seemed like he had to yawn every few seconds, and each yawn just made him sleepier.

He worked as a hostler at the livery stable and also as a part-time deputy for Sheriff Flagg, and he had put in almost a full day's work before the sheriff came by the stable and told him to go home and take a nap because he was going to hold down the night shift on lookout duty at the hotel.

"What lookout duty?" Charlie had asked, not having heard anything about it before that very moment, and the sheriff had explained that from now on, guards were going to be posted atop the hotel and the bank to keep an eye out for Joshua Shade and his gang . . . at least until Shade was caught, tried, and hanged like the no-account buzzard he was.

Cyrus hadn't given Charlie any choice in the matter, and since Charlie needed the money from the deputy job to go along with what he earned at the stable, he'd said sure. He had long since given up on the idea of ever making enough so that his wife would actually be happy, but he didn't see any reason to make things worse than they already were.

He wasn't used to going to sleep at five in the afternoon, though, so he hadn't really gotten much rest before going to the sheriff's office to get a Winchester and a pocketful of shells, then climbing up here. So by midnight, it was all he could do to stay awake.

The roof was flat, with a little wall about two feet high that ran all around it. Charlie figured that if he could sit down with his back propped against that wall, he could catch some quick shut-eye.

But Sheriff Flagg had warned him specifically about that very thing. "Don't you go sittin' down and dozin' off, Charlie," he'd said. "Remember, the fate o' the whole town could be in your hands."

Charlie sighed, yawned, and looked north and east. Down at the bank, on the other side of the street at the far end of the next block, Harlan Eggleston was watching to the south and west . . . although Charlie didn't know what the hell Cyrus Flagg expected them to be able to see in the dark like this. A little moonlight spilled over the landscape, but not much.

Anyway, as far as Charlie could remember, Joshua Shade and his gang always attacked a town in broad daylight. They weren't going to be showing up here tonight. Still, he would do what Cyrus told him. He always did.

The ladder that leaned against the back wall of the hotel rattled a little as someone started up it. Charlie turned toward it, frowning a little. The sheriff had told him that he'd be up here until four o'clock in the morning, when somebody would come to relieve him. It wasn't anywhere close to four yet.

But whoever was coming up the ladder called softly, "Hey, Charlie! You up there?" so it had to be somebody who knew him. Maybe Cyrus had changed his mind and was sending his relief early.

That would be just fine with Charlie. He could still get home and get a few hours of sleep before he had to get up and go to work at the livery stable.

Carrying the Winchester slanted across his chest, he walked over to the ladder and looked down. All he could see in the moonlight was a hat rising toward him as its wearer climbed the rungs.

"Yeah, I'm here," he said. "Who's that?"

"Sheriff sent me to take over for you," the man replied without really answering the question, and Charlie was so glad to hear that, he didn't really think about it. He just let the rifle hang at his side in his left hand and grinned.

"I'm mighty glad to hear that," he said as the man reached the top of the ladder. "I'm so sleepy I can barely keep my eyes open, and Cyrus said we have to stay alert. Here, lemme give you a hand."

He stepped closer as the man seemed to struggle a little getting over the wall around the edge of the roof. Charlie's hand was out to help.

But then the man looked up, revealing his face under the broad-brimmed hat, and Charlie realized he'd never seen the hombre before. He wasn't from Arrowhead or one of the nearby ranches. Even in the dim light, Charlie could tell that. This fella had a bushy black beard and squinty eyes and didn't look friendly at all.

Before Charlie could ask him who the hell he was and what he was doing here, the man's arm whipped up and around, and Charlie stepped back with something hot and wet suddenly flooding down his chest. He tried to yell, but no sound came out.

He dropped the Winchester and reached for his throat with both hands. Blood cascaded over them. He felt it pumping out through the huge slash his fingers found.

Charlie's knees hit the rooftop as his legs folded up underneath him. He finally managed to gurgle a little as he swayed there. The night was warm, almost hot, but he felt cold now as he struggled to accept the fact that his throat had just been cut wide open by the bowie knife clutched in the stranger's hand.

The struggle was a short one. With another gurgle, Charlie toppled forward and died.

Ed Callahan had thought about going the other way when he left Arrowhead with his mule earlier that night, instead of returning to the foothills of the Gilas north of town.

But Joshua Shade had warned him about that, putting an arm around Ed's shoulders and saying in that soft, persuasive voice, "Now, you don't want to be led astray by any foolish ideas, Brother Ed, like not coming back to tell me what you find out. If you do that, I'll have to come looking for you, and you know the Lord will lead me right to you."

Ed didn't doubt it for a second. Shade was downright spooky, the way he seemed able to peer right through a man. Like he knew everything the other fella was thinking and feeling.

"So you find out anything you can that you think will help us, and you come right back here and tell me. Will you do that?"

And God help him, he'd nodded and said, "I s-sure will, Rev'rend. I'll be back."

He had kept his word. He had spent several hours hanging around Arrowhead, talking to folks. He'd found out about the guards Sheriff Flagg had posted on top of the bank and the hotel. He'd even seen Charlie Cornwell and Harlan Eggleston climbing up on those buildings to take the night watch.

Nobody seemed to notice when he left town and headed for the foothills. No one in Arrowhead had ever paid him much mind to start with, and this evening was no different.

When he got back to the spot overlooking the town where he'd left Shade and the rest of the outlaws, he didn't see anybody. At first, he had thought that he was lost, that he'd come to the wrong place.

Then, like phantoms, they had materialized out of the shadows, surrounding him and making his blood run cold. Joshua Shade stepped forward, rested both hands on Ed's shoulders, and said, "Tell me, Brother Ed, what have you found out?"

Ed spilled his guts, of course. What else was he going to do? Lie to this outlaw, this . . . demon? Run the risk of having Joshua Shade pursuing him like a hound from Hades for the rest of his life?

Hell, no!

And when he was done, Shade had squeezed his shoulders and said, "Good work, my friend. The Lord will be pleased that you've provided so much assistance to His humble servants."

"Wh-what are you gonna do now?"

"Bring God's message to Arrowhead, of course. Help the sinners to repent and put the things of this world aside."

Ed bit back the groan of despair that tried to well up his throat. He knew good and well what Shade was going to do. He and the rest of the gang were going to raid the town, looting and raping and killing. They might even burn it down.

There was nothing Ed could do to stop them, so he might as well save his own life, he told himself. He clung to that thought as he sat down on a rock and waited. Shade didn't want him to leave yet.

"You should stay, Brother Ed," he'd said. "Stay and witness the fruits of your handiwork."

That was just about the last thing Ed wanted to see right now, but Shade didn't give him any choice.

A couple of men rode off toward Arrowhead, and after what seemed like forever to Ed, a light suddenly flared to life and moved back and forth three times. Somebody had lit a match and signaled with it.

Mere seconds later, the same sort of signal was repeated from the other end of the settlement. Shade put his hands on his hips and said, "Excellent! The sentries have been taken care of."

Murdered, that was what he meant, Ed thought, and again he struggled to keep from groaning.

Shade turned toward him and motioned for him to get up. Ed stood and swallowed as the outlaw leader approached him.

"We'll be going now," Shade said. "Would you like to accompany us, Brother Ed, or would you rather receive your reward now?"

"R-reward?" Ed repeated. "You didn't say nothin' about no reward."

"You didn't think the Lord would allow your work to go unrewarded, did you?"

Ed rasped calloused fingertips over his beard-stubbled

jaw. He felt bad about what was about to happen to the folks in Arrowhead, mighty bad, but . . . well, since there was nothing he could do about it . . . he might as well get *something* out of the deal, hadn't he?

"If it's all right with you, Rev'rend, I'll, uh, take whatever you got for me and go on my way. I don't care how much it is neither. I'll take whatever you want to give me."

Shade shook his head. "Oh, it's not money, brother. It's a heavenly reward."

With that he brought his hand up and plunged a bowie knife into Ed's belly. Ed cried out in agony as he felt the razor-sharp blade being tugged across his stomach, opening him up so that the coils of his guts spilled out through the wound as Shade stepped back. Ed tried to stuff them back inside, but failed. They slipped out of his hands and uncoiled onto the dirt at his feet. He staggered, fell, lay there gasping as his life ran out.

The last thing he was aware of was Joshua Shade's voice.

The son of a bitch was *praying*.

Chapter 6

Matt Bodine's eyes snapped open in the darkness. He didn't know what had awakened him, but he had a feeling it couldn't be anything good. His instincts wouldn't have roused him from slumber otherwise.

He sat up in bed. A little moonlight filtered in around the curtain over the hotel room's single window. The window was open to let in some fresh air, and the curtain swayed in and out with the currents of the night breeze.

Before turning in, Matt had hung both gunbelts over the back of the chair next to the bed, so that the holstered Colts were within easy reach. He swung his legs out of the bed and stood up, plucking one of the irons from leather at the same time.

In bare feet, wearing only the bottoms from a pair of long underwear, Matt padded over to the window and used the Colt's barrel to ease the curtain aside so that he could look out.

His room was at the rear of the hotel, as was Sam's next door. The windows looked out on an alley.

Nothing was moving in that alley, Matt saw as he

peered down from his window. He judged that the hour was after midnight, and the town was quiet and peaceful.

Well, maybe not so quiet *or* peaceful, he thought a second later as he heard a gurgling sound from somewhere overhead. It was followed by a thump on the roof.

That wasn't right. Matt stuck his head out the window.

To his right, no more than a couple of feet away, a ladder leaned against the hotel. That would be the ladder used by the lookout Sheriff Cyrus Flagg had posted up there.

Sam's window was on the other side of the ladder, and at that moment, Sam poked his head out, too, and looked toward his blood brother.

"You hear something?" Sam asked in a half whisper.

Matt nodded and gestured with the thumb of his free hand toward the roof. Sam brought his right hand into view, holding a six-gun. He gestured with the barrel, pointing upward.

Matt nodded and swung a leg over the windowsill.

His brain was working swiftly. Given the fact that something was going on up there on the roof, it made sense that what he had heard that woke him up was somebody climbing the ladder, since it was right outside his window.

That in itself wasn't suspicious; someone sent by the sheriff could have been going up there to relieve the man on duty and take over as lookout.

But coupled with the noises he had heard, the choked gurgle followed by a thump, the situation didn't seem near that innocent.

In fact, it was downright ominous, Matt thought as

he clung to the edge of the window with one hand and reached for the ladder with his foot.

With the lithe agility he'd been blessed with since birth, he swung over to the ladder. In absolute silence, he started climbing toward the roof. As he looked up, he saw a flare of light. Someone had just lit a match. He smelled the faint tang of brimstone from the lucifer.

Matt smelled something else, too, a metallic, coppery scent that he recognized.

That was the smell of freshly spilled blood—and a lot of it.

Matt's head rose above the level of the short wall that ran around the roof. He saw a man standing several yards away with his back turned, holding a lit match over his head that he moved back and forth three times.

Between Matt and the hombre with the match lay another man, facedown in the middle of a dark, spreading pool.

Matt didn't need anybody to explain to him what had happened here. The varmint with the match had cut the throat of the other man. That was the only thing that would have produced so much blood.

The dead man had to be the guard Sheriff Flagg had posted up here.

Which meant the killer, in all likelihood, was one of Joshua Shade's men . . .

In the back of Matt's brain, he realized that Shade must have managed to sneak some scouts into the settlement after all, or else he wouldn't have known about the guard on top of the hotel.

That guess was confirmed a second later when, from the corner of his eye, he saw another match

being waved back and forth at the far end of the next
block, from the roof of the bank.

He didn't stop to think about that consciously,
though. Instead, he went into action, swarming up
and over the wall and onto the roof. Almost noiselessly, he lunged past the dead man at the outlaw who
had just sent that signal with the match.

Not quite noiselessly, though, because a bare foot
scraped on the rooftop and warned the killer. He
started to swing around as he dropped the now-
burned-out match and clawed at the gun on his hip.

Matt's arm was already raised, and he struck first
before the man could drag iron. The Colt in Matt's
hand smashed down on the man's head, crumpling
his hat and maybe denting his skull.

The outlaw's knees unhinged, dropping him like a
poleaxed steer. He fell in a limp heap next to the man
he had killed a couple of minutes earlier.

Matt whirled as he heard a noise behind him, but it
was just Sam climbing from the ladder onto the roof.
"What the hell happened here?" Sam demanded.

"This fella just killed the guard Sheriff Flagg posted
up here," Matt explained as he gestured with his gun
toward the man he had knocked out. "He was using a
match to signal somebody in the hills when I walloped him."

"Shade," Sam said in a flat, hard voice.

"Yeah, that's what I figure, too. Another of his men
sent a signal from the top of the bank. They were letting Shade know that the lookouts were taken care of."

"That means Shade is about to attack the town."

"That's right," Matt said. "You go warn folks."

"What are you going to do?"

"See if I can catch up with the hombre who sent the

signal from the bank." Matt started toward the ladder, then paused. "You might use this gent's belt to lash his hands behind his back. Wouldn't want him coming to and joining the party later on."

"How come I get that job?"

Matt was already swinging a leg over the roof and onto the ladder. He grinned and said, "Because I'm closer to the ground."

Then he started down the rungs as fast as he could go, skipping some of them and practically bouncing off of the ladder as he descended.

For a second, he had considered stopping at his room to get his trousers, rather than running around Arrowhead in his long underwear, but he'd decided not to take the time to do that. Modesty was one thing; catching the son of a bitch who had no doubt murdered the lookout on top of the bank was another.

Anyway, he had five rounds in the Colt he clutched in his hand, with the hammer resting on an empty chamber as it usually did. If five bullets weren't enough for him to deal with one man, then he was in a lot more trouble than a pair of pants could fix.

As soon as his feet hit the dirt in the alley, Matt sprinted toward Main Street. When he reached it, he turned to his right, toward the bank. At the end of the block, he took a left-hand jog, since the bank was on the opposite side of the street from the hotel.

Nobody was on the street at this time of night, although lights still glowed from some of the saloons and a few horses were tied at the hitch rails.

Matt darted into the alley behind the block of buildings where the bank was located. He made no sound except the soft slap of his feet against the dirt.

That was enough to warn the man who had just reached the bottom of the ladder leaning against the rear wall of the bank, though. Matt could barely see him in the shadows, but he recognized the movement as the man spun toward him.

Matt dropped into a crouch and ran forward. At that same instant, Colt flame bloomed in the darkness as the man loosed a wild shot at him. The bullet whined past Matt's head.

The revolver in Matt's hand roared as he returned a shot of his own. In the flicker of illumination from the muzzle flash, he saw a man in the charro jacket and broad-brimmed, steeple-crowned sombrero of a Mexican.

The man staggered against the wall, but he didn't drop his gun. He pulled the weapon up from its momentary sag and fired again, flame lancing from the barrel.

This slug came close enough for Matt to feel its warmth as it whispered past his cheek. Might have been nice to take this hombre alive, he thought, but he reminded himself that there was already one prisoner on top of the hotel.

So he didn't take any chances. He pulled the trigger three times, and all three bullets hammered the outlaw against the wall. The man hung there for a second, finally dropping his gun, and then pitched forward.

Matt ran lightly toward him and bent to retrieve the fallen Colt. As he straightened, he heard shouts along Main Street, along with the clamorous ringing of a bell. The bell was probably meant to summon Arrowhead's volunteer fire company, but tonight it served as a warning of a danger that might be even greater than an out-of-control blaze.

Matt had no doubt in his mind that at this very minute, Joshua Shade and his band of ruthless killers were sweeping toward Arrowhead like a plague of locusts.

Chapter 7

Sam knew that Matt was right about tying up the unconscious outlaw, so he pulled the man's belt off, jerked his arms behind his back, and lashed the wrists together with it. He didn't worry about how rough he was being either, or about how uncomfortable the hombre would be when he came to.

The smell of blood filled Sam's nostrils, and it seemed to him that the killer was getting off lightly.

When he was finished with that, he pulled the man's revolver from its holster and then hurried over to the ladder. Climbing down with a gun in each hand was awkward, but Sam managed.

If Joshua Shade was about to launch one of his infamous raids on Arrowhead, Sam knew that he might have need of both weapons before this night was over.

About the time his feet hit the ground, he heard a couple of shots from down the street. By the time he had run around the hotel to the front porch, several more shots had blasted out.

Sam was worried about Matt, but he knew his blood brother could take care of himself. Spotting a big brass bell hanging from the roof over the hotel porch, he ran to it and began ringing it, not with the ringer attached to it, but rather with the two guns in his hands, batting the bell back and forth and making it peal loudly.

At the same time he shouted, "Wake up, wake up! Outlaws! Outlaws! Joshua Shade!" He let out a shrill, yipping war cry that would have done his Cheyenne father proud, and then loosed a shot into the air.

Between the yelling, the war cry, the bell ringing, and the shots, that was plenty to alert the citizens of Arrowhead that something was very wrong. Men poured out of the saloons, abandoning their drinks and their poker games, to run into the street and shout questions at each other. The hotel doors swung open behind Sam, and the proprietor hurried out with a shotgun in his hands.

The man swung the Greener's barrels toward Sam, who called quickly, "Don't shoot! It's me, Sam Two Wolves!"

The hotelman recognized Sam and blurted, "What the hell's going on?"

"Joshua Shade and his gang are about to attack the town," Sam replied, thinking as he did so that he and Matt were going to look mighty foolish if that turned out not to be the case. They would be the two little boys who cried wolf, like in the old fairy tale he remembered his mother reading to him.

In this case, a murdering, crazed lobo wolf named Joshua Shade.

Sam didn't think they were wrong, though. No other explanation made sense, considering the murder of the lookouts and the signals sent from atop the hotel and the bank.

Sheriff Cyrus Flagg ran out of the sheriff's office in

a nightshirt that flapped around his thick calves, testifying that he'd slept in the back room of the office. He had a Winchester in his hands. The men on the street had started to stream toward the hotel, so he joined them.

"In the name o' all that's holy and half that ain't, what's goin' on here, Two Wolves?" the lawman demanded of Sam as he came to a stop in front of the hotel.

"Your lookouts have been murdered, Sheriff," Sam replied, his face grim. He didn't know for sure that the sentry on top of the bank was dead, but it seemed pretty likely considering the signal that had been sent from there.

"Murdered!"

Sam nodded. "Matt and I think that Joshua Shade is about to attack the town."

That brought cries of fear and alarm from the men gathered in the street. "What're we gonna do, Sheriff?" one of them asked Flagg.

The sheriff thought for a second, then said, "Spread out all over town. Bang on doors and tell folks to get ready, if they ain't already. Make it quick, though, and then hunt some cover. It won't be long until Shade and his bunch are here, I reckon."

"We'll give those owlhoots a lot hotter welcome than they're expectin'!" one man said.

Sam wasn't so sure of that. Even up in the hills, Shade might have heard the shots and realized that the townspeople were aware of the threat.

Would that be enough to make him call off the attack?

Sam didn't know, and the citizens of Arrowhead couldn't afford to take that chance. They had to be as ready for trouble as they could get in the next few minutes . . . because it was probably already on the way.

More than forty strong, the gang swarmed down out of the hills with Joshua Shade in the lead. He was bare-headed, and the wind whipped his longish hair around his lean face.

Beside him rode his second-in-command, a heavily mustached outlaw named Willard Garth. As they galloped toward Arrowhead, Garth raised his voice and asked, "What about those shots we heard, Joshua? You think they know we're comin'?"

"It doesn't matter, Brother Willard," Shade replied. "The Lord has told me that tonight is the night we need to deliver His message to that sinful town up ahead, and that's exactly what we're going to do!"

"And clean out the bank while we're at it, eh, Boss?" Garth said with a wolfish grin.

"It takes money to do the Lord's work!" Shade said, then gave a maniacal howl of laughter.

Even if the settlers knew they were coming, it wouldn't matter. There wouldn't be time for them to mount an effective defense before the raiders were right on top of them. The gang still had enough of an element of surprise, even if the men sent into town to kill the lookouts had been discovered.

Besides, Shade and Garth knew that the citizens of Arrowhead didn't represent any real danger. They were storekeepers, blacksmiths, and clerks. There might be a few tough cowboys from the nearby ranches in the saloons, but when you stopped to think about it . . .

Just how many real fighting men could there be in a place like this anyway?

Sam was about to go looking for Matt when he spotted his blood brother running along the street toward the hotel. Matt reached the porch and bounded up onto it.

"I suppose you were responsible for those shots I heard a couple of minutes ago?" Sam said.

Matt grinned humorlessly. "Who else?"

"What about the lookout on top of the bank?"

"Dead," Matt said as even the bleak grin disappeared. "Throat cut just like the other fella. Poor son of a bitch probably died before he even knew what was goin' on." He looked around at the men running here and there in the street as they got ready for the attack. "Looks like you did a good job spreadin' the word."

"It's not that hard to do with shots going off." Sam jerked his head toward the hotel lobby. "Come on. It'll take Shade a few minutes to get here. We've got time to get dressed and get the rest of our guns."

"Good idea," Matt agreed. "I feel half naked with only one Colt."

"You *are* half naked," Sam pointed out as they went into the hotel. "So am I."

"What'd I tell you?"

They hurried through the lobby, getting spare keys from the hotel owner as they did so since the doors of their rooms were locked and the keys were inside with the rest of their gear. The proprietor was standing behind the desk, lining up shotgun shells on top of it. He was a mild-looking little man, but his voice held a note of fierceness as he explained, "If any of those owl-hoots get in here, I'll give them a buckshot reception!"

"Well, nobody can say you're not hospitable," Matt told him.

A minute after he and Sam entered their rooms, they emerged into the hallway again, stamping their feet to settle them in their boots. The blood brothers were dressed now, had their hats on, and their gun-belts strapped around their waists. Each carried a fully loaded Winchester.

"We'd better take the high ground while we can," Matt said. "You want the hotel or the bank?"

"Let's both take the hotel," Sam suggested. "If the gang was holed up in the hills, they'll reach this end of town first. Might be a good idea to pull the ladder up once we're up there, too. We can always let it back down after the fight's over."

"Assumin' we're still alive," Matt said.

"I always assume that."

They went out the back door of the hotel this time. The ladder was still there in the alley, propped against the wall. Matt went up first, and as he reached the top of the ladder and swung a leg over onto the roof, he heard something that sounded a little like distant thunder.

Hoofbeats. A large group of riders was galloping toward Arrowhead, and the men weren't far off now.

Sam was right behind him, and he heard the hoof-beats as well as he stepped onto the roof. "Sounds like a big bunch."

"Yeah," Matt agreed. He trotted over to the front of the building, looked down, and saw Sheriff Flagg in the street. Cupping his free hand next to his mouth, Matt called, "Better get inside, Sheriff! Here they come!"

Flagg waved his Winchester in acknowledgment of the warning and hurried toward the sheriff's office. Matt and Sam stood at the edge of the roof, peering northward into the darkness.

"You see 'em?" Matt asked after a moment.

"Not yet," Sam replied, "but they're coming. The hoofbeats are louder now."

Matt looked down again. The street was pretty much clear now, the townspeople having scattered to hunt cover. He worked the Winchester's lever, jacking a cartridge into the rifle's firing chamber.

"Let 'em come," he said.

Chapter 8

Matt and Sam moved to the corners of the hotel fronting the street and knelt behind the little wall. It wouldn't provide much cover, but it was better than nothing.

The hoofbeats still sounded like thunder, but now it was as if the storm was about to roll into the town. Torches suddenly flared to life in the hands of some of the approaching riders, and from the intensity of the flames, Matt and Sam knew that the torches had been soaked in pitch.

"Drop those men with the torches!" Matt called to Sam. "They're gonna try to set the town on fire!"

As the outlaws reached the end of Main Street and began to sweep into the settlement, the blood brothers opened fire, concentrating their shots on the men wielding the torches. With each crack of a Winchester, one after another of Shade's men fell, dropping the torches to be snuffed out in the dust of the road.

The raiders returned the fire, sending a hail of lead from their six-guns at the hotel roof. Matt and Sam were forced to duck as the bullets chewed at the wall.

Then the outlaws raced on past the hotel as more gunfire began to erupt up and down the street. The town's defenders were shooting from the cover of the buildings, but they didn't seem to be doing much damage, Matt saw as he poked his head up again.

A bare-headed man in a long black coat whirled his horse and galloped back to the spot where one of the torches had fallen. It was still burning, and scarcely slackening his mount's speed, the man bent down from the saddle, reached out with a long arm, and snatched the torch from the ground. He whirled it over his head and threw it at the window of a hardware store as he dashed past. The window shattered under the impact, and the torch landed inside.

Matt bit back a curse as he looked through the broken window and saw flames leaping up. He snapped a shot at the man who had thrown the torch, thinking that he might be Joshua Shade. Whether that was true or not, Matt's bullet missed as the man jerked his horse around and headed down the street again.

The outlaws fought with the precision of a well-trained military unit, some of them staying together and sending volleys of lead ripping into the buildings they passed. Others split off from the main group.

Matt saw one man leap his horse onto the porch in front of a saloon; then the outlaw rode on through the batwings into the saloon, flames spewing from the muzzles of the guns in his hands as he charged in. That scene was repeated in several places up and down the street as the battle began spreading through the town.

Two of the riders headed for the hotel. Sam killed one of them with a shot that drove him backward out of the saddle, but the other man reached the porch with his horse. Both of the blood brothers heard the rending crash as the horse slammed through the doors, followed a second later by the boom of the hotel keeper's shotgun, interspersed with the flatter reports of a revolver.

The six-gun kept blasting, but the shotgun was silent after the first charge went off. Matt and Sam knew that couldn't be good.

"Damn it, the way they spread out we can't do enough from up here!" Matt called. "We need to be down there!"

"I'll get the ladder!" Sam said.

"No time for that!"

Holding the Winchester slanted across his chest, Matt stepped up onto the wall and leaped down onto the roof that extended out over the hotel porch. The roof had a little slope to it, so he slid down it to the edge and then rolled over it, catching hold with one hand to break his fall.

He hung there for a second, one hand holding him up while the other lifted the rifle and triggered it at an outlaw galloping past. The owlhoot's bullet burned along the arm Matt was using to hang on to the porch, and forced him to let go so that he dropped the last couple of feet to the ground.

Matt's slug, though, punched into the raider's body, bored through a lung, and burst out the other side in a spray of blood. The man went spinning out of the saddle and slammed to the ground, bouncing once before he lay still in death.

Matt had gone to one knee when he landed. He stayed there and socketed the Winchester against his shoulder. It cracked again and again until the hammer clicked. The rifle was empty.

Surging to his feet, Matt grabbed the Winchester's

heated barrel with both hands and swung the weapon like a club as he leaped toward one of the mounted raiders. The man didn't see him coming in time to get out of the way, and the rifle's stock shattered under the impact of the blow—along with the varmint's skull.

Matt tossed the broken rifle aside and palmed out both Colts. He had both of them smoking as he zig-zagged across the street. Behind him, the outlaw who had ridden into the hotel lobby emerged on horse-back through the broken doorway and swung his pistol toward Matt's back.

Before the gun could erupt, another shot rang out. The desperado's hat flew off his head as a slug from Sam's .45 cored through his brain and exploded out the other side in a fist-sized exit wound. He toppled out of the saddle and sprawled limply on the hotel porch. His spooked horse leaped into the street and went sun-fishing off.

Sam had followed Matt's lead and was hanging from the end of the porch roof, the smoking six-gun still in his other hand. He dropped the rest of the way and ran past the man he had just killed into the lobby.

The hotel man was slumped against the front of the desk, blood staining his white suit and turning it sodden. He had been shot at least three or four times. He lifted pained eyes to Sam; then his head fell forward as he died.

There was nothing Sam could do for the man now, so he wheeled around and charged back out into the street. Matt was across the street in front of the hard-ware store, which was still burning inside. When both Colts were empty, Matt jammed them back in their holsters and kicked the store's door open. He ran

inside and began looking for something he could use
to beat out the flames before they got too big.

Sam crouched on the hotel porch and fired at the
raiders as they galloped past until his revolver was empty.
Then, instead of reloading, he ran into the hotel again
and grabbed the shotgun the proprietor had dropped.
A number of shells were still lined up on the counter.
The hotelman hadn't gotten a chance to use them.

Sam snatched the shells and stuffed them into the
pocket of his buckskin shirt. He broke open the
Greener, saw that only one barrel had been fired, and
pulled out that shell to replace it with a fresh one.

Then, even though the man could no longer hear
him, he told the proprietor, "I'll try to put these to
good use, sir," and ran out of the hotel.

Bloody chaos had ensued, filling the town. A score
of gunfights were going on, scattered from one end of
the street to the other. Only one building seemed to be
on fire so far, which was a blessing, but the blaze could
still spread.

Sam felt the heat of a bullet against his cheek, and
swung around to see who had fired it, lifting the shotgun as he did so. One of the outlaws was almost on top
of him, about to trample him under the hooves of a
charging horse. At the same time, the man was swinging his gun down for another shot at Sam, just in case.

Sam threw himself out of the way of the horse, but as
he was falling he thrust the Greener's twin barrels at the
man and tripped both triggers. With an awesome roar,
the shotgun erupted and sent both charges of buckshot
smashing into the outlaw. At this range, it almost blew
him in half. What fell from the horse and landed in the
street near Sam barely looked human anymore.

Sam pulled two more shells from his pocket as he

scrambled to his feet. He broke the shotgun, shucked the empties, crammed the fresh shells into the barrels.

"The vengeance of the Lord will be upon you!" someone screamed nearby.

Sam whirled and saw another man on horseback charging toward him, the hatless, long-haired, black-suited hombre who had led the charge into the settlement. Sam raised the shotgun and fired, but at the last second the rider hauled back hard on the reins and caused his mount to rear up on its hind legs. The horse took the blast, not the man riding it. With a shrill scream of agony, the mortally wounded animal toppled over backward, taking its rider with it.

The man sprang agilely out of the saddle, though, and avoided being crushed. As he caught his balance, he jerked two guns from their holsters and raised them toward Sam, who hadn't had time to reload the shotgun.

The black-coated outlaw wasn't going to give him the time either. When Sam saw that, he did the only thing he could. He threw the Greener at the man as hard as he could.

The shotgun hit the outlaw in the arms and threw his aim off as the pistols exploded. The bullets whined past Sam as he followed the shotgun. He crashed into the man and bore him over backward, knocking him off his feet. Both men went down.

But Sam landed on top, and as he dug a knee into the man's belly, he sledged a left and a right to the face. The outlaw went limp, stunned by the powerful blows. Sam plucked the guns from his hands.

He surged to his feet and spun toward the sound of more footsteps running toward him. His fingers were taut on the triggers.

He stopped without firing, though, as he recognized Matt's face, now grimy from smoke. Behind him, smoke still came from inside the hardware store, but no flames were visible anymore.

"You all right?" Matt asked.

"Yeah," Sam said. "How about you?"

"Burned my hands a little using a blanket I found to slap out that fire, but other than that I'm fine."

The shooting had started to die away, and as the blood brothers looked around they saw that the raiders were fleeing, having encountered a lot fiercer resistance in Arrowhead than they must have been expecting. Several bodies were scattered around the street, so not all of the varmints had gotten away.

The one sprawled senseless at Sam's feet certainly hadn't. Matt looked down at him and said, "You know who you've got there?"

"Joshua Shade?" Sam said.

"That'd be my guess. He's dressed like a preacher, and he sure had a crazy look about him when he was leadin' the charge into town."

Clouds of powder smoke still drifted through the street. Sheriff Cyrus Flagg emerged from one of them and ran up to Matt and Sam, the long nightshirt still flapping around his legs. He was wearing his plug hat now, too.

"You boys all ri—" he started to ask, then stopped short as he stared down at the stunned man. "Son of a *bitch*! You know who that is?"

"Joshua Shade?" Matt and Sam said in unison.

Flagg swallowed hard and nodded. "It sure is." He blinked in amazement. "You boys not only saved our town, you just captured the most notorious owlhoot in the whole territory!"

Chapter 9

Matt and Sam each took an arm and hauled Joshua Shade to his feet. They half carried, half dragged the outlaw down the street to the sheriff's office and jail.

They wanted to make sure that Shade was locked up securely before they did anything else.

Shade began to regain his senses as they entered the squat, solidly constructed stone building. He groaned and shook his head, causing the long brown hair to flop in front of his narrow face.

Then he jerked his head back so that the cords stood out on his neck, and cried, "Unhand me, foul demons! How dare you lay hands on the Lord's servant?"

Matt and Sam just tightened their grips on him, and Matt growled, "A lobo wolf is more the Lord's servant than you are, you crazy son of a bitch."

Shade jerked and flailed and began to spew curses, spittle flying from his mouth as he did so. He was no match for the blood brothers' strength, though, and they were able to manhandle him across the room to the cell block door that Sheriff Flagg hurried ahead to throw open.

The cell block itself was small, with two cells on each side of a short corridor. The doors were made of thick beams, with a small barred window in each one.

All the doors were open, indicating that the cells were empty at the moment. Matt and Sam wrestled Shade into the first one on the left. The walls were solid stone and appeared to be thick and massive, like the door. There was only one window, also small and barred.

Matt and Sam threw Shade onto the cot attached to the wall. The cot was the cell's only furnishing other than a chamber pot shoved underneath it.

Shade sprang to his feet as Matt and Sam backed out of the cell. He was frothing at the mouth like a rabid dog.

As Flagg slammed the door, Shade threw himself against it on the other side and clawed at the bars in the little window. He pressed his face against the bars as if trying to force his whole head through them. That distorted his crazed features even more.

"You can't lock me up!" Shade screamed. "I've come to do God's work! Release me, you filthy heathens!"

"Shut up or I'll toss a bucket o' water through that window," Flagg said.

"You can't silence the voice of the Lord! You foul abomination! All of you will burn in Hell for your sins!"

"Maybe, but you'll be there before us," Flagg said. He turned to Matt and Sam. "I'm much obliged for your help, fellas. The whole town is. You've done enough already, capturin' Shade like that, but you reckon you could help me take a look around town so I can see just how bad the damage really is?"

"Sure, Sheriff," Matt said.

"Sinners! Unholy sinners!" Shade screeched from the cell as they went into the sheriff's office again.

"Grab a couple o' Greeners," Flagg said as he waved toward a rack of shotguns on the wall. "Liable to need 'em if any o' those wounded owlhoots are still alive."

"We can't just finish them off," Sam said.

Flagg shook his head. "No, that ain't what I meant. Just in case they don't give us a choice, though."

"Never hurts to be prepared," Matt said as he went to the rack and took down one of the double-barreled weapons.

Sam had left the hotel keeper's shotgun in the street, but he still had several shells in his pocket. He used two of them to load the Greener he took down from the rack, while Matt picked up a handful of the shells that Flagg dumped onto the desk from a box.

Well armed again and ready for trouble, the three men left the sheriff's office. A gun popped from down the street, causing them to swing in that direction and raise their weapons, but a man called, "Don't worry, Sheriff! One of these snakes was still alive and reached for his gun, but he won't trouble nobody no more."

Flagg's mouth tightened in a grimace. "Damn it, Kincaid, you better be tellin' the truth," he said. "I won't have anybody takin' the law into their own hands in my town."

For the next fifteen minutes, Matt, Sam, and Flagg made the rounds of the settlement. When they were done, the inventory of their findings included five dead outlaws; five dead citizens of Arrowhead, including the hotel proprietor; eight more townies wounded; a heavily fire-damaged hardware store; and hundreds of bullet holes. Few of the buildings on Main Street had escaped without any damage. It would take folks a while to patch up everything that needed patching up.

Even so, the town had fared much better than the other settlements that had been raided by Joshua Shade and his gang. The bank and the other businesses hadn't been looted, the women were safe, and the whole town hadn't been burned to the ground.

"We were lucky," Flagg said in acknowledgment of that fact. "Mighty lucky that you fellas were here in town when Shade decided to hit us. He'd have taken us by surprise and gotten the upper hand, probably wiped the place out, if not for the two of you."

Matt shrugged. "We don't like owlhoots, so we were glad to help, Sheriff."

"What will you do with Shade now?" Sam asked.

Flagg rubbed his bearded jaw and frowned in thought. "I know what folks'd like to do."

"Drag him out of the jail and string him up to the nearest tree?" Matt suggested.

"Yeah, I'm afraid so."

"Can't blame 'em for feelin' that way," Matt said. "A varmint as ornery as Shade has got it comin'."

"But that wouldn't be legal," Sam argued. "He has to have a trial."

"Oh, he'll have a trial, all right," Flagg said. "I ain't gonna put up with any lynch law in my town." He cast a worried look up and down the street, where people were gathering and talking together in angry voices. A couple of men spat on the corpse of a dead outlaw.

The sheriff went on. "Folks are workin' themselves up into a bad state, though. They may not want to listen to reason."

"Do you have any deputies?" Sam asked.

"A couple o' part-timers. Arrowhead's a pretty

peaceable place most of the time." Flagg frowned at Matt and Sam. "Say, you fellas wouldn't consider—"

Matt raised a hand to stop him. "We're not lawmen, Sheriff. We helped out a badge-totin' friend of ours over in Texas a while back, but that was enough deputyin' to suit us for a long time."

"And we were never actually sworn in over there," Sam added. "It was all unofficial."

"That'd be fine with me," Flagg said. "All I need is somebody to make sure nothin' happens to Shade before his trial."

Matt asked, "How long do you reckon that'll be?"

"The mood the town's gonna be in, it better be as soon as possible. We got a justice o' the peace here, but no judge who could preside over a trial like the one Shade's gonna have." Flagg scratched at his beard and then thumbed his plug hat back on his head. "Reckon I'll have to send word to Tucson to get a judge out here. Probably take a week, maybe a little less."

"Which means you'll have to guard Shade for that long," Sam said. "And lynch mobs aren't the only danger. Once his men realize that he's in jail, they might decide to come back and get him."

"Most of them got away," Matt said. "There's still a good-sized bunch of killers out there. Probably be a good idea to get some more lookouts posted, Sheriff."

"Yeah, you're right," Flagg agreed. "Wish I had a couple o' good men to watch the jail, though."

The blood brothers looked at each other. Matt sighed and said, "I don't reckon we have much choice, do we?"

"Not really," Sam said. He turned to Flagg and went on. "All right, Sheriff. We'll give you a hand."

"Unofficially," Matt added.

"I don't care about that," Flagg said with a sigh

of relief. "I'm just much obliged to you boys for your help."

"To tell you the truth, I sort of lean toward stringin' Shade up myself," Matt muttered.

"You're not the only one," Sam said as he nodded toward the sheriff's office. "Looks like we've already got trouble."

Matt and Flagg turned and saw the same thing Sam did—a large group of men heading toward the jail, carrying rifles and shotguns and talking in loud, angry voices.

"Looks like we're about to start earnin' our wages," Matt said, then went on in a dry voice. "Oh, yeah, we're not gettin' paid for this, are we? We're riskin' our lives for a no-good, murderin' skunk just because it's the right thing to do."

"Hell of a note, ain't it?" Flagg said as he lifted his rifle and started toward the mob.

Chapter 10

The men had almost reached the door of the sheriff's office when Flagg pointed his rifle in the air and pulled the trigger. The crack of the Winchester made the men stop in their tracks. Some of them whirled around and started to raise their weapons, but they froze when they saw the muzzles of two shotguns pointing at them.

"What the hell, Sheriff!" one of the townies yelled.

"Back away from there!" Flagg rumbled. He jerked his rifle in a slashing motion to emphasize the order. "That's my jail, by God, and nobody sets foot in there without my say-so!"

"There's a rumor you got Joshua Shade locked up in there, Cyrus," another man said. "A couple fellas saw you and those drifters draggin' him into the jail."

"Don't you worry about who I got locked up," Flagg snapped. "That's the law's business. Now, I want you all to break it up and go on about your business . . . except for a couple of good men who are willin' to serve as lookouts on top of the bank and the hotel."

Some uneasy muttering came from the crowd.

"That's where Harlan and Charlie were, and they wound up dead," one of the men said.

"That's not gonna happen again."

"How do you know that, Sheriff?"

"Because Shade's men know that we're ready for 'em now. They'll have more sense than to try to attack the town again tonight."

"But they might some other time," another man declared, "because they know that Shade's a prisoner!"

"If we go ahead and hang him, they won't have any reason to come back here!"

Cries of agreement went up from most of the men.

Sam's voice rose powerfully to cut through the hubbub. "What about vengeance?" he asked. "If you lynch Shade, you'll just give his men even more reason to come back to Arrowhead!"

That reasoning quieted the mob for a moment. Flagg took advantage of the opportunity to say, "I'm gonna send a rider to Tucson first thing in the mornin'. We'll have a judge out here in less'n a week, so we can give Shade a proper trial . . . and *then* hang him!"

The sheriff was no longer making any pretense that Shade might not be in the jail. He had just admitted it, for all intents and purposes.

But the mob had been convinced of that already, so the admission didn't really make any difference.

"You sure he's gonna hang?" a man asked.

"He's got to be found guilty first," another pointed out.

"Hell, we got dozens o' witnesses who saw him lead that charge into town, shootin' all the way," Flagg said. "He's been seen in other towns, too, raidin' and killin'. No jury's gonna find him innocent. You know that."

More nods and mutters of agreement came from the crowd.

"So go on home," Flagg continued, "unless you want to volunteer to take a shift on lookout duty."

Several men stepped forward, and Flagg picked two of them to climb up on the hotel and the bank.

"We gotta get poor Charlie and Harlan down from there, too," Flagg said. "Maybe some of you boys could help out with that."

The local undertaker already had his wagon parked in the street, and he and a helper were loading up the bodies of the outlaws that had been left behind.

The crowd in front of the jail began to disperse. Matt, Sam, and Flagg watched them go.

"Looks like you may not need our help after all," Matt said.

"You did a good job of talking some sense into their heads, Sheriff," Sam added.

Flagg shook his head sadly. "They listened to me for now, but once they get back in the saloons and take on a snootful o' Who-hit-John, they'll get mad again. They'll egg each other on until sooner or later they decide not to wait for the judge. Might not happen tonight, but sooner or later they'll make another try for Shade."

"If they do, we'll be here to stop them," Sam said.

"But I'm gonna hate like hell to maybe have to shoot some honest folks just to protect a crazy polecat like Shade," Matt added.

"You and me both, Bodine," Sheriff Flagg agreed with a sigh. "You and me both."

"They were waitin' for us!" one of the outlaws raged. "We got the signal to come in, but the bastards were still waitin' for us!"

"You ain't tellin' me anything I don't already know," Willard Garth growled. "And you all should've knowed there was a chance o' that happenin', since we heard those shots beforehand. Somebody caught our boys after they got rid of the lookouts that old desert rat told us about."

"The reverend should've known that," a man named Jeffries said. He was more educated than most of the gang, but just as ruthless. "We never should have attacked the town."

"Don't you say nothin' bad about the rev'rend!" Gonzalez said. "He's made us all rich men!"

In truth, they weren't all that rich, Garth thought, but they had done all right for themselves. And it was Joshua Shade's planning, as well as his sheer audacity and his ability to inspire the men, that had made it all possible. Gonzalez was right about that.

The members of the gang had scattered as they fled from Arrowhead, rendezvousing in the hills where their last camp had been, according to the plan laid out by Shade before the attack. Shade didn't like the idea of acknowledging the possibility of defeat, but he was too smart not to plan for it in case it happened.

However, this was the first time one of their raids had not gone exactly the way Shade had told them it would. The men were upset because some of their fellow outlaws had been killed and their leader had been captured.

Garth himself had seen Shade being disarmed and knocked out, but hadn't been able to get to him because of the heavy gunfire from the townspeople. He assumed that by now they had locked Shade up in the local jail, but he didn't know that for sure.

He was confident that Shade was still alive, though.

He couldn't bring himself to believe that the reverend would come to such an ignominious end as to be killed by a bunch of pathetic townies.

Jeffries said, "The question now is, what are we going to do about this, Garth? Those yokels are liable to try to lynch the boss."

"And they got to pay for what they did to us!" Gonzalez added.

"I know, I know." Garth took off his high-crowned hat and wearily scrubbed a hand over his rough-hewn face. He didn't like having to do a lot of thinking, which was the main reason he had starting riding with Joshua Shade in the first place. Over time, he had risen to the position of Shade's segundo because he was tough and trustworthy, not because he was all that smart.

Now the rest of the men were looking to him to figure out their course of action, and it was an uncomfortable feeling. He took orders well, and he could give them, too, when somebody else came up with them. He could ride all day and all night when he had to, and he didn't mind killing without mercy.

But he wasn't a leader.

Not by choice anyway.

Even in the moonlight, Garth could see ambition gleaming in Jeffries's eyes as the man crowded his horse forward. "Well, how about it?" Jeffries prodded.

Garth knew what Jeffries was thinking. Jeffries sensed an opening. He thought that *he* should be in charge now that Shade was a prisoner down in that backwater cow town.

Garth was damned if he was going to let that happen, no matter how uncomfortable he was in the role.

"They're ready for us down there," he said harshly. "We go chargin' back in tonight, they'll cut us to ribbons. We got to wait. Bide our time and see what's gonna happen."

"You mean leave the rev'rend a prisoner?" Gonzalez shook his head. "I don't like that, Garth."

"I don't like it either," Garth snapped, "but we don't have much choice. We'll get him loose, but we got to wait until the time is right."

"How are we going to know that?" Jeffries asked.

Garth chewed on his mustache where it hung over his lips. "I wish the boss hadn't killed that old prospector. We could've sent him back in to spy for us, like he did before."

"Maybe what we need to do," Jeffries said, "is to find another spy."

Gonzalez looked over at him. "Where we gonna do that?"

"There are ranches around here," Jeffries said with a shrug. "Find a small one where it's just a man and his family, maybe a hand or two, and take it over. A man will do whatever you tell him to when it's a matter of protecting his wife and kids."

That was a good idea, Garth realized. He wished he had thought of it himself. But he couldn't afford to ignore the suggestion just because Jeffries had come up with it.

"All right," he said. "That's what we'll do. Half a dozen men ought to be plenty. The rest of you stay here and patch up any wounds you got during the ruckus in town."

Jeffries and Gonzales volunteered to go with Garth, who quickly picked out three other men to accompany them. The six of them mounted up and rode off into the night.

"I don't like the way you said the rev'rend made a

mistake by killin' that old man," Gonzalez grumbled. "He thought he was doin' the right thing."

"I didn't see any reason not to kill that desert rat either . . , at the time," Garth said. "It just goes to show you that nobody can think of everything, at least not all the time."

"The rev'rend can," Gonzalez insisted.

If that was true, thought Garth, then Shade wouldn't be sitting in some little cow country jail right now. He kept that sentiment to himself, though. No point in making the Mexican even proddier than he already was, or in encouraging Jeffries to be even more ambitious.

He was going to have his hands full running the gang, Garth told himself. He just hoped that he would be up to the job until they freed Joshua Shade so that he could take his rightful place as the boss outlaw once again.

Garth hoped that day came soon, too.

The dogs barking woke Tom Peterson. His wife Frannie stirred in the bed beside him. They were spooning, and it felt good when her rump moved against him.

He couldn't think about that right now, though, because the dogs were upset about something. Might be a wolf or a bear had wandered down from the mountains and was nosing around the stock.

Better get up and check, Tom told himself. It would be a lot more pleasurable, though, to just lie here, maybe wake Frannie up the rest of the way for a little slap an' tickle. The young'uns were sound asleep in the loft.

With a sigh, Tom moved away from his wife and swung his legs out of bed. Wearing long underwear, he stood up and moved across the darkened room to twitch aside the curtains over the window. Frannie was mighty proud of those curtains, having bought the material for them at one of the mercantiles in Arrowhead.

A lantern was burning in the little shed next to the barn where Felipe slept. The old vaquero was the only hand Tom had hired. He and Felipe took care of things around the spread by themselves, helped a little by Tom's boys, who were eleven and eight and turning into pretty fair hands themselves.

Felipe would see what had the dogs so stirred up, Tom told himself. He turned to go back to bed.

Before he could get there, he heard one of the dogs give a yelp of pain.

Frowning, Tom swung toward the door instead of the bed. No matter how much he wanted to, he couldn't ignore the fact that something was going on. He took down the Henry rifle from the pegs beside the door and levered a round into the chamber. Then he pulled the latch string and pushed the door open.

As the door swung back, Tom heard Felipe's voice start to rise in a startled shout. It was cut off a second later, and the abruptness of it made Tom's heart thud heavily with fear. He rushed outside, holding the gun ready.

Something cracked across his ankles. He cried out in pain and dismay as he felt himself toppling forward. The impact as he hit the ground jolted the Henry out of his hands. He reached for it, only to have a boot come down hard on his fingers. He yelled in pain.

"Tom?" Frannie's sleep-fuzzed voice came from inside the house. "Tom, what's going on out there?"

He wanted to call out and warn her, but someone grabbed him by the hair, jerked his head up, and pressed the keen blade of a knife against his throat.

"Not a sound, Señor," a voice hissed in his ear.

A second later, Frannie cried out, and only the knife at his throat kept Tom from moving. He felt a warm trickle of blood down his neck, and knew that the least bit more pressure would send the blade slicing deeply into his flesh.

"Get him up," a rough voice ordered.

A hand tugged on Tom's long underwear, urging him upright. The knife remained at his throat as he climbed to his feet. To his horror, he saw his wife in the moonlight with a man standing behind her, one arm around her throat and the other hand holding a gun to her head.

"Do what we tell you, hombre," the man said, "and nobody'll get hurt. But if you give us any trouble, we'll just kill everybody on this spread and move on."

"But not before we have some fun with this pretty little wife of yours," another man said as he came forward, and as Tom's eyes gazed around wildly, he saw several other shapes emerge from the darkness. He was surrounded. Helpless, not only because he was outnumbered, but because these strangers were threatening Frannie.

"You savvy what we're sayin'?" demanded the man with the gun pressed to her head.

Tom's mouth had gone bone-dry, but he nodded, and after a second had worked up enough spit so that he was able to say, "I savvy. Just tell me what you want, mister. I'll do anything. Just don't hurt my family."

The gunman chuckled. "You're a smart hombre. Now listen close . . ."

Chapter 11

A door at the far end of the corridor in the cell block led to the room that Sheriff Cyrus Flagg called home. He had a folding cot, though, that he carried into the office and set up for the blood brothers.

"One o' you fellas can get a little sleep while the other one stands watch," he told Matt and Sam. "I'll take my turn, too."

"It's after midnight," Sam pointed out. "Not that long until morning. Why don't you go ahead and get some rest, Sheriff? Let Matt and me worry about watching the jail until morning."

Flagg stifled a yawn. "You sure?"

"We're sure," Matt told him.

"All right then. I can't tell you boys how much I appreciate your help."

Flagg opened the cell block door, and Shade, who had finally quieted down, immediately began haranguing him again through the window in the cell door, clutching the bars as he did so.

Flagg slapped the Winchester's barrel against the

bars, which made Shade let go of them and jump back.
The outlaw began yelling even louder.

"Keep it up, Shade," the sheriff growled. "I might
just toss the keys out the front door and let the folks
in town do whatever they want to you."

"Sinners, filthy sinners!"

Flagg shook his head and walked on back to his
quarters, closing the door firmly behind him. Matt
closed the cell block door. Shade kept yelling.

Matt ignored him and said to Sam, "What was the
idea of volunteering us to stay up the rest of the night?"

"The sheriff's a lot older than we are," Sam pointed
out. "I'm sure he needs the sleep more than we do."

"I wouldn't be so sure of that." Matt yawned himself. "But there's nothing we can do about it now. You
can take first watch, though."

"Fine." Sam went behind the desk and sat down,
while Matt pulled his boots and gunbelts off and
stretched out on the cot. He placed the shotgun on
the floor within easy reach.

A few minutes later, Shade stopped yelling, and
soon after that, Matt was sound asleep.

When he woke up, sunlight was slanting through
the front window of the sheriff's office. Matt sat up
abruptly and said, "What the hell! How come you
didn't wake me up for my turn on watch?"

Sam still sat behind the desk, with his feet propped
on it now as he leaned the chair back against the wall.
"I wasn't all that sleepy," he said, "so I didn't see any
point in it." He grinned. "After the way you complained
last night, I didn't want you being too tired and cranky
this morning."

"Cranky! Why, I'll cranky you, you—"

Shade must have heard them talking. He started

yelling again. Matt and Sam heard the door at the other end of the cell block corridor open, and Sheriff Flagg shouted, "Shut up in there!"

"The word of God will not be silenced!" Shade screeched back at him.

He was still carrying on when Flagg came into the office a few minutes later. The sheriff wore his overalls again and looked more like a farmer than a peace officer.

"Mornin', fellas," he said with a friendly nod for Matt and Sam. "I reckon the rest of the night was quiet?"

"It was," Sam said, not pointing out that Matt had slept through it, too. "I heard a little loud talking from the street a few times, but no one tried to get in." He nodded toward the window. "We had the shutters closed most of the night, but we figured it was all right to open them this morning."

"Sure enough," Flagg agreed. "I'll go down to the hash house and see about gettin' some breakfast sent up for the two o' you . . . and for Shade, too, I reckon, although I hate to waste good food on a varmint like that. Wouldn't be right to let a prisoner starve, though."

"I suppose not," Matt said grudgingly.

"I'll see about gettin' a message sent off to the court in Tucson, too," Flagg promised. "Anything else you boys want in particular?"

To be on the trail again, Matt thought, but that was going to have to wait a while. At least until Flagg received word that a circuit judge was on his way to Arrowhead.

Flagg left, and came back a short time later with a cloth-covered tray containing platters of flapjacks, biscuits, and thick slices of ham. Matt had coffee boiling in the dented old pot on the stove by then. Shade's yells still came from the cell block, but the three men just ignored him as they ate breakfast.

"I did some askin' around town while I was out," Flagg said. "Nobody's talkin' about lynchin' Shade."

"At least not that they would admit to the sheriff," Sam pointed out.

"Yeah, well, there's that," Flagg admitted. "I got pretty good instincts, though, and I don't think anything's goin' on right now."

"But you believe it'll build back up," Matt said.

Flagg nodded. "I do. Hear that?"

He opened the door, and the blood brothers both heard the sound of someone hammering in the distance.

"You know what that is?" Flagg asked.

Matt and Sam shook their heads.

"That's Cassius Doolittle nailin' together coffins in the yard behind his undertakin' parlor. There's gonna be a big funeral here in town this afternoon, for Charlie Cornwell, Harlan Eggleston, Yancy Baker, Bob McCall, and Rufus Nicholson. Those are all the fellas killed by those outlaws. Every time one of those boys is buried, folks are gonna look at each other and ask themselves why Joshua Shade is still drawin' breath when he ought to be danglin' at the end of a rope. They won't be able to come up with a good answer for that question either, except that it's the law . . . and after a while they just won't give a damn."

That afternoon, Sheriff Flagg attended the mass funeral in the church at the edge of town while Matt and

Sam remained at the jail. Later, when the last coffin had been lowered into the newly dug graves in Arrowhead's cemetery, and while the undertaker and his helpers were busy shoveling dirt into the holes, Flagg returned to the sheriff's office.

He still wore the dusty, somewhat threadbare black suit he had worn to the funeral, with a gunbelt strapped around his ample belly under the frock coat. As he hung his hat on a nail near the door, he commented, "Shade's quiet for a change."

"He's been quiet all afternoon," Sam said.

"Reckon he finally wore himself out from all the carryin' on," Matt said. "Any problems at the funeral or the buryin'?"

Flagg shook his head. "Not really, but I could tell that folks are mighty upset. Stan Hightower and all his hands were there, and Stan's wife Margery never stopped cryin'. I didn't like the look on Stan's face."

"We don't know who those people are, Sheriff," Sam reminded him.

"Oh, yeah." Flagg went over to the stove and poured himself a cup of the coffee that was left from that morning, which was probably strong enough by now to get up and walk off under its own power. "Margery is Rufus Nicholson's daughter, and her husband Stan owns the Diamond H. One of the biggest spreads in these parts. So Stan's pretty much used to gettin' whatever he wants around here."

Matt propped a hip against a corner of the desk and frowned. "That sounds like trouble brewin'."

Flagg sighed, sipped the coffee, and nodded. "Yeah, I heard Stan talkin' after the service at the cemetery about how it's a waste o' time waitin' for a judge to come all the way from Tucson. He said why bother with a trial when Shade's just gonna hang anyway."

"And I'll bet people listened to him, didn't they?" Sam said.

Flagg shrugged. "Like I told you, Stan's one o' the big skookum he-wolves around here. Folks want to stay on his good side. And if he rides into town with a dozen tough, gun-hung cowboys right behind him, ready to back his play, some of the good citizens o' Arrowhead will find it mighty easy to fall in with 'em."

"When do you think this is liable to happen?" Matt asked.

"Wouldn't surprise me if it was tonight."

"We'll just have to put a stop to it then," Sam said.

"You're talkin' three men against forty or fifty," Flagg pointed out.

"I'll admit, those aren't very good odds. But we have the law on our side."

Matt grunted. "That won't stop a bullet . . . not unless you've got a big thick law book stuck in your pocket." He turned to Flagg. "You could always just step aside and let them have Shade."

Flagg scratched his beard and nodded, then said, "Yeah, but let me ask you somethin', Bodine. If you'd done swore an oath to uphold the law, would *you* step aside?"

"The things that Shade has done, I might, yeah."

"No, you wouldn't," Sam said. "I know you, Matt. You're too stubborn to ever do anything like that."

Matt had to grin. "Well, you're probably right about that. But we didn't swear an oath, now did we?"

"We told the sheriff we'd help him. That's giving our word. It's the same thing."

"Damn it, Sam! I hate it when you're right." Matt looked at Flagg. "We'll stick, Sheriff."

"Nobody'd think any less of you if you didn't . . ." Flagg began.

"We would," Sam said.

"We'll stick," Matt said again.

Chapter 12

The settlement had been so crowded because of the mass funeral held that afternoon that no one had paid any attention to Tom Peterson as he mingled with the townspeople and talked to everyone he could. Most of the folks in Arrowhead knew Tom, so they didn't think anything of it when he asked about what was going to happen to the notorious prisoner who was locked up in the town jail.

Now as he rode back toward his hardscrabble ranch, fear filled Tom. Frannie and the boys and little, seven-year-old Abigail had been out there at the ranch alone with those outlaws all day, and there was no telling what might have happened while he was gone.

He'd had a long talk with Beau and Chad before he rode out that morning and told them to cooperate with the owlhoots. The boys were scared, but they were also mad that anybody would ride in and take over like that bunch had done. Tom didn't want them trying anything that might get them killed.

He didn't even allow himself to think about what might have happened to Frannie while he was gone. As long as they hadn't killed her, anything else could be gotten over, or at least put in the past. That's what he'd been telling himself all day, to the point where he almost believed it.

Maybe nothing had happened. That man Garth seemed to be in charge of the gang, and he kept a pretty tight hand on the reins as far as Tom could see. He had told Tom all they wanted was to know everything he could find out about Joshua Shade. Since Tom had information to report, that gave him a shred of hope.

But it wasn't good news he was going to give to Garth, and that prospect worried him greatly.

Everything looked peaceful as he came in sight of the ranch. A tendril of smoke curled up from the stone chimney, just as it normally would. The outlaws had put their horses in the barn the night before, so there was no sign of them.

Tom rode up to the house, reined his mount to a halt, and swung down from the saddle, nervously eyeing the house as he did so. Normally, he would have tended to his horse before doing anything else, but he was too anxious to do that. He dropped the reins and hurried to the door.

As he jerked it open and stepped inside, a cold ring of metal was pressed to the side of his head, just in front of his right ear. Tom stopped short, knowing that it was a gun barrel prodding him.

"Take it easy, sodbuster," the outlaw called Jeffries drawled. He was the one Tom feared the most, since he'd made no secret of how he felt about Frannie, practically licking his chops every time he looked at her.

Jeffries went on. "If anybody happens to be watching, we don't want you acting like anything's wrong."

"Sorry," Tom breathed. His eyes were adjusting to the dimness inside the house now, and to his huge relief he saw Frannie, Abigail, and the boys all sitting at the table, apparently unharmed. Wide-eyed with fear, but not hurt.

The six outlaws stood or sat around the room. Jeffries, Garth, and the Mexican, Gonzalez, had their guns drawn. Garth pouched his weapon, though, and motioned for the others to do the same.

"What about it?" Garth demanded as he came toward Tom. "Is Joshua still alive?"

Tom forced his head up and down in a nod. "He's alive. Sheriff Flagg's got him locked up, just like you thought."

"What are they gonna do with him?"

"The sheriff sent word to Tucson about what happened and asked for a judge to come out so they can put your boss on trial."

"When's that supposed to happen?"

Tom shook his head. "Hard to say for sure. Whenever the judge gets there. A week or thereabouts from what I heard. Maybe a little less."

Gonzalez said, "*Bueno*. That gives us time to get the rev'rend out o' there."

Tom grimaced, and Garth noticed the reaction. "What?" the outlaw asked.

"I don't know if you're gonna be able to bust Shade out of there," Tom replied honestly. "The whole town's worked up over the men who got killed last night, and every able-bodied man is walking around with a gun. The sheriff's got lookouts on top of the hotel and the bank again—"

Jeffries laughed. "That didn't do them much good last time, now did it?"

"Everybody's more alert now," Tom went on. "Plus Sheriff Flagg's got a couple of gunfighters helpin' him out. They're holed up inside the jail with the prisoner."

"Gunfighters?" Garth repeated with a frown. "What gunfighters?"

"Matt Bodine and that half-breed sidekick of his, Two Wolves."

Garth let out his breath strongly enough so that it fluttered the mustache hanging over his mouth. "Bodine and Two Wolves," he said in disgust.

"Who are they?" Jeffries asked. "I never heard of them."

"Bodine's a slick iron artist," Garth replied. "Supposed to be damn near as fast on the draw as Smoke Jensen. And Two Wolves is right behind him. They're a pair o' first-class fightin' men, that's for sure."

Jeffries shrugged. "Two men against all of us. With odds like that, it doesn't matter how good they are."

"Yeah, you can say that all you want, but nobody's gonna want to be among the dozen or more of us they'd kill before they went under," Garth pointed out. "I'm gonna have to do some thinkin' about this."

He winced as if the idea of thinking itself gave him a pain.

Tom took a deep breath. He wasn't going to hold anything back from these men. Complete cooperation was his best chance of getting his family out of this alive.

"That's not all," he said. "A lynch mob tried to take Shade out of the jail last night."

"That don't surprise me none. What happened?"

"The sheriff talked them out of it . . . and I don't reckon anybody wanted to try Bodine and Two Wolves either. But there's a rancher named Hightower who won't be turned away so easy. His father-in-law was one of the men who was killed, and from what I heard in town, Hightower wants to settle the score for the old man."

"Can he do it?"

"He's got a tough crew. And the townspeople are liable to throw in with him. They'll have a better chance of gettin' to Shade than you fellas would."

"Only they want to string him up, not bust him out of jail."

Tom nodded. "Yeah. That's exactly what they want."

Something stirred inside Garth's brain, and it was a moment before he recognized it for what it really was—an idea. "Maybe we ought to let this Hightower hombre do the work for us," he said slowly.

"What you talkin' about, Garth?" Gonzalez demanded. "We can't let no lynch mob have the rev'rend?"

"We can let them do the bustin' him out of jail, though," Garth said. "Then, before they have a chance to lynch him, we swoop in and snatch him away from 'em. Nobody'll be expectin' us to strike right then."

"That might actually work," Jeffries said with a tone of grudging admiration in his voice.

"Once it's dark, we could make our way along the bed of the river that loops around the town," Garth went on as more details formed in his mind. "That way, we can get close enough to keep an eye on what's goin' on without anybody spottin' us."

He looked around as if waiting for someone to argue with him or point out the flaws in his plan, but Jeffries, Gonzalez, and the other three outlaws remained silent.

"All right then," Garth said with a nod. "That's what we'll do. We'd best get on back to the rest of the boys and let them know the plan."

Jeffries waved a hand at Tom. "What about the sod-buster here? We can't let him ride into town and warn everybody about what we're going to do."

"No, o' course not."

Fear leaped up in Tom's chest as the burly outlaw reached for his gun. He knew now that he had been a fool to trust these men, to believe that they would honor their word to leave him and his family alone if he helped them. He lunged toward Jeffries and reached out in a desperate attempt to snatch the man's gun from its holster.

Tom had barely moved when he felt what seemed like a punch in his back. Cold fire speared into his body. He staggered forward, reaching awkwardly behind him as he did so. His fingers brushed the hilt of the knife that protruded from his back. Gonzalez must have thrown it, he thought as he fell to his knees and then pitched forward on his face as the rest of his strength deserted him.

"Good idea, Gonzalez," Garth said as Tom struggled to hang on to consciousness. "We'll use knives on 'em. Quieter that way."

Frannie and the kids were screaming, but the sounds were far away and fading now in Tom's ears. The pounding roar of his own pulse rose until that was all he could hear.

Then it stopped. He heard that, too, as he died, but that was all. He missed all the terrible sounds of what happened to his family after that, and the swift rata-plan of hoofbeats that came through the open door as the killers rode away afterward.

Once those hoofbeats had dwindled away to nothing, the ranch was quiet again . . . quiet with the eerie hush of death.

Chapter 13

Shade hadn't eaten the breakfast that Flagg had brought him that morning, nor had he touched the food on the tray the sheriff carried into the cell at midday. Both times, Matt and Sam had stood just outside the cell door with rifles trained on the prisoner as Flagg took the food inside.

When it came time for supper, Flagg said, "Damned if I'm gonna waste more o' the town's money on feedin' that vicious son of a bitch when he don't eat none of what I bring him."

"There's food in there if he wants it bad enough," Matt pointed out.

"I'll stay here for a while. Why don't you boys go get you something to eat? I'm sure you wouldn't mind bein' out o' this place for a while."

The blood brothers looked at each other. Matt shrugged and said, "Might as well. We can get back here in a hurry if there's any trouble."

"That's right," Flagg agreed. "If you hear a scattergun go off, though, I'd be obliged if you'd come a-runnin'."

"I could use a cold beer, too," Matt said as they left

the jail. He grinned. "And I'll bet that girl Amelia at the Ten Grand would be mighty pleased to see you again, Sam."

"I think we should just get the beer and then something to eat," Sam said.

"Whatever you say," Matt replied with a chuckle.

Archie Cochran was behind the bar again when they entered the Ten Grand this evening. He lifted a hand in greeting and started drawing two beers without being asked as Matt and Sam headed for the bar.

As he set the foaming mugs in front of them, Archie said, "On the house, boys. After what you did last night, I'm not sure your money's good in here anymore."

"Is that your decision to make?" Sam asked.

Archie laughed. "I own the place, so it damned well better be!"

Matt took a long swallow and sighed with satisfaction as he lowered the mug to the bar. "We're much obliged," he said.

"Nothin's too good for the men who captured Joshua Shade." A worried frown briefly crossed the bartender's face. "Of course, some folks in town aren't so happy with you boys. They figure Shade would be rottin' on the end of a rope by now if it wasn't for you backin' up Sheriff Flagg."

"No one has the right to take the law into their own hands," Sam said.

"Maybe not under normal circumstances . . . but I reckon most folks feel like these ain't normal circumstances. A lot of people are grievin' tonight."

"Like Stan Hightower?" Matt suggested.

Archie cast a nervous glance from side to side. He leaned forward over the bar and lowered his voice as he said, "You didn't hear it from me, but I've got a pretty good idea that Stan's not gonna wait for that judge to get here. I don't want to see old Cyrus get hurt. What he ought to do—what you boys ought to do, too, if you're still helpin' him out—is to take a ride out of town for an hour or so this evenin'. It'd all be over by the time you got back."

"We can't do that, Archie," Sam said. "Neither can the sheriff."

Archie sighed. "Yeah, I figured as much. But I didn't think it'd hurt anything to mention it."

Matt and Sam finished their beers, then left the saloon. They walked down the street to the hash house where Sheriff Flagg had been getting their meals. The food had been good so far, so they didn't see any reason to change horses in midstream.

They were polishing off platters of thick steaks and mounds of German potatoes when they heard a racket from the street. A large number of riders were passing by outside.

Matt and Sam looked across the table at each other. Matt said, "I don't reckon we ought to wait for the sound of a shotgun blast, do you?"

"Not hardly," Sam agreed. "Let's go."

Matt dropped a greenback on the table to pay for their meals, and they headed for the door . . . but not before casting regretful glances at what was left of their food. As they emerged from the café, they looked toward the sheriff's office and saw that the riders had reined to a halt in front of the blocky stone building.

One man edged his horse to the forefront of the group and yelled, "Open up in there, Sheriff! Nobody has to get hurt here!"

Quite a few townspeople had heard the commotion and were now heading toward the jail. Most of them were grim-faced men who carried rifles or shotguns, Matt and Sam noted.

They exchanged worried glances. The situation was developing just as Sheriff Flagg and Archie Cochran had predicted it would. The members of the lynch mob that had been turned back the night before were ready to join Stan Hightower and his men for another stab at hanging Joshua Shade.

"We should've brought those Greeners with us," Matt muttered as they started walking toward the jail.

"We'll have to make do with what we have," Sam said.

As they got closer, they saw that the men who had ridden into town with Stan Hightower were all tough, competent-looking hombres. They bristled with hardware, too. Each man was armed with a rifle and at least one handgun.

If it came to shooting, both Matt and Sam knew that they couldn't stand up to those odds for very long. And some innocent folks would be killed, too. Although you could argue that if they were all that innocent, they wouldn't be joining lynch mobs, Matt thought.

Still, with all the hell Shade had raised, all the innocent folks *he* had killed, it was easy to get carried away with the desire for vengeance.

"Damn it, Cyrus, open up!" yelled the man who had to be Stan Hightower. "Don't make us bust in there!"

The inside shutters had been closed over the windows, Matt noted as he and Sam drew closer. Now one of the shutters was pulled back a little and the barrel of a rifle thrust through the opening. Guns came up in the hands of Hightower's punchers in response to the threat.

"Go home, Stan!" Sheriff Flagg shouted from

inside the jail. "You know good an' well I can't let you have Shade!"

"He doesn't deserve to have a good man like you protecting him!" Hightower replied.

"Maybe not, but he's my prisoner and I ain't lettin' anything happen to him! You and your boys just turn around and go home! Margery's already grievin'. You don't want to make it worse on her."

"I don't see how hanging that murdering bastard Shade could make it any worse on her!" Hightower replied.

"Because she'll be a widow, too!"

Hightower stiffened and sat up straighter in the saddle as the implications of Flagg's words obviously hit him. "Hold on there, Cyrus," he said. "You and I have always been friends."

"That was before you came stompin' up to my door and told me to turn a prisoner over to you! I got this rifle pointed right at you, and the first man takes a step toward this door, I'm pullin' the trigger!"

A man in the crowd shouted, "Don't let him talk to you like that, Stan! He wouldn't dare shoot you, and you know it!"

Hightower might have his doubts that Flagg would shoot, but he couldn't be sure of that. And having a gun pointed directly at him had a wonderful way of clearing the fog of emotion from a fellow's mind.

"Hold on now," Hightower said as he gestured toward the men in the crowd. "Don't go doing anything foolish."

"Shade killed your own wife's pa," a man argued. "You can't let him get away with that."

From inside the jail, Flagg called, "He won't get away with it! He'll hang! But it'll happen legal-like!"

"You can't stop us by yourself, Cyrus!" another man shouted.

Matt nodded to Sam and shucked his irons. Beside him, Sam drew his Colt as well. They eared back the hammers on the weapons, and even in the noisy street, the men closest to them heard those ominous metallic sounds.

"Oh, hell!" one of those men exclaimed as he glanced over his shoulder. "It's Bodine and Two Wolves! They're behind us!"

That news flashed through the crowd like wildfire. Men turned and started to reach for their pistols or lift their rifles they held, but they froze as they found themselves staring down the menacing barrels of the blood brothers' revolvers.

"I've got six in each wheel, gents," Matt said into the sudden silence, "and so does Sam here. That's eighteen shots. Tell me . . . which eighteen of you want to die?"

"You can't kill a man with every shot!" one of the mob blustered.

"Care to bet *your* life on that, amigo?" Matt drawled as a reckless grin played around his wide mouth.

Hightower turned his horse and forced his way through the crowd until he confronted Matt and Sam. Glaring at them, he said, "I've always heard that you two were law-abiding men. Why are you taking the side of a vicious murderer?"

"Because we *are* law-abiding men," Sam replied. "We want to see Shade hanged just as much as you do, Mr. Hightower, but you should leave it to the law to do it."

"The law!" Hightower made a slashing motion with his hand. "You can't count on the law! Out here the only real law is what a man carries on his hip!"

"I reckon that's always been true," Matt said. "But

things have started to change. I don't like it all the time either. In the long run, though, there's nothin' we can do about it, because nothin' stays the same forever."

Hightower stared at them for a long moment, then said, "You really think the law will take care of Joshua Shade?"

"I do," Sam said.

"So do I," Matt said.

Hightower hesitated a moment longer, then sighed and nodded. "All right. I know Cyrus Flagg is an honest man, and I'll trust him—and you boys—for now." The rancher's voice hardened. "But the law had better do its job . . . or the rest of us will take care of it ourselves."

"You mean there's not gonna be a hangin'?" one of the men asked in a disappointed tone.

"Not tonight," snapped Hightower. "We'll see about tomorrow or next week." He lifted his reins. "Come on, boys. Diamond H, follow me!"

Loud mutters of discontent came from the crowd, but it began to disperse rapidly once Hightower and his punchers had galloped off. Matt and Sam lowered the hammers on their guns, but didn't holster the weapons until everyone had drifted off to the saloons or their homes.

The jail door swung open. "Get in here while the gettin's good," Flagg urged from inside.

The blood brothers went into the jail. Flagg slammed the door behind them, lowered the thick bar across it, and heaved a sigh of relief. Back in the cell block, Shade was yelling, but the three of them had learned not to pay any attention to that.

"How long do you reckon we can keep dodgin' this particular bullet?" Matt asked.

"Until the judge gets here, I hope," Flagg replied. "Once folks see that Shade's gonna get what's comin' to him, I think all this lynch fever will settle down."

Matt grunted. "Yeah, well, I've got a hunch it's gonna be a *long* week."

In the deep gully cut by the San Francisco River, about a quarter of a mile from Arrowhead, Willard Garth asked, "Damn it, when's the shootin' gonna start?"

Gonzalez, who was the stealthiest of them all now that the men who had slipped into the settlement the previous night to dispose of the lookouts were dead, said in a tone of disgust, "There ain't gonna be no shootin'. That mob of gutless gringos broke up and went home because they were afraid of Bodine and Two Wolves and the sheriff."

"No lynching?" Jeffries asked.

Gonzalez put his sombrero on and shook his head. *"Nada."* Using the shadows for concealment, he had slipped into the town on foot and gotten close enough in an alley to see and hear everything that went on during the confrontation in front of the jail.

Jeffries turned to Garth. "Now what the hell are we going to do? We're in the same situation we were in before. We can try to break Joshua out of that jail—"

"And get the gang shot to pieces in the process," Garth interrupted. "I know, damn it, I know."

It wasn't fair. He had come up with a plan all on his own, a plan that actually might have worked, and now it was ruined because a bunch of cowards wouldn't stand up to an old sheriff and a couple of cheap gunslingers.

He became aware that all the men were staring at him in the moonlight, waiting for him to make a decision. All he could think of to say was, "We'll just have to wait for a better time."

"And how will we know when that is?" Jeffries asked. "We can't just waltz into town and ask somebody what's going on."

"We'll find somebody to, uh, to spy for us . . ."

"Like we did before?" A cold laugh came from Jeffries. "Maybe we'd better stop killing our informants so quickly."

"But the last ones died so *good*," Gonzalez said.

"Don't worry none about that," Garth said. "Ain't never gonna be a shortage of folks to kill."

Chapter 14

Despite Matt's ominous prediction, the next few days passed relatively peacefully in Arrowhead. There was still considerable muttering going on in the town about how Joshua Shade ought to be taken out and strung up, Flagg reported when he came back to the jail from his forays outside a couple of times a day, but without somebody powerful like Stan Hightower to back them up, the men who would have been eager to form a mob settled for grousing in their beer.

The part-time deputy Flagg had sent to Tucson arrived back in Arrowhead five days after he left, bringing good news with him.

"The judge is about a day behind me," he told Flagg as he lowered his weary body into one of the chairs in the sheriff's office. "He'll be here sometime tomorrow, and he said he'd hold the trial right away."

Flagg sighed in relief. "And we'll have Shade strung up as soon as the trial's over, I'm bettin'. But at least it'll be legal."

Shade had quieted down considerably the past couple of days. He sat on the bunk in the cell, constantly muttering to himself. Matt and Sam didn't know if he was praying, calling down curses on his enemies, or just raving maniacally, but any time one of them stepped into the cell block, day or night, he could hear the soft voice from Shade's cell.

The outlaw had started eating, too. The blood brothers supposed it was so he could keep his strength up for whatever he was doing in there.

Now, after hearing that the trial was imminent, Sheriff Flagg said to Matt and Sam, "I reckon you boys will be glad when this is all over and you can be on your way."

"We were in no hurry to get anywhere," Sam said,

"Just driftin'," Matt added.

A knock sounded on the thick front door. All four men in the office tensed at the sound, but they relaxed as they realized how unlikely it was that a lynch mob would knock so politely. Flagg went to the door and called through it, "Who's there?"

"It's Matthew Wiley, Cyrus."

Flagg grunted in surprise and turned to look at Matt and Sam. "The mayor o' Arrowhead," he said by way of explaining who Matthew Wiley was. "Wonder what he wants."

"Only one way to find out," Matt drawled.

He and Sam had their hands on their guns as Flagg unbarred the door, just in case this was some sort of trick. Flagg swung the door open and said, "Come on in, Mayor. What can we do for you?"

Wiley was a thin, pale, fair-haired man in a brown tweed suit. Matt and Sam knew from talk they had heard that he owned the bank, which was not surprising since political power always followed the money.

"I saw Deputy Johnson ride past the bank," Wiley

said with a nod toward the man who had just returned from Tucson, whose name was Randy Johnson. Wiley pulled a handkerchief from his pocket and mopped his forehead with it. As he put it away, he went on. "Does that mean the judge is on his way?"

Flagg nodded. "It does. With any luck, by the time the sun goes down tomorrow, this whole ugly business will be behind us."

"That's just it," Wiley said. "The town council and I have been talking about it, and we're afraid that the trial won't bring an end to our problems."

Flagg frowned. "You ain't afraid that Shade'll be found not guilty, are you, Mayor? There's too many witnesses against him for that to ever happen."

"No, that's not it." Wiley began to pace worriedly. "But what's going to happen *after* we've hanged him? What will his gang do then? Will they try to avenge him by attacking the town?"

Matt had been leaning casually against the desk with his arms crossed over his chest. Now he straightened and said, "No offense, Mr. Mayor, but wait just a doggoned minute. We had to stand up to lynch mobs twice, and now you're sayin' you don't *want* Shade to be hanged?"

Wiley reached for his handkerchief again. "That's not what I'm saying at all. After what Shade and his gang did to our town, I'd like to see that son of a bitch dancing at the end of a rope as much as anybody would. But I'm not sure it would be the wisest thing for Arrowhead if it happens here."

"Because you're afraid of his gang," Flagg said.

"It's not just me," Wiley said. "All the businessmen in town are worried, and with good reason."

Sam said, "You can't be suggesting that we just . . . let him go."

Wiley shook his head. "Not at all. We can go ahead and have the trial, find him guilty and sentence him to hang, but I think the sentence ought to be carried out somewhere else."

"Like where?" Matt asked.

"I don't know. Tucson perhaps?"

With a frown, Flagg sat down behind the desk. "I don't know," he said slowly. "I figured we'd just take care o' things right here. I was about to go tell Cassius Doolittle to start hammerin' together a gallows."

"The town council and I just don't think it's wise," Wiley insisted.

"Well, I reckon we'll have to wait and see what the judge says," Flagg said with a sigh. "If you can talk him into it, I'll go along with whatever he decides."

"Thanks, Cyrus. That's all we're asking."

Wiley left the office, and Matt barred the door after him. He shook his head and looked disgusted as he turned back to the others.

"You can't blame them for feeling that way," Sam said, knowing what his blood brother was thinking. "They're worried about their businesses, their homes, and their families. They've been through one attack by that bunch, and they don't want to have to go through another."

"I suppose." Matt shrugged. "And in the end it doesn't really matter where Shade gets hanged, as long as he winds up at the end of a rope."

"You can count on that," Flagg said.

The next day dawned bright and hot. The air was so clear that Willard Garth had no trouble seeing with the naked eye what was going on in the town from the top of the hill where he hunkered about half a mile away.

He used a spyglass anyway, just to give himself a better view. He was careful to stay in the shade of a scrubby pine tree, though. He didn't want the sun to reflect off the glass and maybe warn the townspeople that somebody was watching them.

"Have they started building a gallows?" Jeffries asked. He was sitting below the top of the hill with his back propped against another pine tree. His legs were stretched out in front of him, with the ankles crossed casually.

"No, no gallows," Garth replied. A frown creased his forehead. "I thought they would've started by now."

"Maybe they're just going to hang Joshua from a cottonwood limb, or something like that," Jeffries suggested.

"They ain't gonna hang him at all," Garth snapped. "We see anything like that fixin' to happen, and we'll be down there on top o' those damn townies before they know what's goin' on."

They had been unsuccessful at finding anyone else they could force to go into the settlement and spy for them. Garth had made the same mistake Shade had made before him—he had gotten rid of prisoners when they might have still been of some use to him.

But brooding over that misjudgment wouldn't do any good. All they could do now was wait to see what happened . . . and hope that they got a chance to free Shade before it was too late.

The rest of the men, except for Gonzalez, had gathered at the bottom of the hill to wait for Garth's orders. They were playing cards, checking over their guns, or just sitting on rocks and logs.

Gonzalez had ridden off a short time earlier to check on some dust he had seen rising in the distance to the northeast. Garth had agreed when Gonzalez told him he wanted to go have a look.

Garth was still peering through the spyglass when Jeffries suddenly muttered, "What the hell?" A commotion started down the hill among the other men.

Garth moved back so that he would be below the level of the hilltop before he stood up and turned to see what was going on. Up a draw that led to the bottom of the hill, a covered wagon trundled along. Gonzalez rode beside the wagon, his gun out and covering the man at the reins.

A grin creased Garth's rugged face. A woman with a baby in her arms sat beside the driver of the wagon.

Gonzalez had found them another spy, a man who would be willing to do anything they asked in an effort to save the lives of his wife and child.

Of course, in the end, it wouldn't do the poor bastard a damned bit of good . . . but he didn't have to know that just yet.

Jeffries had gotten to his feet, too. "That Mexican's got a nose for trouble," he said with a grin of his own.

"Yeah, and now we got somebody to go into Arrowhead and find out what's goin' on down there," Garth agreed. The two outlaws strode down the hill to join the others.

The wagon had come to a stop by the time they got there. The outlaws crowded around it, leering at the young woman on the seat, who was quite pretty and had blond curls peeping out from under her sunbonnet.

She probably would have been even prettier had she not been so pale and frightened-looking.

"Look what I found, Garth," Gonzalez crowed with a

big grin on his face. "These pilgrims were bound for Arrowhead. Gonna make a fresh start for themselves, *sí!*"

Garth studied the face of the young sodbuster, who was as scared as his wife but also had anger lurking in his eyes.

"Forget about tryin' anything funny, mister," Garth warned him. "You wouldn't have a chance, and then there's no tellin' what might happen to that wife and young'un o' yours."

"What do you want?" the man asked tightly. "We don't have any money, if that's what you're after. It took all we had to outfit for the trip West. But if there's anything in the wagon you want, it's yours if you'll just let us go."

"You'll be goin', all right," Garth told him. "Right on to Arrowhead, in fact. But you'll be goin' alone, and on one of our horses, not in this wagon."

"Why shouldn't he take the wagon?" Gonzalez asked. "As long as we keep the señora and the *niño* here, he got to come back."

"People might notice a fella drivin' into town in a wagon and then leavin' a little while later," Garth said. "But the town's crowded today. They won't pay no attention to a man on horseback who wanders in for a while and then wanders back out again."

Jeffries nodded. "That's a good point. I think you're getting smarter, Willard."

Garth felt like backhanding the smug son of a bitch, but he controlled the impulse. Instead, he reached up, grabbed the pilgrim by the shirt, and jerked him off the wagon seat. The woman screamed as Garth flung the man on the ground.

Garth pulled his gun, pointed it in the man's face, and eared back the hammer. "You listen to me, and listen close," he said. "I'm gonna tell you what to do, and if you do it, you and your family will be all right."

Knowing smiles passed among several of the outlaws. They were well aware that Garth was lying to the young man, and were looking forward to everything that would happen later on, when they were through with the poor bastard.

The man didn't seem to notice, though. He just nodded and said, "A-all right. Just tell me what you want, and I'll do it. You don't have to hurt anybody."

Garth nodded, lowered the hammer on the revolver, and slid it back into leather.

"Here's what we need you to find out," he said.

Chapter 15

"Lot of people in town today," Matt commented as he and Sam stood on the porch in front of the sheriff's office, their Winchesters canted over their shoulders.

"You know how it is in these frontier settlements," Sam said. "Anything that breaks the monotony is a big deal. The trial of the most notorious outlaw in the territory is bound to attract a great deal of attention."

"And the hangin' will attract even more, wherever they do it. Everybody in the territory wants to see Joshua Shade get what's comin' to him."

Sam knew that was true. Public hangings were like holidays in most frontier towns. People would come from miles around. Kids would run around and play, shouting and laughing. If Arrowhead had a band, it would probably play a few rousing patriotic songs. There might even be a speech or two before the main event.

Sam had read stories in Eastern newspapers calling such hoopla over a man's execution barbaric. What those soft-handed Easterners failed to understand was that a hanging was a reminder, however fleeting, that such a thing as law and order actually existed. In a land where swift, brutal death could strike without warning—from outlaws, from Indians, from nature itself—it did folks some good to see that every now and then, justice was served . . . even if it was a harsh, unforgiving justice.

What else could people expect in a harsh, unforgiving land?

Sam didn't feel any sympathy for Joshua Shade. The man was a vicious lunatic, and Sam reserved his sympathy for all the people Shade and his gang had hurt along the way.

Now that the feeling had spread through the town that it would be better if Shade *wasn't* hanged here, the worry that a lynch mob might try to take him out of the jail had eased. Matt and Sam didn't have to stay barricaded behind the building's thick walls around the clock except for when Flagg brought in their meals.

Flagg came up to the blood brothers and gave them a friendly nod. "Been down at the town hall makin' sure there'll be enough chairs for everybody. Of course, there won't be, the way folks'll pack in there. But at least there'll be places for the judge and the lawyers and the defendant to sit."

"You actually found a lawyer to represent Shade?" Matt asked.

"Yeah, old Colonel Wilmont said he'd do it. I don't know how he intends to defend a varmint like Shade, but that's his problem." Flagg thumbed back his hat. "My problem is I need somebody to ride out and meet the judge to make sure he gets into town all right. I got to worryin' that Shade's bunch might try to stop him."

"That would just postpone the trial," Sam pointed out. "It wouldn't really change anything."

"Yeah, but who knows how an outlaw thinks?"

"You want us to take care of that chore?" Matt asked.

"I was thinkin' you might," Flagg admitted. "Randy and me and my other deputy can hold down the fort here. I got half a dozen other volunteers who'd be glad to pitch in if I needed 'em, too. I don't reckon we're gonna have any trouble here, though. Stan Hightower's passed the word to all the other ranchers in the area to let the trial go on as planned, and Mayor Wiley's done the same thing here in town. We may have a few hombres gettin' drunk to celebrate what's gonna happen to Shade, but I reckon that'll be about all."

Matt lowered his rifle so that the barrel smacked into the palm of his left hand. "All right," he said. "After the last few days, it'll feel good to get out and move around some, won't it, Sam?"

"I'm sure our horses will appreciate the opportunity to stretch their legs," Sam agreed.

Flagg told them which trail the judge would be coming in on. They headed for the livery stable and saddled up their horses. Since they didn't know exactly how far out of town they would have to ride to meet the judge, they filled their canteens and took some biscuits left over from breakfast to tide them over in the middle of the day if necessary.

The horses were skittish and high-spirited from being cooped up, as Sam had predicted. He and Matt felt pretty much the same way. As soon as they were well clear of town, they put the animals into a hard gallop to ease some of that tension.

After half a mile, the blood brothers reined their mounts back to a slower pace. Matt grinned over at Sam and said, "I don't know about you, but I feel a mite better."

Sam returned the grin. "So do I. I'll feel even better, though, when this is all over."

"We headin' on out to California, like we talked about?"

"I suppose so. It's been a while since we were there."

"Lots of pretty girls in California," Matt said. "I'm not sure any of 'em are any prettier than Miss Amelia, though."

"I haven't even *seen* Amelia in almost a week," Sam pointed out. "We've been too busy guarding Shade."

"Well, there's a good reason to pay a visit to the Ten Grand tonight, don't you think?"

"We'll see," Sam said with a shrug.

They were headed south by southwest, following the main trail from Arrowhead to Tucson. The judge would be traveling by buggy, Flagg had told them, so they were on the lookout for such a vehicle as the mountains fell into the distance behind them and they rode through rolling hills dotted with scrub brush and sparsely grassed.

Around mid-morning, they spotted some dust rising in the distance ahead of them. "You reckon that's him?" Matt asked. "Whoever it is, looks like they're movin' along at a good clip."

"Could be," Sam replied. He was about to say something else, but then both young men reined sharply to a halt as they heard faint popping sounds.

"Gunshots!" Matt said.

"I'm afraid you're right," Sam said. He dug his heels into his horse's flanks and sent the animal leaping ahead again. Matt was right beside him.

The dust came closer, and so did the gunshots. As Matt and Sam leaned forward in their saddles, they spotted a buggy bouncing and careening along the trail toward them, being drawn by a pair of black horses.

About fifty yards behind the buggy and rapidly closing the gap were four men on horseback. Smoke plumed from the guns in their hands as they fired after the fleeing vehicle.

"That must be the judge!" Sam called over to Matt above the rolling drum of hoofbeats.

"And I'll bet those are some of Shade's men after him!" Matt replied.

They shucked their Winchesters as they raced closer. Splitting up, Matt galloped down the left side of the road, Sam the right. As soon as they had swung out far enough so that they could fire past the buggy without any danger of hitting its occupant, they brought the rifles to their shoulders and opened up.

The pursuers tried to peel off from the chase, but they were too late. One man went backward out of his saddle as if punched by a giant hand as a slug from Matt's rifle slammed into his chest. Another slewed around under the impact of one of Sam's slugs, but he managed to stay mounted. The other two kept coming, firing frenziedly.

Matt and Sam flashed past the buggy, which hadn't slowed down. They caught glimpses of the man at the reins, who wore a black suit and hat and had a jutting gray beard.

Then all their attention was on the two men still trying to kill them. Guiding their horses with their knees, they angled toward the middle of the trail again. Bullets whipped past their heads.

One of the gunmen suddenly rose in his stirrups and bent over at the middle, hunched against the burning pain of a bullet in his guts. He fell sideways. His right foot hung in the stirrup, and even after he slammed into the ground, the running horse continued to drag him.

The last of the would-be killers wheeled his horse around and tried to flee, giving up the fight. The turn was too sharp, though, and the horse lost its footing. With a shrill whinny of fright, the horse fell and rolled, and both man and animal disappeared in the cloud of dust that was kicked up by the fall.

Matt and Sam slowed their mounts and approached cautiously. As the dust settled, they saw the horse that had fallen struggle upright. The animal appeared to be a little shaken up but not seriously hurt.

The same couldn't be said of its former rider, who'd had a couple thousand pounds of horse roll over on him.

"He's gotta be busted to pieces inside," Matt said. "We'd better check on the other varmints first."

"Yeah, one of them got away," Sam said.

"No, he didn't." Matt pointed, and Sam saw that the wounded man had ridden only a couple of hundred yards before finally toppling out of the saddle. He now lay motionless next to the trail while his horse cropped grass nearby.

It didn't take long to confirm that three of the men were dead. The only one still alive was the unlucky gent whose horse had rolled over on him . . . and he probably wouldn't be among the living for very long, Sam saw as he dismounted and knelt beside the man.

Crimson worms of blood had crawled from the man's nose and mouth, and the grotesque, misshapen look of his body testified to how many bones were broken. His internal organs were probably crushed, too.

But somehow he managed to open his eyes, gaze imploringly up at Sam, and gasp, "H-help me!"

"I'm sorry, but there's nothing I can do for you," Sam said.

"I . . . I'm dyin'!"

"More than likely," Matt said from horseback. "But if you want to blame somebody, blame the son of a bitch who got you into this mess—Joshua Shade."

The injured man blinked. "Sh-Shade?" he husked.

Sam frowned and leaned forward. "Aren't you part of Shade's gang? Weren't you trying to stop the judge from reaching Arrowhead?"

"Didn't know he was . . . a judge . . . and I heard of Shade . . . but never met him. My pards and I . . . we thought the old fella looked like . . . like he might have money . . . we figured to rob him . . ."

Sam's frown deepened as he studied the dying man's face. This hombre wasn't much more than twenty years old, if that. The other three had been young, too. And the ragged trail clothes they wore made them look more like down-on-their-luck cowboys than hardened desperadoes.

"Matt, I don't think they're part of Shade's bunch," Sam said as he glanced up at his blood brother. "This was just a holdup we came along and interrupted."

The young man struggled to say, "We never meant to . . . hurt anybody . . . just tryin' to . . . scare the old man and make him stop . . ."

"Well, what do you know about that?" Matt said. "Just some would-be owlhoots with the bad luck to pick the judge as their first victim."

"*If* that was the judge in the buggy," Sam said.

Matt nodded toward the trail. "We can ask him. Here he comes."

Sam turned to look, and saw the buggy rolling toward them. His attention was drawn back to the man beside him by a gasped plea.

"W-water! Can I have . . . some water?"

"Sure," Sam said. It wouldn't do any good, but at this point, it wouldn't hurt anything either. He straightened and stepped over to his horse to untie the canteen from the saddle horn.

"Don't bother," Matt said.

"It won't hurt anything to give him a drink—" Sam began.

"No, I mean, don't bother. It's too late."

Sam looked again and saw the injured man's eyes glazing over in death. He shrugged and left the canteen where it was.

A moment later the buggy rolled to a stop at the edge of the trail. The distinguished-looking gent at the reins asked in a deep voice, "Are all the brigands dead?"

"Yes, sir, they are," Sam replied. "Would you be the judge who's going to Arrowhead to preside over the trial of Joshua Shade?"

"I am. Judge Julius Stanfield, at your service, young man. I'm very fortunate that you and your friend came along just as those highwaymen jumped me."

"Nothin' lucky about it, Your Honor," Matt said as he thumbed back his hat. "The sheriff in Arrowhead sent us out to meet you and escort you to the settlement. My name's Matt Bodine. This other fella is Sam Two Wolves."

Judge Stanfield's rather bushy eyebrows rose in surprise. "Bodine and Two Wolves, eh?" he said. "I've heard of you. Always wondered if you two young hellions might appear before me in court someday."

"Not us, Judge," Sam said.

"We're peaceable men," Matt added dryly.

"Hmmph. Yes, I can see that," Stanfield said. "Again, my thanks." He pointed a gnarled finger at the dead hombre. "Did that man and his companions have any connection to Joshua Shade?"

"That's what we figured at first, too," Sam said. "But he claimed they were just trying to rob you, and since he knew he was dying, I don't see what reason he would have had to lie about it."

"Indeed. What are we going to do with the bodies?"

"Round up their horses and tie them over the saddles so we can take them back to Arrowhead, I reckon," Matt said. "Either that or leave them for the buzzards and the wolves."

"I think not," Stanfield said. "Even miscreants such as these deserve proper burials."

"Yeah. Let's get busy, Sam."

Within ten minutes, they had the four dead men strapped onto their saddles. Matt and Sam each led two of the horses with their grisly burdens as they followed the buggy toward Arrowhead.

"Miscreants," Matt said under his breath. "You and the judge ought to get along fine, Sam. You talk the same language."

"That of well-educated men, you mean?" Sam asked.

"No, I figure His Honor there savvies Cheyenne, too." Matt chuckled. "Of course I meant he went to college, too."

"You're not as uneducated as you like to make out, Bodine."

"Maybe not, but you'd never catch me at some faculty tea party neither."

"Not that you'd ever be invited to such a gathering."

"Thank the Good Lord for that."

They continued bantering as they rode along, but that didn't keep them from watching the landscape around them with keen, alert eyes. They weren't out of danger yet, and they knew it.

In fact, the threat of Joshua Shade still hung over Arizona Territory, and it would continue to do so . . .

Until Shade himself dangled at the end of a hang-rope.

Chapter 16

It was just about the noon hour when Matt and Sam rode back into Arrowhead behind Judge Stanfield's buggy. Matt eased his horse up alongside the vehicle and pointed out the squat, stone jail.

"That's where Shade is," he said.

"I'll see Shade soon enough," Stanfield said. "Where's the courthouse?"

"Well, there's not one," Sam said from the other side of the buggy. "Sheriff Flagg was figuring that you'd hold court in the town hall, which is right down yonder."

He pointed out that building.

"All right, let's go have a look," Stanfield said. "I'll see if it's suitable."

As they drew up in front of the town hall, the commotion that was growing in the street because of the judge's arrival—and the dead men on the horses being led by Matt and Sam—brought Flagg hurrying from the jail.

"Howdy, Judge," he said as Stanfield was looping the reins around the buggy's brake lever. "I'm Sheriff Cyrus Flagg. I don't think we've met."

"No, I've only recently been assigned to this circuit," Stanfield said. He climbed down from the vehicle and shook hands with the sheriff. "Let's have a look inside, shall we?"

Flagg hung back as Stanfield strode on into the building. He waved a pudgy hand at the corpses and asked Matt and Sam in a low voice, "What the hell happened? Are those some o' Shade's men?"

"Nope," Matt replied. "Just some young saddle tramps who decided to turn owlhoot."

"It was an unfortunate decision," Sam added. "For them."

"They tried to hold up the judge just as you boys came along and met him?" Flagg guessed.

"That's right."

Flagg shook his head. "Trouble's like a bunch o' rocks rollin' downhill. Once it starts, it just keeps pickin' up steam."

He went on into the town hall after Judge Stanfield, and Matt and Sam took the bodies to Cassius Doolittle's undertaking parlor. The undertaker, a round-faced man with thinning brown hair and a jolly smile, said, "My business has sure increased since you fellas hit town."

"It's not our doing," Matt said. "Well, I guess in a way it is . . . but we haven't gone looking for any of this trouble."

"Actually, we did," Sam said. "Remember how we stuck our heads out of those windows in the hotel when we heard something odd on the roof?"

"Well, yeah, but it's a good thing we did."

"No doubt about that," Doolittle agreed. "The citizens of Arrowhead are lucky to have you two around right now."

They stabled their horses and returned to the town hall just as Flagg and Judge Stanfield were emerging from the building. Stanfield declared that the hall would be satisfactory for the trial.

"We'll begin the proceedings at one o'clock," he said. "Is that all right with you, Sheriff?"

"Whenever you want to commence tryin' that skunk is fine with me, Your Honor," Flagg replied. "The sooner he's convicted and out of my jail, the better."

Stanfield frowned. "There's such a thing as the presumption of innocence in this country, you know."

"Well, no offense, Your Honor, but if you'd been here the night Shade and his bunch raided the town and saw all the suffering they caused, you wouldn't presume anything except that he's a low-down rattlesnake in human form."

Stanfield grunted, but didn't say anything else except, "I'd also like to clean up a bit, if someone will point me toward the hotel."

"Right down here, Your Honor," Sam said. "Matt and I will escort you."

"Why would I need an escort here in town? Surely I'm in no danger here."

"You wouldn't think so," Flagg said, "but there are a heap of folks in town today because word's got around about the trial. Some of 'em are strangers to me, and we can't be sure that none of 'em are part of Shade's gang."

A worried look crossed Stanfield's face, as if he hadn't considered that possibility. He nodded and said, "Very well. In that case, I'd be glad for you and Mr. Bodine to accompany me, Mr. Two Wolves."

They started toward the hotel, with Matt and Sam being as watchful here on the main street of Arrowhead as they had been out on the trail. In a situation this volatile, there was no telling when or where danger could strike, so the blood brothers wanted to be ready in case it did.

Both of them noticed the weary-looking man on horseback plodding slowly down the street, but he wasn't even armed so they didn't pay that much attention to him. From the looks of him, he was no threat at all.

Ike Winslow saw the two men striding along the street, flanking a distinguished-looking gent with a beard, and wondered if they were Matt Bodine and Sam Two Wolves. The outlaw called Garth had told him about Bodine and Two Wolves. They were gunfighters who had aligned themselves with the townspeople and were helping to bring Joshua Shade to justice.

From what Ike had seen of Shade's gang, the man probably deserved hanging. Anyone who could lead such a group of brutal hardcases had to be even worse himself.

A shudder went through Ike as he thought about his wife Maggie and son Caleb being in the hands of those varmints right this minute. All he could do to help them was follow the orders Garth had given him and hope to heaven that they weren't being mistreated.

Ike had never felt more helpless in his life than when that bandit Gonzalez had charged up out of an arroyo and stuck a gun in his face. He hadn't even had time to reach for the old single-shot rifle behind the wagon seat. Gonzalez had ordered Maggie to take it out and cast it aside, then forced Ike to drive at gunpoint toward the place where all the other outlaws were gathered.

His fear had grown even stronger as he saw those rough, ruthless men crowding in around the wagon and leering at Maggie. Working on the farm they had lost back in Ohio had toughened Ike's muscles, but even so, he knew he was no match for even one of those men, let alone twenty-five or thirty of them. They could do whatever they wanted to and he couldn't stop them.

They hadn't molested Maggie while he was still there, however, and so he clung to a shred of hope that they would leave her alone if he did as he was told. They had given him a horse, told him to ride on into Arrowhead as if he were just a saddle tramp.

Then, when he had found out what the situation was with their boss, Joshua Shade, he was to drift out of town again, making sure that no one noticed him leaving. Garth had promised that as soon as he returned, they would let him and Maggie and Caleb go on their way.

Ike didn't really believe him, but he had to hope that Garth was telling the truth.

What else could he do?

If things were similar here to the way they were back in Ohio, the best place in town to hear all the gossip would be one of the saloons. He reined the horse to a halt in front of the biggest one he saw, a place called the Ten Grand. With his pulse pounding in his head, he dismounted, looped the reins around the hitch rail, and went inside.

The saloon was crowded, with men lining the bar and occupying most of the tables. Young women with painted faces and gaudy, low-cut dresses circulated

among them, delivering drinks and bawdy comments.
Laughter and loud conversation filled the room.

Ike paused just inside the batwings and took a deep
breath of the boozy air that was also scented with saw-
dust, tobacco, and human sweat. He steeled himself
and made his way to the bar, finding a place among
the men crowded there.

He ordered a beer from the jolly-looking bartender
who greeted him. "Town's boomin' today, looks like,"
he said as the bartender placed a foaming mug in
front of him.

"Well, of course it is," the man replied with a grin.
"Joshua Shade's going on trial today. This is the biggest
day in Arrowhead's history, my friend."

"Joshua Shade?"

The bartender's grin disappeared and was replaced
with a frown. "You never heard of Joshua Shade? He's
the worst outlaw in these parts. The worst in the whole
territory."

Ike realized he might have made a mistake by pretending ignorance of Shade. He tried to correct it by
saying, "I've, uh, been up in Colorado for a while. Just
rode down this way to look for work."

The bartender's forehead smoothed as he nodded.
"In that case, I reckon it was just luck that brought
you here on the big day, friend. Stick around for the
festivities."

"Festivities? Is this fella Shade gonna be hanged
after the trial?"

Garth and the other outlaws had known that Shade
was going to be put on trial, and the crowds gathering
in town made them suspect that today was the day. Ike
had picked up that much from listening to them talk
with each other. They had wanted Ike to confirm that,

though, along with finding out when the hanging that was bound to follow the trial would take place.

"Well, you're assuming that he's gonna be found guilty." The bartender chuckled. "Which, of course, he is. But I don't think the hangin's gonna be here. There's talk that Shade will be taken somewhere else for the sentence to be carried out. But we'll be celebrating anyway, let me tell you, just knowing that he's gonna get what's comin' to him."

That was news to Ike, so it would be to Garth and the other outlaws, too. And probably welcome news, because it would mean they would have more time and opportunity to rescue Shade before his neck was stretched. Ike was certain that was what they planned to do, even though they hadn't said as much while he was around.

To be sure what was going to happen, he would have to stay in town longer. If he went back now, he couldn't tell the outlaws anything that they didn't already suspect. So even though he hated the idea of leaving Maggie and Caleb alone with those bastards any longer than he had to, he didn't have much choice.

"Anything else I can do for you?" the bartender asked. He had other customers along the hardwood demanding attention.

Ike shook his head and lifted his mug of beer. "No, thanks, I'm fine," he said.

It was probably the biggest lie he had ever told in his life.

Chapter 17

Matt and Sam came into the sheriff's office and nodded to Randy Johnson, who had been left in charge at the jail.

"We're supposed to take Shade over to the town hall for the trial," Matt said.

Johnson nodded as he stood and picked up the shotgun that lay on the desk in front of him. "We'll go along with you," he said, referring to himself and the other two guards who were posted just outside the building.

Matt got the keys from the nail on the wall, unlocked the cell block door, and then swung the door open. Shade was at it again, ranting and raving inside the cell.

His voice was hoarse and not as strong as it had been when he was first locked up. He had slept some during his incarceration, but not much. Nor had he eaten all that well. He had to be getting a little weaker by now.

That was all right, Matt thought. Shade was less likely to cause trouble that way.

With their rifles at the ready, Matt and Sam went into the corridor between the cells. Johnson stood just outside the door with the shotgun in his hands.

Matt unlocked the door of Shade's cell and stepped back quickly, leveling the Winchester at the door. "Come on out of there, Shade," he called.

Shade kept talking. He wasn't praying now. Instead what came out of his mouth was the vilest profanity as he heaped curses on the whole town and everyone in it. Matt reached out with the rifle and used its barrel to shove the door open.

"Come on out," he said again, "or we'll have to come in and get you. And we won't be gentle about it."

Shade spewed more obscenities. He seemed to have forgotten all about his claims of being a man of God. If he ever really had been, those days were far behind him now.

He came toward the door, raising his arms so that his clawlike hands were extended toward Matt and Sam, who kept their rifles trained on him. Shade's long hair was tangled and matted, as if he had been running his fingers through it constantly all the time he had been locked up in there. His eyes seemed to be sunken even deeper in their sockets, and they blazed with an unholy fire.

Shade's steps were unsteady as he emerged from the cell. Matt didn't trust that the outlaw was really as weak and shaky as he appeared to be, though. Shade could be pretending, hoping to catch them off guard.

"Randy," he said to Johnson, "get those shackles and leg irons Sheriff Flagg has in the cabinet."

At the mention of the restraints, Shade's head jerked up. He threw himself at Matt with a speed and ferocity that he hadn't seemed capable of a second earlier.

The blood brothers were expecting that, though. In fact, Matt had spoken in the hope of goading Shade into revealing his true colors.

Before Shade could reach Matt, the barrel of Sam's rifle came down on his head with a solid thud. Shade stumbled and went to his knees. Matt took a quick step to the side and planted a booted foot in the middle of Shade's back, driving him facedown onto the stone floor.

He kept that foot there while he and Sam each grabbed one of Shade's arms and forced them over his head. Johnson rushed in and snapped the shackles into place around Shade's wrists. Once those heavy cuffs with their six-inch length of chain between them were secured, Johnson took the pair of leg irons that was draped over his shoulder and fastened them around Shade's ankles.

The blow to the head had stunned Shade enough so that he was quiet while the restraints were being put on him. His senses came back to him, though, and he started cursing again as Matt and Sam each grasped an arm and lifted him to his feet. The outlaw was slender enough so that the blood brothers were able to handle him without much trouble.

"You reckon we'd better gag him before we take him out?" Matt asked Sam.

"It might be a good idea," Sam said. "Otherwise, the ladies out there are going to hear things that they don't have any business hearing."

They took off their bandannas. Matt wadded his into a ball and shoved it into Shade's mouth, jerking his hand back as the outlaw tried to bite his fingers. Sam used his bandanna to tie Matt's into place.

"We'll have to buy new ones," Matt commented. "I don't want that bandanna back after it's been in the mouth of a hydrophobia skunk like Shade."

"Ask over at the general store," Johnson suggested.

"I'll bet the owner would replace 'em free of charge after everything you fellas have done to help the town."

With Shade gagged, shackled, and in leg irons, Matt and Sam led him out of the jail. When they reached the street, Shade quit cooperating, and they had to drag him toward the town hall, where his trial would take place. Johnson and the other deputies surrounded them, shotguns held at the ready.

A hush fell over the crowd in the street as Matt, Sam, and the other men emerged from the jail with their prisoner. Folks stared wide-eyed at the notorious bandit leader, their expressions a mixture of curiosity, anger, and nervousness. Joshua Shade was probably the most hated man in the territory, as well as the most feared.

People stood aside to create a lane through which Matt and Sam dragged Shade. He grunted, but couldn't force any coherent words past the gag, and his struggles didn't avail him anything against the strong grip that the blood brothers had on him. They reached the town hall, forced him up the steps and inside the building.

The jury had already been agreed on by the lawyers, and the twelve men were seated in a row of chairs against the wall. All the other chairs were full already except for one at a table up front.

Matt and Sam recognized the elderly, white-bearded man sitting at the table as Colonel J.B. Wilmont, who was going to handle Shade's defense. At another table sat Mayor Wiley and the town prosecutor, a slender, fair-haired man named Finch.

Sheriff Flagg was waiting beside the empty chair at the defense table. He nodded to Matt and Sam as they manhandled Shade up to the table.

"No need to sit him down yet," the sheriff told them. "Just hang on to him for a minute, if you would."

Flagg turned and shouted over the talking that filled the room, "Everybody hush up! All rise for the Honorable Julius Stanfield!"

As the spectators came to their feet, Stanfield emerged from a door in the back of the room and walked to the table that would serve as his bench. He carried his gavel with him. He took off his hat and placed it on the table, then banged the gavel.

"Be seated. This court will come to order."

Matt and Sam each put a hand on Shade's shoulder and forced him down into the empty chair. As soon as they let go of him, though, he bolted up again, grunting and thrashing and staring in pop-eyed hate toward the judge.

Stanfield banged the gavel down on the table several times and said, "Sheriff, take whatever steps are necessary to restrain the prisoner so that we can have order and decorum in this court!"

"Yes, Your Honor." Flagg turned to Johnson. "Randy, go get a rope!"

"No need." The voice came from Stan Hightower, who was in the front row of the spectators. "There's a lariat on my saddle, and my horse is right outside. I'll fetch it."

Flagg nodded for the rancher to go ahead. Hightower left the town hall, and returned a moment later with a coiled reata of braided horsehair. He handed it to Flagg, who wrapped the rope around Joshua Shade as Matt and Sam forced him back down into the chair.

When that was done, Judge Stanfield frowned at Shade and declared, "I dislike being forced to these measures, sir. It's undignified, and I don't like such things in my courtroom. But you've forced us to this point." He whacked the gavel on the table again. "Counsel is ready to proceed?"

Finch got to his feet. "The prosecution is ready, Your Honor."

Wearily, Colonel Wilmont rose. He had flinched away from Shade as the prisoner was being secured, and it was obvious he didn't like the job he had been handed. Matt would have been willing to bet that Wilmont's belief in and devotion to the legal system was the only reason he had let himself be dragged into representing Shade.

"Counsel for the defense is ready, Your Honor," Wilmont said.

Stanfield nodded. "I'll listen to opening statements, if either side cares to make one. Mr. Finch?"

"Yes, Your Honor." Finch launched into a speech that lasted several minutes, all of it devoted to declaring what a vicious, bloody-handed owlhoot Joshua Shade was. He wasn't saying anything that everyone in the courtroom didn't already know, but that didn't stop him from saying it anyway.

When Finch was done, Colonel Wilmont got up again and said, "The defense has no opening statement, Your Honor."

Stanfield nodded. "Very well. Mr. Finch, call your first witness."

"I call Sheriff Cyrus Flagg, Your Honor."

Flagg took the witness stand—which was a ladder-back chair at the end of the table where Judge Stanfield sat—and told what he knew about the events of the night when Shade and his gang had raided Arrowhead. Colonel Wilmont had no questions for him.

Following Flagg's testimony, Finch called half a dozen other leading citizens, all of whom had witnessed the atrocities committed by Shade's men. Even though all the spectators knew what had happened, they listened in rapt attention as that violent night was recreated in the words of the witnesses.

It was all a little boring to Matt, who had never been long on patience to start with. Finally, Finch called Matt himself to the stand to testify about how he and Sam had discovered one of Shade's men on the hotel roof after the outlaw had killed Charlie Cornwell, the lookout.

"You and Mr. Two Wolves were still on the roof of the hotel when the rest of the bandits attacked the town?" Finch asked.

Matt nodded, feeling a little ill at ease with the eyes of everyone in the room on him. "Yes, sir, that's right."

"In your own words, tell us about the battle that followed."

Matt wondered briefly whose words he would use, if not his own, but he didn't voice that thought. Instead, he did as Finch asked and described the parts he and Sam had played in the defense of the settlement.

After Finch thanked Matt and Wilmont said he had no questions for the witness, Stanfield told Matt to step down. Finch said, "I could spent the rest of the day and all day tomorrow calling witnesses who would tell the same story, Your Honor, and I see no point in that. The prosecution rests, having proven its case."

"That will be up to the jury to decide, Counsel," Stanfield said with a frown.

This was a waste of time, Matt thought. Everybody knew Shade was guilty. Everybody knew he deserved to be hanged. They were just going through the motions.

Stanfield was determined to do everything legal and proper, though. The judge turned to Wilmont and said, "Colonel, you may call your first witness."

Shaking his head with its mane of white hair, Wilmont rose to his feet and said, "The defense has no witnesses, Your Honor."

Stanfield leaned forward sharply, his frown deepening. "Colonel, as an attorney, I'm sure you need no reminder that your client has a right to the best possible defense you can give him, regardless of the circumstances or your own personal feelings about the case. You have asked no questions of the prosecution's witnesses, and now you say you intend to call no witnesses of your own?"

"That is correct, Your Honor." Wilmont stood straight, his shoulders square. "I cannot present witnesses to call the facts of the case into question, because they are so clear-cut and because the testimony of the prosecution's witnesses cannot be refuted. Therefore, our defense will consist solely of my closing statement."

"Your client won't even testify on his own behalf?"

Wilmont shook his head. "I deem it inadvisable, Your Honor, considering the inflammatory statements he's been known to make. I fear he would simply prejudice his own case that much more."

"Very well," Stanfield said, although it was clear that he didn't like this unorthodox course of action from the defense. "Does the defense rest?"

"It does, Your Honor."

Stanfield looked at Finch. "I'll hear closing statements."

There wasn't much Finch could say other than what had already been said. He repeated what a varmint

Joshua Shade was, although in more high-flown language, and sat down. Wilmont rose again.

The elderly lawyer clasped his hands behind his back and gazed at the jury. "Gentlemen, take a good look at my client. He's wearing shackles and leg irons, and he's been gagged because otherwise he would have subjected this courtroom to a stream of profanity and obscenity and threats the likes of which none of us need to hear. We all know what he's done, the deaths he's been responsible for, the deaths he has carried out with his own hands, the suffering he has inflicted on the citizens of this territory. I deny none of that. But I would have you ask yourselves a question . . . Why? Why has Joshua Shade done these things?"

One of the spectators in the back of the room called out, "Because he's loco!"

Laughter burst from the crowd.

Wilmont turned as Stanfield hammered for order. "That is exactly correct!" Wilmont said, raising his voice to be heard over the clamor. "He's as crazy as an animal with a belly full of locoweed! You wouldn't hold an animal responsible for its actions if that happened! Neither should you hold Joshua Shade responsible for his. He should be locked up someplace where he can't hurt anyone else, not executed!"

Angry shouts of disagreement came from the crowd, and Stanfield had to bang the gavel for several minutes before order was restored. When it was, Wilmont said, "That's all I have to say, Your Honor," and sat down.

"Well, that's an . . . unusual . . . defense, Counselor," Stanfield said, "but if you feel it's the best one you have—"

"It's the only one we have, Your Honor."

"Very well." Stanfield turned to the members of the

jury. "You can now begin your deliberations, and continue them until you have reached a true verdict."

The men glanced at each other for a second. Then the one at the end of the row closest to the judge's bench stood up. "I reckon we're done, Your Honor."

Stanfield sighed, clearly not surprised. "In that case, what say you?"

"We find the defendant guilty of murder, robbery, assorted banditry, and anything else you want to charge him with, Judge. Matter of fact, we find him guilty as hell!"

"A simple verdict of guilty will be entered into the record," Stanfield said. He turned back to the defense table. "Does the defendant have anything to say before I pass sentence on him?"

Shade struggled against his ropes as if he were trying to stand up, and frenzied grunts came from behind the gag.

"I don't suppose it matters now, does it?" Wilmont said with a sigh.

Flagg motioned for Matt and Sam to take the gag off of Shade. "Leave him tied in the chair, though," the sheriff warned.

Sam untied the bandanna around Shade's head. Matt pulled the gag out of the outlaw's mouth. Shade's chin lifted defiantly as he yelled, "The Lord will strike you down! He will visit plagues and abominations on this town and everyone in it! You'll all die screaming for mercy! Rivers of blood will run in the streets, and your women will cry over the broken bodies of their children!"

From there, the tirade descended into profanity again, until Flagg motioned for Matt to stick the gag back in Shade's mouth. Matt did so, shutting him up.

"That was an inspired defense, Counselor," Stanfield told Colonel Wilmont. "Unfortunately, the jury has reached its verdict, and now I shall pass sentence on the defendant. Normally, I would have him rise to hear this, but under the circumstances . . ." Stanfield cleared his throat. "It is the judgment of this court, the defendant Joshua Shade having been found guilty, that he shall be hanged by the neck until dead, and that this sentence shall be carried out immediately in this jurisdiction."

Mayor Wiley leaped to his feet. "But, Your Honor," he protested, "we don't *want* him to be hanged here!"

"Then you should have thought of that before you put on this trial," Stanfield snapped. "You tried him here, you can hang him." He lifted his gavel to signal that court was adjourned.

Before the gavel could fall, though, a new voice spoke up over the clamor, saying, "Just a moment, Judge. Could I have a word with you?"

The crowd parted, and a tall man in a dark suit strode forward. He was middle-aged, with a face tanned to the color of saddle leather and a nose like the beak of a hawk jutting out over a dark mustache that framed a wide mouth.

"Who in blazes are you?" Stanfield demanded.

The newcomer moved the lapel of his coat aside so that the badge pinned to his vest was visible. "Deputy United States Marshal Asa Thorpe," he said, introducing himself. "I've come for Joshua Shade."

Chapter 18

The courtroom exploded with noise in response to that dramatic announcement. Judge Stanfield had to hammer the gavel on the table for a full minute again before everybody settled down enough for him to make himself heard.

"What do you mean by that, Marshal?" he demanded.

Thorpe had stood there calmly during the excitement. Now he reached inside his coat and said, "I meant just what I said, Your Honor. I have here a court order signed by a federal judge placing Joshua Shade in my custody."

"You can't have him!" Stanfield snapped. "I've already pronounced sentence on him."

"I didn't make myself clear, Your Honor. I'm not here to interfere with these proceedings or to set aside the verdict reached by this court, with one exception." Thorpe strode forward and placed the document he had taken from his coat on the table in front of the judge. "The federal government wants Shade to be hanged at Yuma Prison."

Sam leaned over to Matt and muttered, "This is unusual."

Matt grunted. "What do you expect from the government?"

Stanfield leaned forward in his chair to study the paper Thorpe had placed in front of him. "What's the meaning of this? Why would the Justice Department do such a thing?"

Thorpe shrugged. "I have no idea, Your Honor. All I know is that I happened to be in Tucson after wrapping up another case, and I received a telegram from the chief marshal ordering me to accompany you here to Arrowhead and take charge of the prisoner if he was convicted. But when I went looking for you, I found that you'd already left, so I had to follow you instead."

"This is highly irregular . . ."

Thorpe stuck his thumbs in the pockets of his vest and said, "My guess is that Washington wants to have a hand in Shade's execution because he's stolen a couple of army payrolls. Those were federal crimes. They could have me take him in for a new trial in those cases, but I reckon they figure since he can only hang once, there's no point in going to that much trouble and expense. They'll let the Territory of Arizona take care of it . . . as long as they get some of the credit."

Stanfield tugged at his beard. "This document appears to be in order," he said with a frown. "And since it doesn't void the verdict of this jury, or affect anything except the place of execution . . ."

"We didn't want Shade hanged here anyway, Your Honor," Mayor Wiley put in.

Stanfield nodded. "Irregular or not, I suppose I have no choice but to honor this court order and place Joshua Shade in your custody, Marshal, to be taken to Yuma Prison and hanged at the earliest possible opportunity." The gavel came down with a sharp crack. "This court is adjourned!"

Sheriff Flagg turned to Matt and Sam and said, "Keep an eye on Shade. Me and the deputies'll clear the place out before we take him back to jail."

They didn't have to try very hard to do that. Many of the spectators were already pouring out of the town hall, headed for the saloons and a chance to rehash the day's events over a drink.

The news of Shade's conviction and the U.S. marshal's arrival spread rapidly. These were the biggest doings the town of Arrowhead had seen in a long time, maybe ever. By the time Matt and Sam left the town hall, once again dragging the shackled, gagged Joshua Shade between them, the street was crowded with excited citizens who wanted to see the notorious outlaw being taken back to jail.

Once again, Flagg and his deputies surrounded Matt, Sam, and Shade as the procession made its way along the street. But this time, they had the marshal with them, striding alongside with his right hand resting on the butt of the Colt holstered at his hip. Thorpe's cold-eyed gaze was enough to make most folks step aside.

Shade had stopped trying to talk. He hung limply in the grasp of the blood brothers as they hauled him along. They took him into the jail, and didn't remove the gag until they had him back in his cell with the shackles and leg irons off.

Even then, Shade didn't say anything. His expression had turned dull and lifeless, as if all the fight had finally gone out of him.

Maybe he was thinking about the hangrope that

was waiting for him, Matt mused as he slammed the cell door closed.

Once they were all in the sheriff's office, Flagg offered Thorpe a cup of coffee. The federal lawman smiled for the first time since his arrival in Arrowhead and nodded.

"Much obliged, Sheriff. That sounds good. Why don't you introduce your deputies to me?"

Flagg poured the coffee and carried out the introductions of Johnson and the other men, leaving out Matt and Sam. Thorpe nodded toward them and asked curiously, "What about these two hombres?"

"You said to introduce my deputies, and they ain't sworn in or nothin'. Reckon you'd have to call 'em volunteers. But their names are Matt Bodine and Sam Two Wolves."

Thorpe's eyebrows rose in surprise. "Bodine and Two Wolves, eh? I've heard of you. I'd bet there aren't very many lawmen west of the Mississippi who *haven't* heard of you."

"You make us sound like some sort of desperadoes, Marshal," Matt said.

Thorpe shook his head. "Not necessarily. But you have to admit, hell seems to have a way of breaking loose wherever you two happen to be."

"If not for these boys, I expect Shade and his bunch would've laid waste to our town," Flagg said.

"Really? I'd like to hear about that," Thorpe said as he perched a hip on a corner of the desk.

Matt and Sam weren't given to boasting about anything they had done, so Flagg explained how they had discovered Shade's gang was about to raid Arrowhead and had warned the town. When the sheriff was done, Thorpe nodded.

"Sounds like these folks owe you a debt of gratitude, all right," he said. "From everything I've heard about you, though, you boys like to drift. What are you doing still here?"

"After being partially responsible for Shade getting locked up, we wanted to see what was going to happen," Sam explained.

"And we didn't figure it'd hurt anything if we gave Sheriff Flagg a hand either," Matt added.

"Darn right it didn't hurt anything," Flagg chimed in. "It's been good havin' these two hombres around. Might not have been able to stop those lynch mobs without 'em."

Thorpe sipped his coffee. "Then I suppose the federal government owes you its gratitude, too," he said to Matt and Sam. "And a reward for capturing Shade, if you care to claim it."

Matt stiffened. "We're not bounty hunters. You can keep your damn blood money."

Anger sparked in Thorpe's eyes. "I never said you were bounty hunters. But if you've got a reward coming to you—"

"We're fine without it, Marshal," Sam said as he moved between Matt and Thorpe in an effort to defuse the sudden tension in the room. "All we really want is for justice to be done."

"It will be. You can count on that. Shade will hang just as soon as I can get him to Yuma."

Flagg scratched his beard. "I was wonderin' about that," he said. "How do you intend to get him there?"

"The railroad's well south of here. I'll need a wagon to transport him that far, and then we'll take the train the rest of the way."

"Reckon we can supply you with a good sturdy wagon. You'll need some men to go with you, though."

Thorpe shook his head. "I have my own shackles and leg irons for the prisoner. I can handle one man without any trouble."

"One man, sure," Flagg said, "but what about twenty-five or thirty?"

"Shade's gang?" Thorpe asked as a frown creased his forehead.

"That's right. They're still on the loose, and they're liable to come after him."

"How long has Shade been locked up here, almost a week?"

Flagg nodded. "That's right."

"And you haven't seen hide nor hair of his gang during that time, have you?"

"Well . . . no."

Thorpe put out a hand. "There you go. They've abandoned him. Someone else has taken over the leadership of the gang, and they've moved on to greener pastures. You know owlhoots have no loyalty to anything except their own best interests. The concept of honor among thieves is just a myth."

Matt and Sam weren't so sure about that. The glance they exchanged said as much.

Flagg tugged at his ear. "I dunno," he said slowly. "From everything I've heard, Shade's men would follow him right into hell. I can't see 'em just ridin' off and forgettin' about him."

"Then why haven't they tried to rescue him?"

Matt spoke up. "Because they know everybody in town has been waitin' for that very thing to happen? Even a bunch of outlaws have to be smart enough to know that they'd be ridin' into a real hornet's nest if they tried to bust him out of this jail."

"But if Shade's being taken all the way across Arizona Territory by only one man," Sam said, "they might see that as a perfect opportunity to rescue him."

Thorpe shook his head. "They're not going to be foolish enough to interfere with the federal government."

"They stole army payrolls, didn't they?" Sam pointed out. "They didn't seem too afraid of the federal government then."

Thorpe glared at them. "What are you suggesting that I do then?"

"Take some guards with you," Flagg said. "I'll bet you'd have half a dozen volunteers from around here at least."

Matt and Sam looked at each other again, and then Sam said, "And we'd ride along, too."

Without hesitation, Thorpe snapped, "Absolutely not. How would it look if a deputy United States marshal had to enlist the aid of a couple of notorious gunfighters to help him do his job?"

"Like he had enough sense to know when he was outnumbered?" Matt said.

Thorpe shook his head stubbornly. "No, I won't do it," he insisted. "I suppose it wouldn't hurt anything to take some other men with me . . . but not these two."

"I think you're makin' a mistake," Flagg said. "Bodine and Two Wolves are two o' the best fightin' men you'll ever see."

"And as I pointed out, men like them *attract* trouble. Shade's gang will be more likely to leave us alone if Bodine and Two Wolves don't come with us."

Matt opened his mouth to tell Thorpe that he was as loco as Colonel Wilmont had made Shade out to be.

But before he could get the angry words out of his mouth, Sam closed a hand around his arm and said, "Come on, Matt."

Matt turned to his blood brother in surprise. "But this stiff-necked star packer—"

"If that's the way Marshal Thorpe feels about the situation, then we'll just have to honor his decision," Sam said. "He's the law. It's up to him to handle things however he wants to."

Matt stared at Sam in disbelief. It wasn't like Sam to cave in like that to some damn fool.

But it was true that Thorpe was now the top dog around here when it came to the law. If the marshal wanted to, he could order Flagg to lock up the two of them until he had left Arrowhead with Joshua Shade. Matt didn't want that to happen.

"All right," he said in disgust. "Have it your way, Thorpe. Just don't look for any help from us if you find yourself facing Shade's whole gang."

"That's not going to happen," Thorpe said with confidence that bordered on arrogance. He turned back to Flagg. "But if you can find me some good men, Sheriff—men who *aren't* trigger-happy gunslingers— I'll interview them and deputize several of them to come with me."

Matt started for the doorway. "Come on, Sam," he said. "Let's get out of here before I say something I regret."

Sam followed his blood brother out of the jail. They hadn't gone very far down the street when Sam chuckled.

"What the hell's so funny?" Matt asked. "Not that damn fool lawman, that's for sure."

"Actually, I was thinking that Thorpe really doesn't know you very well."

"Of course he doesn't. I just met the loco hombre an hour ago!"

"No, I mean he can't have heard all that much about us, or he'd never think that Matt Bodine would go along with a bad idea so easily." Sam paused. "Or me either, for that matter."

Matt frowned. "You mean . . ."

"I mean that we're going to make sure Joshua Shade reaches Yuma so that the sentence of hanging can be carried out."

"Whether that varmint Thorpe likes it or not?"

"Exactly," Sam said. "Whether Marshal Thorpe likes it or not."

Chapter 19

Ike Winslow's heart pounded heavily in his chest as he approached the place where he had left the outlaws. Dusk hung over the landscape now. He had waited until it started to get dark before leaving Arrowhead, thinking that his departure might more easily escape notice that way.

Not that anyone had paid much attention to him anyway. He had drifted around the town for hours, nursing beers in several different saloons and talking to anybody who'd pass the time of day with him.

There had been no shortage of people who wanted to talk either. Everyone seemed excited about the trial, the verdict, and the sentence that had been handed down. More than one person had gone on at length about how that son of a bitch outlaw Joshua Shade was finally gonna get what he had coming to him.

Ike had no fondness for owlhoots, so it would have been just fine with him, too, if Shade wound up on the end of a rope . . . if not for the fact that Maggie's and Caleb's continued survival depended on Shade staying healthy.

Ike knew quite well that if anything happened to Shade, the gang would have no reason to keep his wife and son alive.

For that reason, he would do anything in his power to help them, even though in the back of his mind he had already realized that once Shade was free, the outlaws would have no further need of him and his family.

He would deal with that ominous prospect when he came to it, he told himself. For now, he had to concentrate on following orders.

Two shadowy forms suddenly materialized out of the twilight. "Hold it right there," one of them rasped. Ike saw guns pointed at him. "Is that you, pilgrim?"

Ike recognized the voice of the outlaw called Garth. "It's me," he said. "I found out what you wanted to know."

"That's good, pilgrim, mighty good," Garth said. "Get down off that horse and tell us all about it."

An unaccustomed surge of defiance that took him as much by surprise as it must have the outlaws prompted Ike to say, "I'm not telling you anything until I know that my wife and son are all right."

The other man stepped forward. Ike had already recognized the big sombrero, even in this dim light, so he wasn't surprised when he heard Gonzalez's sinister purr.

"Let me teach this foolish gringo a lesson about how he ought to talk to us, Garth," Gonzalez said. "I'll make him tell us everything he knows."

"Back off," Garth growled. "If you cut him up, he won't be any good to us anymore if we still need him. I've learned my lesson." He motioned with the gun in his hand. "Come on, Winslow. Your wife and kid are fine. I'll take you to them."

Ike dismounted then and followed Garth, leading his horse. Gonzalez fell in behind them, and Ike could hear the Mexican muttering in Spanish. Ike didn't speak the language, but he was willing to bet that whatever Gonzalez was saying, it wasn't anything good.

Garth led the way to a depression ringed by trees where the rest of the gang had gathered. Ike's wagon was parked there as well. His eyes searched desperately in the fading light for Maggie and Caleb, but he didn't see them.

"Where are they?" he asked, unable to keep the fear from making his voice tremble.

"In the wagon, pilgrim," Garth told him. "Nobody's bothered them. Here, gimme that horse and go take a look for yourself."

Ike handed over the reins and ran to the wagon. When he'd seen the vehicle, he'd hoped that Maggie and Caleb would be in there, but now he had to see them with his own eyes before he would believe it.

"Maggie!" he called when he was still twenty feet from the wagon. "Maggie!"

"Ike!" She scrambled from the wagon bed over the back of the driver's seat. Her fair hair shone under her bonnet, even in this bad light. "Oh, Ike!"

By the time he reached the vehicle, she had scrambled down to the ground. She threw herself into his arms, and he wrapped his arms around her and held her tightly, so tightly that it seemed nothing could ever pry them apart.

The leering drawl of the owlhoot called Jeffries managed to do that, though. "Well, ain't that touching?" He lounged next to the wagon with one shoulder leaned against the sideboards. He held his gun casually in his hand.

Ike stepped back and rested his hands on Maggie's shoulders. "Did they hurt you or Caleb?" he asked. "Did they lay a hand on you?"

She shook her head. Tears ran down her cheeks. "We're all right," she told him. "Caleb's sound asleep in the wagon. He's fine, Ike." She clutched him closer for a second. "Oh, when can we get out of here?"

"Maybe . . . maybe as soon as I tell them what they want to know."

From behind him, Garth said, "Be a good idea if you went ahead and did that, pilgrim."

Ike hated to let go of Maggie, so he kept his arm around her shoulders as he turned to face Garth again. "They had their trial this afternoon, just like you thought they would."

Garth nodded and said, "With so many people in town today, I figured that must be what was goin' on. How'd it come out?"

"You know what the verdict was. Guilty."

Garth nodded again. "Yeah, that ain't no surprise. What are they gonna do with the boss? They don't have no gallows built yet."

"That's because they're not going to hang him there in Arrowhead," Ike said. "A deputy U.S. marshal showed up just as the trial was over with a court order that gave him custody of Shade."

"You call him Rev'rend Shade," Gonzalez ordered, emphasizing the command with a snarl.

"Reverend Shade." Ike nodded, although referring to that bloodthirsty monster as a man of God rubbed him the wrong way. Ike had never been a particularly religious fella, but he believed in the Lord and knew that Joshua Shade wasn't doing His work, regardless of what the crazy owlhoot claimed.

"Go on," Garth urged. "What's this U.S. marshal gonna do with the boss?"

Ike thought the outlaw sounded a little worried now, as if he didn't like the idea of clashing with a federal lawman.

"He's going to take Reverend Shade to Yuma Prison. The hanging will take place there."

"Yuma! Hell, that's clear across the territory! Why in blazes would the law want to take him all the way over there to hang him?"

Ike shook his head. "I don't have any idea. From the gossip I heard about what went on in the courtroom, Marshal Thorpe doesn't know either. All he knows is that he's got his orders, and he intends to carry them out."

"Thorpe, eh?" Jeffries said. "So that's the fella's name?"

"Yeah. Asa Thorpe."

Garth looked around at the other bandits. "Anybody heard of this fella Thorpe before?"

"I have," one of the outlaws said. "He's supposed to be a pretty tough hombre."

"But he's just one man!" Gonzalez said. "We can take the rev'rend away from him, no trouble!"

Garth rubbed his jaw. "I don't know Thorpe, but he'd be a damned fool to try to take the boss all the way across the territory by himself. I'm surprised he don't have a cavalry patrol with him, or a posse of deputies."

"I heard he's going to deputize some men and take them with him," Ike said.

"What about Bodine and Two Wolves?" Jeffries asked.

Garth nodded. "Yeah, those two are supposed to be

hell on wheels, and they're the ones who captured Joshua in the first place. Are they goin' along?"

Ike shook his head again. "No, Marshal Thorpe didn't want them going. From what I heard, he thinks they're gunfighters and doesn't want them along."

Jeffries snorted contemptuously. "There's your answer, Garth. This so-called marshal *is* a damned fool."

"Maybe, maybe not. But he'd be smarter to take those two hellions with him. We'll take advantage of the fact that he ain't."

Ike saw Garth studying him. He didn't like the look on the outlaw's face, what he could see of it in the fading light, and he tightened his arm around Maggie's shoulders. Now that he had accomplished their bidding, were they going to kill him and his family?

"Listen, I've done what you asked," he said quickly. "I found out everything there was to find out. You promised you'd let us go if I helped you."

An evil, leering smile spread over Gonzalez's face, and cold steel whispered against leather as he began to draw the big knife at his hip. Maggie sobbed and shuddered against Ike's side.

He would fight, he told himself, but he knew it wouldn't do any good. In the end, these bastards would do whatever they wanted to.

"Put that pigsticker away, Gonzalez," Garth snapped.

"But the gringo's right," the Mexican protested. "We don't need 'em no more."

"I'll decide what we need and what we don't need, and I reckon the pilgrim here can still be of some use to us."

Sensing how close he and his wife and son had just come to death, Ike said, "Whatever it is you want from me, I'll do it. I swear."

Garth turned his head toward the other outlaws and said, "Somebody get the pilgrim a six-shooter."

"Wait a minute," Jeffries said. "You're going to give him a gun?"

"That's right. He can't volunteer to go along with that U.S. marshal unless he's armed, now can he?"

Ike stared at the man in disbelief. "You . . . you want me to go along as one of the deputies?"

"That's right," Garth said. "That way, when the time comes for us to make our move, we'll have you right there amongst 'em to help us."

"But what can I do? I'm just a farmer!"

"You can point a gun and pull the trigger, can't you?" Garth smiled savagely at him. "That's what you're gonna do, Winslow. The marshal won't know you're with us, so you stick close to him. And when the shootin' starts . . ."

One of the outlaws brought a coiled shell belt with a holstered Colt attached to it. Garth shoved the weapon into Ike's stunned hands.

"You take this hogleg and blow that son of a bitchin' badge toter's head off," Garth said.

Chapter 20

Matt and Sam were in the Ten Grand that evening, nursing beers and talking with Archie Cochran, when Sheriff Flagg came into the saloon. The sheriff looked around, spotted the blood brothers leaning against the bar, and came over to them.

"Evenin', Sheriff," Matt greeted him. "I hear you've got one more night to guard your prisoner. Then he's not your responsibility anymore."

"Yeah, that's what I wanted to talk to you fellas about," Flagg said.

"You want us to spend the night at the jail like we've been doing?" Sam asked. "I'm not sure how Marshal Thorpe would feel about that."

"Yeah, he made it pretty clear he doesn't have much use for us," Matt said.

"Listen," Flagg said, lowering his voice, "I know Thorpe's a pure-dee jackass, but I got to talk to you boys anyway. Private-like."

Matt and Sam both drained their beer mugs. There wasn't much beer left in them anyway.

"We'll take a walk outside," Sam suggested as he

placed his mug on the bar. Matt's empty glass thumped down beside it.

The three men left the saloon together and walked toward the sheriff's office. When they were out of earshot of the Ten Grand, Flagg said, "Thorpe let it be known around town that he's not leavin' with Shade until tomorrow mornin', but that ain't true."

"He's sneakin' out of town tonight, under cover of darkness," Matt guessed.

"That's right."

"Maybe he's not as foolish as we thought after all," Sam said.

"I wouldn't say that. He's still bound an' determined not to take you two with him. But I got me a hunch that you're goin' anyway."

"You think so?" Matt asked.

"You been mixed up in this whole deal so far," Flagg said. "I just can't see you turnin' your backs on it now."

"Well . . ." Sam began, "it probably wouldn't be a good idea for us to tell a lawman that we're going to defy the wishes of a United States marshal."

Flagg gave a disgusted snort. "Don't you fellas know me better'n that by now? I don't give a hoot in hell what Thorpe thinks. I just want Joshua Shade to make it to Yuma so's he can dance at the end of a rope where he belongs!"

"All right," Matt admitted. "We thought we might trail along, just to see what happens."

"You'd better go get your horses ready to ride then, because Thorpe intends to pull out in less'n half an hour. I didn't find out about it until just a little while ago, and I come to find you fellas as soon as I could."

Matt and Sam both felt urgency gripping them. Thorpe's ruse was actually fairly smart. If the outlaws were somewhere in the hills, keeping an eye on the settlement, they wouldn't be able to see him slip out of town with his prisoner because of the darkness.

Even if the gang had spies in town, which neither of the blood brothers would have doubted for a second, it was possible they wouldn't find out that Thorpe and Shade were gone until the next morning. That would give the federal lawman a good head start.

"How many deputies is he taking with him?" Sam asked.

"He's got nine men lined up to ride with him. There'll be eight outriders all the time, and a shotgun guard on the wagon box with the driver. Thorpe's plannin' on handlin' the shotgun himself, I think. One of the fellas goin' with him says he's a good hand with a wagon team."

"Can you vouch for all the men goin' along on the trip?" Matt asked.

"Well . . . all but a couple of 'em. But the two I don't know don't look like any owlhoots I ever seen."

Matt and Sam glanced at each other. They didn't know if whoever had assumed command of the gang in Shade's absence was smart enough to try to plant somebody among the deputies, but it was a possibility. There probably wasn't much one man could do against nine, though.

"I hope Thorpe's got enough sense to keep an eye on the two you don't know," Sam said, giving voice to the worry that he and Matt shared.

"I'll say somethin' to him before he leaves town. He ain't the friendliest fella I ever met, and he's right full of himself, no doubt about that. But I don't think he's dumb. He'll keep his eyes open for tricks."

"So will we," Matt promised.

* * *

Their gear was still in their hotel rooms, even though they hadn't used those rooms since their first night in Arrowhead. It didn't take long for them to gather up those few things and head for the livery barn where their horses were stabled.

Sheriff Flagg had told them that Thorpe had the wagon parked behind the jail and would be taking Shade out the rear door, then swinging wide around town to intersect the main trail southwest of the settlement. It was a decent enough plan and stood a chance of fooling the outlaws . . . assuming that Thorpe wasn't right about the rest of the gang deserting Shade.

Matt and Sam weren't going to believe that unless and until the journey to Yuma went off without a hitch.

The elderly hostler was surprised to see them. "You boys leavin' town in the middle of the night?" he asked as Matt and Sam began saddling their mounts. The old man had come out of the office, which doubled as his living quarters, wearing a nightshirt and scratching his head.

"Thought we'd get a good start while the weather's cooler," Matt explained.

"Well, I'm sorry to see you go," the old-timer said. "You been good customers. Ain't caused me a lick o' trouble." He cackled with laughter. "And things been right excitin' since you boys rode into town. You draw trouble like honey draws flies."

"So we've been told," Sam said.

"Too many times," Matt added.

They drew the cinches tight, secured their saddlebags, and snugged their Winchesters down in the saddle boots. Then they swung up onto the horses.

Matt ticked a finger against the brim of his hat and said, "So long, old-timer."

"Y'all come back any time now, hear?" the man called after them as they rode out.

They went around the barn, through some back alleys, and left town heading south, not following any trail. Once they were well clear of the settlement, they would cut west and pick up the wagon, hanging back so that Thorpe wouldn't realize he was being followed, but still close enough so that they could catch up in a hurry if any shooting started.

According to what Flagg had told them before they bade the portly sheriff farewell, Thorpe didn't intend to follow the main road all the way to Tucson and board the train there. The biggest danger would come while he was transporting the prisoner in the wagon, so the sooner they made it to the railroad, the better. Once they were clear of the hills that ranged around Arrowhead, Thorpe could turn due south and reach the Southern Pacific sooner by heading for a little whistle-stop village near the Dragoon Mountains called Pancake Flats.

"You'll know why when you see the place, too," Flagg had said. "It's as flat as a pancake thereabouts."

Now, as they rode at an easy lope through the night, trusting on their keen sense of direction and their knowledge of the stars to keep them on the right track, Sam said, "Do you think Shade's gang will actually try to rescue him?"

"I'd bet a hat on it," Matt said.

"They haven't shown any signs of it so far."

"That's because they're waiting for the right time. They knew they'd be in for a hard, bloody fight if they tried to bust him out of jail. It's a hell of a lot easier to waylay a wagon out on the trail, even with guards around it."

"Yeah, things have worked out pretty well so far for Shade, haven't they?" Sam mused. "We keep those lynch mobs from getting him, and then instead of being strung up there in Arrowhead as soon as the trial was over, Thorpe shows up to take him all the way to Yuma, giving his gang an even better chance to bust him loose."

Matt frowned as he looked over at Sam. "You think there's somethin' fishy about Thorpe?" he asked. "Like maybe he isn't a real marshal?"

"Oh, I think he's real enough. I got a pretty good look at his badge—"

"Anybody can pin on a badge," Matt pointed out.

"And I took a gander at that court order, too, while Judge Stanfield had it spread out on the table. It was genuine."

"So if Thorpe's really a marshal and that court order was the real thing, then what are you sayin'?"

"Just that it's a mite suspicious, him showing up right when he did," Sam said. "I'd like to know what prompted the Justice Department to come up with this business of taking Shade to Yuma."

"Well, when we get done here, I reckon you can just ride on up to Washington and ask," Matt said.

"I wouldn't mind going to Washington one of these days. There are a lot of things there that could use some straightening out."

"Amen, brother," Matt said.

They rode on into the night, angling southwest when they came to the main trail that led to Tucson. Flagg had told them the landmarks to look for where the smaller trail to Pancake Flats turned off.

"There'll be a big rock to the left o' the trail that looks like the head of one o' them Mexican dogs. You know, the ones with the pointy ears. About fifty yards past it is a lone pine tree. The Pancake Flats trail is just past that pine."

Now, as they approached a dark, bulky shape beside the trail, Sam pointed at it and said, "That must be the rock Sheriff Flagg was talking about."

"Yeah, you can see the ears stickin' up and the snout stickin' out in front of 'em," Matt agreed. "Looks like a dog's head to me."

Sure enough, just past the big rock, a single pine tree stood solitary watch beside the trail. The blood brothers drew rein beside it and studied the ground in the light of a rising half-moon.

A couple of narrow ruts branched off from the main trail. Sam dismounted and hunkered on his heels next to them, sniffing the air.

"I don't smell any dust," he said. "I don't think the wagon's come along here yet. We're ahead of Thorpe."

"You sure about that?"

"Pretty sure."

Sam took a lucifer from his shirt pocket and snapped it to life with the thumbnail of his left hand, cupping the right around the flame so that it couldn't be seen from more than a few feet away. He studied the ground for a moment before snuffing out the match.

"Nobody's been over this branch trail for days," he said positively as he straightened. "Let's get over there behind the rock and wait."

The dog-head rock was big enough to shield them completely from the road. They had been there for about fifteen minutes when the thudding of hoofbeats and the creaking of wagon wheels announced the approach of someone coming along the trail from Arrowhead.

Matt and Sam put their hands over their horses' muzzles to keep the animals quiet as the group of riders neared. Invisible in the deep shadows next to the rock, they watched as the first outriders came into view, followed by the wagon and more men on horseback ranged around it.

The wagon had an enclosed bed with a couple of small windows in its sides and one in the back. Slats had been nailed over those windows to form bars. They weren't as secure as iron bars, of course, but they would do for a short trip. Matt and Sam knew that the wagon ought to reach Pancake Flats and the railroad by nightfall the next day.

The temperature inside that wagon would get mighty hot in the middle of the day, Matt and Sam knew, but neither of them felt any sympathy for Joshua Shade. It was going to be a lot hotter where the outlaw was going.

A hell of a lot hotter, in fact.

A saddle horse was tied on to the back of the wagon, plodding along behind it. Two men were on the seat, one handling the reins attached to the six mules pulling the wagon, the other sitting there with the butt of a shotgun propped against his leg and the twin barrels extending skyward at an angle. The rising moon cast enough light for Matt and Sam to recognize Marshal Asa Thorpe as the shotgunner.

"Ever seen the driver before?" Matt asked in a whisper.

"I can't really tell in this light, but I don't think so," Sam replied.

"There's somethin' familiar about him," Matt mused.

"Can't quite place him, though. Reckon I must've seen him around Arrowhead sometime before we left."

"He was one of the men Sheriff Flagg didn't know. I hope the sheriff had a chance to warn Thorpe to keep an eye on him."

"Thorpe's got enough sense to do that—I hope."

The wagon and the outriders all swung onto the trail leading south to Pancake Flats. Matt and Sam watched them go, letting them get well ahead before they led their horses out of the shadows next to the rock and mounted up.

Then they set off at an easy lope, heading south themselves and listening for the sound of gunshots in the night.

Chapter 21

By morning, the wagon had covered several miles without encountering any trouble. Exhaustion and the strain of worrying about his family had taken quite a toll on Ike Winslow, dulling him mentally and physically. He swayed a little on the seat next to Marshal Thorpe as he clutched the reins, slapping them against the backs of the mules from time to time to keep the animals moving.

Thorpe was still as stiff and upright as he had been when the journey started. His head swiveled from side to side almost constantly as he kept a lookout for any sign of trouble. Garth and the other outlaws were going to have a hard time taking him by surprise.

But that was *his* job, Ike reminded himself. If he wanted to save Maggie and Caleb, he had to kill Thorpe.

He had never killed anybody, hadn't even been in a serious fight since he was a kid. All he'd done for years now was work hard and try to provide for his family.

But a series of bad years on the farm had forced him to borrow money, and then more bad years had kept him from being able to pay it back. And almost before he knew it, the farm was gone, taken away by the bank.

He had been able to scrape together enough money to buy supplies for the trip West. If he hadn't already had the wagon, left over from better times, he wouldn't have been able to afford it.

Maggie had been mighty good about the whole thing. She knew Ike was doing his best, she had told him, and she thought heading West to make a new start was a fine idea. Maybe deep down she didn't really believe those things—Ike suspected that she didn't—but she said them anyway.

Now he had led her right into trouble that might be the end of them all. Lord knows what was happening to her even now. You couldn't expect brutal, ruthless men like Shade's gang to keep their hands off of a young, pretty woman for very long. Sickness roiled Ike's gut as he tried to shove the horrible images out of his head.

He had to concentrate completely on the job he had been given, he told himself. That was all he could allow himself to think about.

Kill Thorpe. Turn into an outlaw like the rest of Shade's men. Even if he somehow survived this ordeal, he would be hunted for the rest of his life as a murderer, a wanted fugitive who had shot down a federal lawman.

That new life he had hoped for when they started West was gone, slipping through his fingers like smoke.

"Rein 'em in," Thorpe said beside him.

Thorpe hadn't said anything for what seemed like miles. The abrupt command took Ike by surprise and made him jump a little. He recovered quickly, hauled back on the lines, and asked, "Something wrong, Marshal?"

"No, we just need to give the mules and the horses a little rest," Thorpe explained. He called to the outriders to halt as well, and then climbed down from the wagon seat, still holding the shotgun. "Better stretch your legs while you've got the chance, Winslow."

Ike had given the marshal his real name when he asked to join the group of volunteers going along with the wagon. He didn't see that it mattered if they knew who he was. He didn't know what he would have done if Thorpe had refused to bring him along, so he emphasized his experience at handling a wagon team. And of course, it was true that he had driven a team of mules hundreds of miles already. He'd had no trouble so far with this team.

Luck had been with him . . . if you could call it lucky to be captured by a gang of desperadoes and forced to help them murder nine innocent men so they could free a monster in human form.

Thorpe went to the back of the wagon, which had a door set into it. A heavy padlock held the door closed. The marshal reached into his pocket and pulled out the key to the padlock, and as Ike dropped to the ground beside the wagon, Thorpe tossed the key to him. Instinctively, Ike caught it.

"Unlock the door," Thorpe said as he stepped back and leveled the shotgun. "We'll give Shade a little air."

Swallowing nervously, Ike went to the door and stuck the key in the lock. He stood well to the side and stretched his arm out to reach the key as he turned it. If Shade tried anything, Ike didn't want to be in the line of fire when that scattergun went off.

He hoped desperately that Shade wouldn't try to

escape just yet, though. If Thorpe was forced to kill the outlaw, then the rest of the gang would call off their rescue attempt . . . and Maggie and Caleb would be lost.

Nothing happened, though, except the door swung open. Training the shotgun on it, Thorpe said, "Come on out of there for a minute if you want, Shade." Without taking his eyes off the door, he added, "Draw your gun, Winslow."

Ike pulled the Colt revolver the outlaws had given him. He let the weapon dangle at his side as he watched the door. The walnut grips felt odd in his hand. He had used a rifle and a shotgun in the past, but he'd never handled a six-gun all that much. He wasn't sure he could hit anything with it except at close range.

Like the width of a wagon seat . . .

Ike caught his breath as Shade appeared in the doorway at the rear of the wagon. His confinement over the past week had caused a pallor to set in on the outlaw's face. His hair was matted and tangled, his eyes sunken and haunted by unknowable demons. His suit was dirty and disheveled. He looked like a lunatic, Ike thought, and from everything he had heard about Joshua Shade, that was an apt description. The man was crazy as a bedbug.

But still dangerous. Ike felt a chill go through him as those haunted eyes swept over him.

Something about the man inspired great loyalty in his followers, too. Ike had heard the way the outlaws had talked about "the reverend." Sure, they respected Shade because the raids he planned were successful and had netted them plenty of loot, and no doubt they feared him as well.

But it was more than that. The fire that blazed

in Shade's eyes got into a man and burned right through him when Shade looked at him. Ike felt it now. He didn't think that he ever would have succumbed to it . . . but at least he could understand why some men did.

"You can walk around a little if you want," Thorpe told the prisoner. "We'll give you some water and something to eat. Just don't try anything funny."

Shade didn't say anything. He just stared at Thorpe with those baleful eyes for a long moment, then turned to look at Ike. Ike had to look away. A dry chuckle came from Shade.

"That's right, boy," he rasped. "Avert your eyes from the avenging angel of the Lord."

Shade had no idea that Ike was working with the gang, and Ike couldn't tell him. He just said, "I'll get the canteen."

"And a little jerky, too," Thorpe said.

Awkwardly because of the shackles and leg irons, Shade climbed down from the wagon bed. There was nothing inside the enclosure but the bare planks, nothing Shade could use to free himself or turn into a weapon. He shuffled along for a few steps, then turned and went back to lean against the wagon. Evidently, that was all the exercise he wanted.

Ike holstered his gun and got the canteen and a strip of jerky from the bag of supplies stashed under the wagon seat. Being careful not to get between Shade and the marshal, he handed them to Shade.

"The blessings of the Lord be upon you, my son," Shade said. Ike thought he detected a hint of irony in the outlaw's voice, but he couldn't be sure.

Shade took a long drink from the canteen, his

prominent Adam's apple bobbing in his thin neck as he swallowed. He smiled as he handed it back to Ike.

"I'll take particular delight in flaying every inch of skin from your body, you foul, fornicating sinner, so that you take days to die screaming in agony."

Ike shuddered as he stepped back. Shade's voice had been as soft and friendly as he uttered that threat as it had been a moment earlier when he asked for the Lord's blessing on Ike. The man was loco, all right. No doubt about it.

"You won't be torturing anybody else, Shade," Thorpe said. "Now take that jerky and get back in there. Lock up after him, Winslow."

Shade did what the marshal told him. Ike was glad when he swung the door closed and couldn't see that evil, smiling face anymore.

But he knew he would have trouble shaking the image from his mind, maybe for the rest of his life . . . however long *that* was.

Ike didn't expect it to be very long.

"When can we have the woman?" Gonzalez asked, for the fourth or fifth time.

"When Joshua's free again," Garth answered, trying to suppress the feelings of irritation that went through him. "I ain't takin' no more chances. I want her safe and sound to use as leverage against that husband o' hers just as long as we might still need him."

Along with the other members of the gang, they were riding along about two miles behind the wagon carrying Joshua Shade. Garth had spotted it earlier through his spyglass when they paused at the top of a long swell that provided a good view of the territory to the south.

Earlier, when the wagon tracks had left the main road and turned south, Garth had studied the map that Shade always used when he was planning their jobs. It hadn't taken him long to figure out what the marshal was doing.

Thorpe wanted to get his prisoner on a train as soon as possible, because that was the fastest and safest way to transport Shade to Yuma. So instead of going all the way to Tucson to catch the train, he had struck out across country toward the railroad, following a meager track that barely qualified as a trail.

"Right there," Garth had said, stabbing a blunt finger at the map he had spread out on a rock. "He's headed for Pancake Flats."

Since then, nothing had happened to change his mind. It was mid-morning now, and the wagon was still headed in the same direction.

Garth turned his head to look at the others. Mrs. Winslow rode double with Jeffries; they had abandoned the wagon back where the gang had been camped before. It wasn't that Garth trusted the dapper gunman not to molest the woman, but he probably trusted him more than he did Gonzalez and the other men.

Mrs. Winslow had her baby in her arms, cradling the kid against her. Garth felt an unaccustomed twinge of pity. He had killed plenty of times in his life—men, women, children, whoever he needed to kill to get what he wanted—but every now and then, such as now, some fleeting, unwanted memories came back to him. Memories of a time before he was a killer and an outlaw, when he'd had a woman and a young'un of his own . . .

With a grimace, Garth turned around to face front once again. Those days were long gone, and good riddance to 'em. They'd ended badly anyway, and he'd just as soon not think about them.

"Hey, Garth," Gonzalez said.

"What?" Garth snapped, his voice abrupt and angry because he figured the Mexican was fixing to pester him again about raping Mrs. Winslow.

Gonzalez had something else on his mind, though. "I think I saw a couple of riders up there, off to the east of the trail."

Garth looked where Gonzalez was pointing and didn't see anything. He reined in and motioned for the others to do likewise. Fishing the spyglass out of his saddlebags, he extended it and lifted it to his eye, squinted through it.

The pepper-eatin' son of a bitch was right, Garth thought as he focused in on a pair of riders. They were too far away for him to make out any details about them, but they were also a good quarter of a mile east of the trail leading to Pancake Flats.

"Just a couple o' cowhands, more than likely," Garth said as he closed the spyglass. "There are some cattle spreads down this way, but they're pretty scattered. Or maybe they're just drifters passin' through these parts."

"You can't be sure of that," Jeffries said.

"You heard what Winslow said. The marshal wasn't takin' anybody with him except some outriders. The whole bunch is with the wagon." Garth tugged on his mustache as he frowned in thought. "But I reckon it wouldn't hurt anything to be sure. The rest of us will ride on ahead and circle around the wagon to the west so's we can set up an ambush. Larkin, you and Glenister go check out those riders over east a ways."

The two outlaws Garth had selected for the chore

nodded in understanding. One of them asked, "What do you want us to do about 'em?"

"Oh, hell, might as well play it safe," Garth said. "Wait until the shootin' starts, then kill both the sons o' bitches."

Chapter 22

During the morning, Matt and Sam had swung gradually to the east as they followed the wagon, so that they wouldn't be directly behind the vehicle. They didn't want Thorpe to check his back trail, spot them, and take them for members of Shade's gang.

Nor did they want the outlaws to realize that they were riding herd on the wagon. With some distance between them and Thorpe's party, even if Shade's men noticed them, they might not think the two of them had any connection to the wagon.

"Do you think the gang will try to take Shade away from the marshal before the wagon gets to Pancake Flats?" Sam asked.

"Well, if I was a no-account outlaw, that's what I'd try to do," Matt said. "Be harder to take him off the train. Not impossible, mind you, but harder."

Sam nodded. "That's what I thought, too. How would you go about doing it?"

Matt rubbed his jaw and frowned in thought. "Well, again, if I was a no-good, murderin' skunk like Shade's men, I reckon I'd try to get ahead of the wagon and set up some sort of ambush."

"You know Marshal Thorpe has to be thinking the same thing," Sam pointed out. "He'll be ready for something like that."

"Bein' ready for something and bein' able to stop it when it starts happenin' are two different things."

Sam shrugged. "I can't argue with that."

"They'll find a good spot with plenty of cover," Matt went on, gesturing as he spoke, "and then try to gun down as many of the outriders as they can in the first volley. Then men on horseback will sweep in and finish off the others."

"There'll be a lot of lead flying around that way," Sam said, playing devil's advocate. "Shade might get hit by a stray bullet."

Matt shook his head. "That wagon looked sturdy enough to stop some of the slugs anyway, and as soon as Shade hears guns goin' off, he'll hug the floor as tight as he can. Chances are he'd come through it without a scratch."

All that sounded feasible to Sam. He said, "So what do we do to stop it?"

Matt grinned. "Bushwhack the bushwhackers?"

"I like the way you think . . . dirty and underhanded."

"I'll give any man an even break, includin' outlaws, when it's just him and me. But when they're plannin' on murderin' innocent folks, they've stepped over a line. They don't deserve any more consideration than a nest of rattlers."

Sam chuckled. "I was just joshing you, Matt. I agree completely."

"I guess we need to get in front of the wagon then."

Sam urged his horse ahead at a faster pace. "That's just what I was thinking."

Only a few minutes had gone by before Matt called over the pounding hoofbeats, "Look yonder!" and pointed westward.

Sam saw the thin haze of dust in the air about a mile away and said, "Riders!"

"Quite a few of 'em, by the looks of it! That's got to be Shade's gang, tryin' to cut off the wagon!"

"Marshal Thorpe's bound to notice that dust."

"Yeah, but he won't know what's causin' it," Matt said. "Could be some cowboys hazin' a jag of cattle from one place to another. Thorpe'll have to keep that wagon movin', dust or no dust."

Sam nodded grimly. The marshal had no choice but to keep going and hope to reach Pancake Flats before the outlaws closed in on him.

"So much for an ambush!" Sam said. "It's a race now!"

"Yeah," Matt agreed, "a race Thorpe can't win in that wagon!"

Without saying anything, both of them veered to the west, angling toward the wagon now. It was likely the marshal was going to need their help before too much more time passed.

Just then Matt felt something whip through the air not far from his head, followed an instant later by the sharp crack of a rifle. He jerked his head around and saw a couple of riders pounding after him and Sam, maybe two hundred yards back.

"Damn!" Matt said. "We've got company!"

Sam looked around, too. "Shade's men?"

"Bound to be. They must've spotted us and sent those hombres to keep us busy while they hit the wagon. The fat's in the fire now, boy!"

So it was. Outlaws closing in from behind, more outlaws about to attack the wagon Matt and Sam had come along to protect . . . No one could have blamed the blood brothers for being discouraged.

But both of them wore reckless, fighting grins on their faces as they urged more speed from their mounts and galloped straight toward their favorite destination . . .

Trouble.

"Damn it!" Willard Garth grated as he heard shots begin to ring out in the distance. "There wasn't supposed to be any gunplay until *we* started the ball!"

"Too late now," Gonzalez said. "Let's go kill those gringo bastards and get the rev'rend out o' there!"

Garth twisted in the saddle. "Jeffries! Take the woman and the kid and fall back! Keep 'em outta the fight!"

Jeffries looked like he wanted to argue, but then he shrugged and hauled his horse's head to the side, peeling away from the rest of the gang. It was unlikely they would need the woman after the next few minutes, Garth thought, but being in command had taught him to hedge his bets.

As Jeffries fell back, Garth and the other outlaws kicked their horses into a run. In the lead, Garth veered his mount slightly to the east on a course that would intersect with that of the wagon.

He wanted to stop the vehicle and get Joshua Shade out of there as quickly as possible. The longer Shade was locked up, the more chance that something bad could happen to him, like being hit by one of the stray bullets that were about to start flying around.

Up ahead, the wagon careened past some boulders and a clump of scrubby mesquite. As the outlaws drew closer, Garth could see that stupid pilgrim Winslow slashing the reins at the mules, driving them on to greater speed.

That was just the opposite of what the bastard was supposed to be doing, Garth thought. By now he should have pulled his gun and plugged that damn marshal! Instead, it looked like he was trying to help Thorpe get away with his prisoner.

Winslow was going to be damned sorry about that, Garth vowed as he leaned forward in the saddle and pounded after the wagon.

Ike had been scared plenty of times in his life, including earlier today. But he had never been as flat-out terrified as he was when bullets started whining through the air near his head. His heart was racing so hard, he felt like it was about to climb right up his throat and burst out of his mouth.

At the same time, he wasn't just frightened for himself. He was scared for Maggie and Caleb, too. He glanced over at Marshal Thorpe, who was saying, "Whip that team up harder, Winslow! Damn it, make 'em run!"

Ike bit back a groan of despair. He knew what he was supposed to do. As Thorpe twisted around on the seat beside him and leveled the shotgun back over the top of the wagon, Ike knew he could slip the gun out of the holster on his hip, raise the weapon, and put a bullet in the marshal's head before Thorpe could stop him.

If he did that, the other deputies might give up the fight and run for their lives, rather than face the outlaws. Joshua Shade would be free, and maybe . . . just maybe . . . he would spare Ike's life, and the lives of Ike's wife and child.

On the other hand, Shade was too loco to predict what he might do. He could have all three of them tortured to death just to amuse himself.

The other problem was that Ike had never even shot at another human being, let alone killed anybody. He had thought that he could do it when he believed that his family's safety depended on him being a killer, but when the time had come, he had frozen just as he started to reach for his gun.

Then Thorpe started yelling at him to whip up the team, and instinctively Ike had obeyed. Now the chase was on, with the outlaws closing in from the right, a huge dust cloud boiling up from the hooves of their galloping horses.

The outriders had swung around so that all of them were now between the wagon and the outlaws who were closing in from the west. Their rifles barked and cracked as they returned the gang's fire.

To Ike's horror, one of the deputies suddenly flung his arms in the air, throwing his rifle away, and toppled out of the saddle. Ike caught a glimpse of blood spurting from the man's throat where a bullet had torn it open, but then the grisly sight was lost in the dust.

Ike suddenly wondered what the outlaws had done with Maggie and Caleb. Had they brought the two of them along, so that they were in danger from the bullets buzzing through the air like lethal bees, or were they somewhere behind the gang in relative safety? Ike wished he could see them again, just one more time, but he hoped they were well out of the line of fire, even if it meant he would never lay eyes on them again in this lifetime.

"Keep those mules moving!" Thorpe yelled at him over the rolling thunder of hoofbeats. The marshal got his knees up on the seat and started crawling out onto the top of the enclosed wagon bed.

What the hell was he doing? Ike glanced over his shoulder and saw that Thorpe had flattened out and drawn his pistol, although he still had the shotgun at his side. Thorpe edged over to the side so that he could reach down to one of the little windows that let light and air into the wagon.

He was going to kill Shade!

That thought sprang into Ike's head. If the outlaws closed in and looked like they were about to stop the wagon, Thorpe planned to shoot through the window and kill the prisoner rather than allow him to be freed.

With Shade dead, the gang would have no reason at all to spare the lives of Maggie and Caleb. Ike couldn't let that happen. He knew now what he had to do. He twisted on the seat and dragged the Colt out of its holster. Thorpe wasn't even looking at him. It would be a simple matter to shoot the marshal.

But as Ike turned, holding the gun in his right hand, the reins slipped out of his left. He made a grab for them, but missed as they fell to the floorboard of the driver's box. The mules were running flat out now, and if the reins slid off the box, Ike would have no way of stopping the team. He lunged after the lines.

At that moment, the wagon hit a rough spot in the trail, jolting heavily as it bounced. Ike was already off balance as he reached for the trailing reins. He felt himself thrown from the seat, and something crashed into his head with stunning force. The pain filled his entire being, washing everything else away, and swept him along with it into oblivion.

Chapter 23

Matt and Sam pulled their rifles from the saddle boots as they raced toward the wagon, closing in from the east as the outlaws closed in from the west. They still had to deal with the owlhoots who were pursuing them, however, and that problem became more pressing as a bullet tugged at the sleeve of Matt's shirt.

"We ought to do something about those varmints behind us!" he called across to Sam as they galloped side by side. "Some of those slugs are comin' a mite too close for comfort!"

Sam nodded. "I was thinking the same thing! On three?"

"One, two, three!" Matt shouted.

The blood brothers hauled back on the reins as the same time, pulling their mounts around in sharp turns that would have sent most horses tumbling out of control. Matt and Sam had trained their animals for this very maneuver, though, and they stayed upright, coming to a dead stop with Matt and Sam facing back toward their pursuers.

Winchesters came up as if synchronized, socketing

themselves against the shoulders of the blood brothers. The outlaws realized they were charging right into the barrels of those rifles and tried to react, but they were too late.

The whipcracks of sound erupted so close together, they might have been mistaken for one shot. Flame spurted from the muzzles of the Winchesters as Matt and Sam fired.

And both outlaws went backward off their horses, punched out of the saddles by the .44-40 slugs that smashed into their chests.

"That takes care of those two," Matt said as he lowered his rifle.

"Let's see what we can do about the others," Sam said.

They grabbed the reins again, whirled their horses, and charged toward the running battle that was going on between the outriders and the rest of Joshua Shade's gang.

The deputies were putting up a valiant fight, Matt saw, but one of them was down already and they had been badly outnumbered to start with. Thorpe never should have tried to transport Shade to Yuma with such a small force accompanying him. By doing that, he was practically asking the outlaws to try to take the prisoner away from him.

But it was too late to change things now. Matt and Sam would just have to hope that the element of surprise would be to their advantage.

As they closed in, Sam called, "Something's happened to the driver! That team's a runaway!"

Matt saw he was right. Thorpe appeared to be alone on the wagon. The marshal was stretched out on the top of the vehicle, firing his pistol toward the outlaws as the wagon careened along.

"It's gonna wreck if it keeps goin' like that!" Matt shouted.

"That's the least of our worries right now!" Sam called back.

That was true. Another deputy pitched off his horse as outlaw lead riddled him. Matt and Sam were close enough to join the fight now, though, and they did so as they came up slightly behind and to the side of the gang.

In a flank attack, they gashed into Shade's men with their Winchesters blasting as fast as the blood brothers could work the levers. That sudden hail of unexpected shots took a heavy toll. Half a dozen members of the gang were down before they knew what was going on.

The rifles clicked on empty after a moment, though, and there was no time to reload. Matt and Sam jammed the Winchesters back in the saddle boots and drew their Colts.

Blinding, choking dust filled the air. Flames spurted from the muzzles of the twin revolvers in Matt's hands as he guided his horse with his knees. He fired right and left as he tore through the gang in a mad dash. Laughter floated around him, the laughter of a man who was never more alive than when he was daring death to reach out and take him.

Sam's attack was more deliberate but no less effective. He skirted the edge of the gang, making for the wagon as he fired at the outlaws he passed. A couple of them fell, and another man reeled in his saddle as he was hit, but managed to hang on.

Sam came alongside the vehicle, and saw Thorpe

start to swing the shotgun toward him. "Don't shoot, Marshal!" he shouted.

Thorpe recognized him and held off on the Greener's triggers. Instead, the lawman twisted back the other way and touched off a blast toward a couple of outlaws who had almost drawn even with the wagon on that side. The buckshot shredded one man and blew him out of the saddle. The other man fell back, pawing at his face where one of the balls had ripped his cheek open and caused a cascade of blood.

Thorpe fired the other barrel a second later, but Sam didn't see where that charge went. He had already pulled ahead, and was now galloping alongside the runaway mules. A glance at the driver's box showed him that that driver was crumpled on the floorboard, either unconscious or dead. He lay near the edge on the far side from Sam, and as the wagon gave another bounce and lurch, the man began to slip off.

There was nothing Sam could do for him except hope that he fell clear of the wagon wheels. The driver slid out of sight and was left behind in the roiling dust.

Sam brought his horse closer to the lead mule on the left side. In the past, he had pulled off the trick he was about to attempt, but it was damned dangerous. Still, there was no other way to stop the madly galloping mules except to shoot one of the leaders, and that would cause the wagon to crash. The reins had slipped completely off the box and were trailing under the vehicle now.

Sam took a deep breath, slipped his feet out of the stirrups, and threw himself from the saddle. For a harrowing instant, he hung in midair between his horse and the mule. Then he crashed down on the mule's back.

A pained grimace twisted Sam's face as he tangled his fingers in the mule's mane and hung on for dear life. Landing like that was guaranteed to be pretty damned uncomfortable on a man's privates, but he would recover. As he settled himself securely on the mule's back, he pushed the pain to the back of his mind and reached for the harness.

"Whoa! Whoa, you jugheads!" Sam shouted as he hauled back on the harness. The mules responded almost instantly to his firm touch and began to slow down.

He didn't want them to slow too much, though. Those outlaws were still back there giving chase, so the mules needed to keep running.

Or *were* the outlaws back there? As Sam twisted his neck to look over his shoulder, he saw to his surprise that the gang had fallen back. From the looks of it, they were peeling off and abandoning the attack. A few rifle shots still cracked here and there, but the gunfire had diminished considerably.

To his great relief, Sam spotted Matt and saw that his blood brother appeared to be all right. Matt rode toward the wagon as Sam pulled back on the harness again and slowed the mules even more.

Marshal Thorpe slid from the top back onto the seat. "What happened to the driver?" he called to Sam.

"Don't know," Sam replied with a shake of his head. "He fell off a ways back. I couldn't tell if he was still alive or not."

Sam checked on the outlaws again as the mules slowed to a halt. The shooting had stopped entirely now, and the dust trailing off to the north made it clear that the outlaws were leaving.

That might be a trick, though. They could always double back and attack again. Because of that, Sam didn't think it would be a very good idea for the wagon to remain stopped for long.

The team really needed some rest after that hard run, though, or else they might collapse. It was a double-edged sword on which the situation was perched right now.

Matt rode up, as glad to see that Sam was all right as Sam had been about him. Behind him, the surviving deputies straggled in, only four of them now.

That meant that four men had been lost in this attack. Four lives lost, more than likely, just so Joshua Shade could have his evil life snuffed out at the end of a hangrope in one place and not another. That knowledge put a bitter taste in the mouths of both Matt and Sam.

Sam slid down from the mule and retrieved the reins that had fallen earlier. He wrapped them around the brake lever while Thorpe was climbing down from the seat.

"I have to check on the prisoner," Thorpe said. He started toward the rear of the wagon, digging for the key to the padlock that held the door closed.

Matt had been reloading his Colts, the first thing he did after any fracas. He snapped the cylinder closed on the second Colt and filled both hands. Pointing the irons at the door, he told Thorpe, "I'll cover you, Marshal."

"Shade, if you're anywhere near that door, stand away from it!" Thorpe bellowed. "If you try anything, we'll shoot to kill!"

He unlocked the padlock, pulled it loose, and stepped back as he raised the shotgun. The door swung open, revealing Joshua Shade huddled at the far end of the wagon bed. For a second, Matt thought the outlaw chief was dead, but then Shade raised his head and glared at them. His eyes were like some crazed animal's.

"Loco as ever," Matt said.

Thorpe gestured with the Greener's twin barrels. "Stand up, Shade. Were you hit during all that shooting?"

"The Lord's hand was upon me," Shade said as he climbed to his feet. He couldn't stand upright in the wagon, but he was able to get up far enough that it was obvious he wasn't hurt. "He shielded me from harm."

"If you had somebody lookin' out for you, it was more likely the Devil," Matt said.

"All right, I'm satisfied," Thorpe told the prisoner. "You can sit down again."

He closed the door and snapped the lock back into place.

Then he turned and looked at the surviving deputies, who were keeping watch in case Shade's gang returned.

"Are the others dead?" Thorpe asked.

One of the men nodded with a stricken expression on his face. "I'm afraid so, Marshal. We checked their bodies to make sure."

"Except for that Winslow fella," another man added. "We didn't find him, and I see now he ain't on the wagon either."

"He fell off," Thorpe said. "You can look again while you're rounding up the horses and loading the dead men on them."

"You're takin' the bodies with you?" Matt asked.

"I'm not going to leave them for the damn coyotes,

if that's what you mean," Thorpe snapped. "They were good men, and they died in service to the law. I'll see to it that they're laid to rest properly."

"I think that's a good idea, Marshal," Sam said. "Matt and I will help."

"That is, if you'll let us go with you the rest of the way to Pancake Flats," Matt added.

"I've lost half my men and it's likely those outlaws will come back," Thorpe said. "So I don't really have any choice but to allow you and Two Wolves to come along, do I, Bodine?"

Matt grinned at Sam. "Always nice to be wanted, ain't it?"

Chapter 24

"What the hell happened?" Jeffries demanded. "You outnumbered them three to one!"

Garth fought down the impulse to pull his gun and blow a hole in the arrogant son of a bitch. "Those two hombres off to the east were Bodine and Two Wolves!" he said, although he didn't think he owed any explanations to Jeffries. "They killed Larkin and Glenister and then hit us from the flank. I never saw anybody who could shoot like those two!"

"How many men did we lose?"

"Ten," Garth answered bleakly. That was more than a third of the gang. "We still outnumber 'em by quite a bit, though. We'll just regroup and go after Joshua again."

The members of the gang were riding slowly south, following the wagon. They had picked up Jeffries and the woman and the kid, then started on the trail again.

The woman still rode double with Jeffries, holding the kid in her arms. She spoke up now, asking, "Mr. Garth, did . . . did you see what happened to Isaac?"

"Your husband?" Garth shook his head. "I don't

have no idea, ma'am. The dust was too thick to see much. For all I know, he's still drivin' that wagon with the marshal."

"He . . . he didn't do what you told him to do?"

Jeffries said, "Evidently not, or Joshua would be free now."

"Last I saw, the marshal was still fine," Garth confirmed.

"Good," the woman said with a note of defiance in her voice. "I'm glad he didn't help you. I knew he couldn't kill a man in cold blood."

Garth reined in and turned to frown at her. "Ma'am, you *do* know that by goin' against us, that husband o' yours has put your life in danger, as well as your kid's. If he ain't gonna help us . . ."

He left the rest of it unsaid, but he was sure Mrs. Winslow knew what he meant. If the pilgrim wasn't going to cooperate, there was no need to keep his family alive.

She had the sense to turn pale and look scared at least.

"Hey, Garth," Gonzalez said suddenly. "Somebody comin'."

Garth turned back around and saw a man staggering across the semiarid landscape toward them. Heat haze blurred him for a moment, but then he came closer and Garth recognized him.

So did the woman. "Ike!" she cried.

"Hang on to her," Garth growled at Jeffries. Then he spurred his horse forward, followed by Gonzalez.

Blood had sheeted down the right side of Winslow's face, giving him a gruesome appearance. He weaved from side to side as he walked, as if he could barely stay on his feet.

Maybe he had been wounded early in the fight, Garth thought. It was even possible that he had hesitated long enough to tip off the marshal and Thorpe had shot him. The important thing was that he was still alive and they might be able to get some use out of him after all.

Winslow stopped and stood there swaying as Garth and Gonzalez reined in. "What happened?" Garth demanded as he dismounted. "You were supposed to plug that damn marshal!"

"I . . . I tried," Winslow said. "I had my gun out . . . but then the wagon . . . the wagon hit a rough spot in the trail . . . bounced so hard it threw me off the seat . . . I hit my head on something . . ." He winced and lifted his hand toward the big gash above his right ear, then lowered it without touching the wound. "I'm sorry. I don't remember anything after . . . after that . . ."

Winslow's eyes rolled up in their sockets and he dropped to his knees. As his wife screamed, "Ike!" he pitched forward on his face.

"Hold her!" Garth yelled at Jeffries. He knelt beside Winslow and rolled the pilgrim onto his back. Winslow's chest rose and fell jerkily, so he was still alive, but he appeared to be out cold.

"I can cut his throat if you want, Garth," Gonzalez offered. "Then we can have some fun with the woman."

"Not until we get Joshua back from that marshal, damn it!" Garth stood up and gestured toward the unconscious man. "We've got extra horses now. Throw him on one and tie him in the saddle."

Jeffries looked over the shoulder of the sobbing Maggie Winslow, who still clutched her infant son to her. "Why do we need him? He couldn't even do a simple thing like killing Thorpe."

"I don't know, but it won't cost us anything to take him along," Garth snapped.

He was getting sick and tired of everybody questioning his orders. Joshua had made it clear that Garth was to be in charge if anything ever happened to him, but Jeffries and Gonzalez didn't seem to remember that, and some of the other men were starting to cast dissatisfied looks in his direction, too.

He needed to do something to remind them that he was the boss, at least for now, and bringing Winslow along was part of that.

The other part was making a daring move to show them that he could come up with a plan. He said, "We're gonna split up."

"Are you sure that's a good idea?" Jeffries asked. "There aren't as many of us as there were when we started out."

Garth knew that, and Jeffries knew he knew it, the smug varmint. Garth said, "That wagon won't get to the railroad until close to nightfall. We've got time to circle around and set up an ambush like I wanted to do all along. A dozen men will do that. The others will push the wagon right into the trap we set up. This time it'll work," he added, hating the sound of the defensive note that crept into his voice. If he could hear it, that meant the others could, too.

But all it would take was freeing Joshua, and killing that marshal—Bodine and Two Wolves, too—to make the rest of the gang forget all about their previous failures. Garth was going to do that if he had to fight to the last breath in his body.

* * *

"You know, Marshal," Sam said, "you didn't seem all that surprised to see Matt and me when we showed up to help you fight off those outlaws."

Unexpectedly, a hint of a smile appeared on Asa Thorpe's face. "That's because I wasn't," he said.

The two men were on the wagon seat, with Sam handling the reins now as the vehicle rolled south toward Pancake Flats. His horse was tied on behind the wagon. Matt had the point about a hundred yards in front, with the remaining four outriders spread out to the sides and behind the wagon.

Sam looked over at Thorpe and said, "You're going to have to explain that."

"I don't have to explain anything. I work for the United States government." Thorpe shrugged. "But I don't suppose it would hurt anything now to admit that things worked out pretty much like I planned, at least where you and Bodine are concerned."

"All right, now I'm *really* curious."

"I've heard a lot about you two young hellions. You can't stay away from trouble. You seek it out, even though you claim to be peace-loving hombres."

"That's not exactly true," Sam said. "But close enough for government work, as they say."

Thorpe grunted, and it was a second before Sam realized that the marshal had just laughed. Thorpe went on. "I knew that if I told you and Bodine you couldn't come along, you'd be bound and determined to do it anyway. I figured that you'd follow along, thinking that you were putting one over on me."

"So when the outlaws attacked, as you were sure they would, we'd be in position to hit them either from the side or from behind, taking them by surprise."

"That's right," Thorpe said with a nod. "And it sort

of worked out that way. We're still here, and Shade's still our prisoner. And we did considerable damage to the gang."

"But not so much that they'll give up," Sam predicted.

Thorpe sighed. "No, I figure they'll be back. It wouldn't surprise me if they hit us again before we reach Pancake Flats."

The sun was lowering in the western sky now. In another hour, it would be dark. If everything went according to plan, the wagon would reach the settlement— and the railroad—about then.

Which meant that if the outlaws wanted to stop them before that happened, another attack would come within the next hour, Sam thought.

"Why do it this way to start with?" he asked, not knowing if Thorpe would answer him or not. "I can understand why the government wants Shade to be hanged at Yuma. They can make a bigger show out of it that way."

"You sound like you know how things like that work."

"My father was Cheyenne," Sam said. "His people have had to deal with the Bureau of Indian Affairs. I do indeed know how petty, hidebound bureaucracies work, Marshal. I don't expect that the Justice Department is any different."

Thorpe grunted again, but Sam didn't think it was a laugh this time.

After a moment, Sam went on. "Why didn't you bring a troop of cavalry with you to escort the prisoner to Yuma? That wouldn't be so unusual, would it?"

"No, I suppose not," Thorpe admitted. "In fact, I

thought about that, and wired the chief marshal's office about it. I was told that no soldiers were available at the moment and that the situation with Shade was too pressing to wait until they were." He paused. "I was also ordered to keep the involvement of local law enforcement and civilians to a minimum."

A frown creased Sam's forehead as he thought about what Thorpe had just said. That explained why the marshal had recruited only a minimal amount of volunteers. He was just following orders.

But why in the hell had the chief marshal given him those orders in the first place? Thorpe's superior had to have known that trying to take Shade across Arizona Territory, with only a small group of deputies to guard him, was bound to attract rescue attempts by the crazed outlaw's gang.

Before Sam could ponder that puzzling question any more, Matt turned his horse and rode back to the wagon. He fell in alongside the seat.

"I don't like the looks of the country up ahead," Matt said. "There are a couple of bluffs flankin' the trail. Be a good spot for an ambush."

"Can we go around them?" Thorpe asked.

Matt shrugged. "Maybe. The terrain looks pretty rugged on both sides of the trail, though. Lots of arroyos and ridges. None of 'em are too deep or too high, but they'd still be hard to get that wagon through 'em." He thought it over and then suggested, "Better slow down and let me scout that cut between the bluffs before you go through there."

"That sounds like a good way to get yourself shot if there *is* an ambush," Sam said.

Matt grinned. "Won't be the first time I've waltzed into a place where I might get myself shot, now will it?"

"Unfortunately, no."

Matt lifted his reins. "I'll be back—" he began.

But before he could finish making that promise, shots blasted out from somewhere behind the wagon, and rifles crashed closer as the remaining outriders began to return the fire.

Chapter 25

Matt twisted in the saddle, looked back to the north for a second, and then said, "They're comin' after us again! Whip that team up, Sam!"

"It's probably a trap," Sam warned.

Matt's grin flashed again. "Hell, I know that. But they're not givin' us much choice, are they?" He dug his heels into his horse's flanks. "Follow me!"

The horse lunged toward the cut between the two bluffs. Matt drew his Winchester from the saddle sheath as he leaned forward in the saddle.

Behind him, Sam slashed the long reins across the rumps of the mules and shouted at them. The balky animals hesitated, as mules were bound to do most of the time, but then they broke into a run and the wagon lurched forward.

Sam glanced back and saw that the outriders were putting up a good running fight against what appeared to be half a dozen or so of the outlaws. That small number confirmed the thought that had flashed through his head as soon as the shooting started behind the wagon.

With nowhere else to go, they were being driven straight toward that cut where the rest of the gang lurked, ready to ambush them. Sam had no doubt of that.

But there was nothing they could do except try to fight their way out of the trap.

Up ahead, Matt saw the wink of muzzle flashes from the slopes on both sides of the trail as he galloped toward them. The bushwhackers were hidden up there behind rocks and brush and any other cover they could find.

Dirt and gravel spurted into the air around the racing horse as bullets plowed into the ground. Matt was moving too fast for the outlaws to draw a bead on him accurately, though. He felt the hot breath of a slug on his face as it passed by his head, but that was as close as any of the shots came.

He lifted the rifle to his shoulder and peppered the right-hand slope with four bullets as fast as he could work the lever and squeeze the trigger. Then he turned and sprayed the left-hand slope with four more shots. He didn't figure he would actually hit any of the outlaws, firing blind like that, but he wanted to make them duck for cover and give them something to think about.

The tactic worked, giving him a couple of seconds' respite, and during that moment Matt's horse, stretched out and running at top speed, dashed into the cut, which was about fifty yards long. The bushwhackers couldn't hit him now from where they were.

Matt slowed his mount, but didn't wait for it to stop before he kicked his feet out of the stirrups and threw himself from the saddle. He lit running and allowed his momentum to carry him into some boulders nestled against the right-hand slope. He stopped and crouched there for a second as the horse continued running through the gap.

The slope was steep but not sheer. Matt was able to scramble up it carrying the rifle in his right hand and occasionally putting his left on the rocks for balance.

The shooting was still going on. When Matt reached the top, he could see the wagon about a hundred yards away, still careening toward the bluffs. He was relieved to see that Sam was still all right, as was Marshal Thorpe. Sam whipped the team and got all the speed out of the mules that he could.

Only two of the outriders were left, though, Matt noted grimly. He couldn't see the other two men because of the dust raised by the wagon, but it was likely they were lying back there somewhere with outlaw lead in them. The two surviving deputies had caught up to the wagon and were right behind it now, still turning in their saddles to fire back at the pursuing outlaws.

Matt paused long enough to throw a couple of shots at the owlhoots pounding along about fifty yards behind the wagon. He was rewarded by the sight of one of the varmints throwing his arms out to the sides and then pitching off his horse. That slowed the others down a little.

Then Matt hurried forward and looked down the front slope of the bluff. From up here he could see several of the bushwhackers as they crouched behind boulders to fire at the wagon.

Matt didn't have any qualms about shooting a man in the back when the bastard was trying to kill innocent people. He drew a bead and squeezed off a round. One of the outlaws was driven forward by the slug that slammed into his back.

Before that man could fall, Matt had turned and homed in on another owlhoot. The man must have heard the first shot and realized that danger now threatened from behind, because he was starting to twist around as Matt's next shot drilled him through the body.

The outlaw dropped his rifle, slumped against the rock he had been using for cover, and started to slide down it as bloody froth from his bullet-torn lungs bubbled from his mouth.

Now the rest of the bushwhackers on this slope knew Matt was behind them, and they whirled to start shooting at him instead of the wagon. That took some of the heat off Sam and the others, Matt thought as bullets started to whine around his head again. He snapped off a couple of shots, and then darted back where the outlaws couldn't see him anymore.

The last glimpse he'd had of the wagon, it had almost reached the cut between the two bluffs. Matt ran toward that gap now, hearing the pounding hoof-beats of the team as he approached it. He reached the edge and never slowed down as he saw the wagon flashing past about a dozen feet below him.

Instead he leaped into the air, sailing out from the bluff and trying to angle himself toward the wagon as he fell.

"Son of a *bitch*!"

Marshal Thorpe let out that shocked yell as Matt came crashing down on top of the wagon right behind him. Matt's momentum made him slide on across the vehicle. He grabbed at the edge with his free hand and dug in the toes of his boots to slow himself. He came to a stop just before he would have toppled off the far side of the wagon.

Matt rolled over onto his belly as he stretched out atop the wagon. He still had a couple of rounds left in the Winchester, so he brought the rifle to his shoulder and sent them toward the outlaws who were now entering the cut. With all the dust swirling around he couldn't tell if he hit any of them or not.

The wagon burst out of the southern end of the gap. Sam yelled at the mules as he lashed them with the reins. Behind the wagon, on the slopes, the bushwhackers who hadn't been cut down by Matt ran to the southern end and fired after the wagon.

One of the outriders cried out and arched his back as a slug tore through him. Matt saw the man topple from the saddle. That meant only one of the nine men Thorpe had deputized was still with them.

But the marshal had Matt and Sam siding him now, and it wasn't far to Pancake Flats. Matt didn't think the gang would follow them all the way into the settlement . . . but he couldn't be sure about that. He reached in his pocket, found more .44-40 shells, and began thumbing them into the Winchester's loading gate.

He didn't need them, though, because the outlaws on horseback fell back, giving up the chase, and within minutes the wagon was out of range of the riflemen on the slopes. This latest attack had done some damage, but the wagon was still moving and Joshua Shade was still locked up inside it.

On the seat, Sam asked Thorpe, "Do you want to stop to check on Shade?"

The marshal shook his head. "No, keep moving. We'll reach Pancake Flats soon, and we'll find out then if he's still alive."

Sam nodded. If any bullets had penetrated the

wagon, Shade might be wounded and slowly bleeding to death in there . . . but if that was the case, it was his own fault for giving up his career as a preacher and becoming a loco, bloodthirsty desperado.

Since the outlaws were no longer giving chase, Sam let the mules slow down a little, but only a little. He intended to keep them moving pretty fast until they reached the railroad.

"Do you know when the next westbound train will be coming through Pancake Flats?" he asked Thorpe.

The marshal shook his head. "Tonight or tomorrow morning, I hope. The sooner we get Shade on a train rolling toward Yuma, the better."

"Amen to that," Matt said as he sat up on top of the wagon. His hat had come off when he leaped from the bluff onto the vehicle, and now it hung behind his head by its chin strap. He tapped Sam's shoulder and pointed. "My horse."

The horse was trotting along the trail up ahead. It stopped in response to the piercing whistle Matt let out, and when the wagon drew closer, Sam slowed the vehicle so that his blood brother could slide over the side and drop to the ground.

Matt went to his mount and sheathed the reloaded rifle. He swung up into the saddle, lifted the reins, and rode out ahead of the wagon once more. The lone remaining guard trailed behind the wagon, his head swiveling on his neck as he checked their back trail frequently for any sign of the outlaws from Shade's gang.

Now that this latest attempt to rescue Shade had failed, Sam's thoughts turned back to the conversation he'd been having with Marshal Thorpe just before the shooting started. He said, "Marshal, doesn't it seem strange that you were ordered to deliver Shade to Yuma practically on your own?"

The lawman shrugged. "That's my job."

"Yes, but the odds against you being able to do it are high, and your boss had to know that."

"I've gotten Shade this far, haven't I?" Thorpe snapped.

"Yes, but you're still a long way from Yuma."

"Not that far by train. It won't take more than half a day to get there once we board."

"You've still got to get on board," Sam pointed out.

"What's your point, Two Wolves?"

"I think something more is going on than just taking Shade to Yuma to be hanged," Sam said. "I haven't figured out what it is yet, but there has to be a reason the government wants things done this way."

Thorpe shook his head. "You're seeing conspiracies where there aren't any," he said. "You're making it sounds like the government *wants* Shade to get away."

Sam looked over at Thorpe and cocked an eyebrow, as if to ask if that might not be the case. Thorpe just snorted in disdain.

A few minutes later, a patch of green appeared up ahead, an oasis of color in the mostly drab brown-and-tan landscape. The terrain had smoothed out so that it was as flat as could be. Thorpe nodded toward the vegetation and said, "That's got to be the settlement. There's a spring there, or so I've heard."

The sun was almost down. Night would fall quickly as soon as the blazing orb dropped below the horizon.

"I just hope we don't have to spend much time there," Sam said.

"You and Bodine plan on going all the way to Yuma, eh?"

"We've come this far. I don't expect we'll turn back now."

"What if I tell you I don't want you coming with me and Shade?"

"The railroads are public conveyances, Marshal," Sam pointed out. "I'm not sure you can stop us."

"I could have the local law lock you up."

"But you're not going to do that, are you?"

Thorpe didn't answer for a moment. Then he shook his head and said, "No, I'm not. I'm no fool, Two Wolves. I know I wouldn't have made it this far with Shade if not for the help I've gotten from you and Bodine. But don't forget who's in charge."

"We won't, Marshal," Sam promised.

But at the same time, he knew that he and Matt were going to do everything in their power to see that Joshua Shade wound up at the end of a hangrope where he belonged.

Chapter 26

Willard Garth was at his wit's end. Twice, he had led the men—*his* men, damn it, as long as Joshua Shade was a prisoner!—against that blasted marshal in attacks that by all rights should have been successful.

And twice those attacks had been beaten back, thanks in large part to the audacity and deadly gun-handling of Matt Bodine and Sam Two Wolves.

Four more men had died during this latest fracas, leaving fourteen members of the gang still alive. A few of those fourteen had minor wounds, but nothing that would keep them out of the next fight.

There *would* be a next fight, Garth vowed to himself as the gang regrouped and the wounded men were tended to. He hadn't come this far, risked this much, just to let Shade be taken to Yuma and hanged. They would free him somehow.

But the task had gotten more difficult now, and Garth knew it as he stared across the flat expanse to the spot where lights were beginning to be visible in the gathering shadows. That was the settlement where Thorpe planned to catch the train. There would be people around, and buildings where the lawman could hole up with his prisoner.

Even worse, a westbound train might come through this evening, and Thorpe could get on it with Joshua. If that happened, Garth would have to figure out some way to stop the train before it reached Yuma.

He looked around and settled his gaze on one of his remaining men. "Hennessy, ride southeast and find a place to watch for a train before it gets to that settlement. If you see one comin', you light a shuck back here to let us know, you hear?"

The outlaw called Hennessy nodded. He mounted and rode off into the looming darkness.

Jeffries walked up and asked, "What now, Garth? Any ideas?"

Garth had an idea, all right, and it involved putting his fist down Jeffries's throat. "I thought I told you to keep an eye on the pilgrim and his woman."

"That sodbuster's not going anywhere," Jeffries said. "Hell, he hasn't even fully regained conscious-ness since he collapsed. If you ask me, his skull's busted and he's going to die before the night's over."

"Damn it, hush that up!" Garth said. "I don't want the woman hearin' it."

"Why not?" Jeffries sneered. "Are you worried about upsetting her?"

An idea had begun to form in Garth's brain. He said, "No, but if she thinks her husband's fixin' to die, she might not cooperate with us."

"She doesn't have any choice about that, does she?"

"If she's gonna do what I want her to, we'll have to trust her. We can't trust her if we don't have her hus-band's life to hold over her, along with the kid's."

Jeffries frowned and asked, "What are you thinking about, Garth?"

"You'll see," Garth said. He didn't feel like explaining himself to Jeffries or anybody else. Instead, he stalked over to where Winslow was now stretched out on the ground with his bloody head pillowed in his wife's lap.

She had ripped some strips from her petticoat and tied them around his head as makeshift bandages. Somewhere along the way, she had lost her bonnet, and her blond hair had slipped out of its bun to hang loosely around her shoulders.

Garth felt a pang of regret as she looked up at him with a stricken expression. He remembered a time when women this wholesome and pretty hadn't looked at him with fear in their eyes.

"He won't wake up," she said. "I can't get him to wake up."

"He'll be fine," Garth told her gruffly. "I've seen plenty o' fellas who got knocked addlepated like he did, and they just need some time to sleep it off. Then they wake up and they're all right again."

"He needs a doctor," Maggie Winslow pleaded.

Garth shook his head. "No doctor. But we'll take good care o' him. You got my word on that."

"You . . . you won't let him die?"

"Not if I can help it." Garth paused, then added, "Not if you cooperate and do what I tell you."

"Anything." Her hands went to the top button of her dress and started to unfasten it even though her fingers trembled. "You can do anything you want."

Garth shook his head and made a curt gesture. "Not that. What I want you to do is ride down to that settlement and find out when the next train headin' west is due to come through."

Her hands dropped away from the buttons. "You . . . you want me to spy for you? Like when you sent Ike into Arrowhead?"

"That's right." That part of his plan had worked, Garth thought. They had known what Thorpe's plans were, even if they hadn't been successful in stopping those plans . . . yet.

He went on. "That ain't all. We'll need to know exactly where Joshua's bein' held and how many deputies the marshal has."

Gonzalez was close enough to have been listening to the conversation. He spoke up, saying, "I saw just one of the gringo deputies left, Garth, if you don't count that Bodine and Two Wolves."

"You'd damned well better count them," Jeffries said. "From the looks of what they've done so far, they're worth two or three good fighting men apiece."

"I want to know about all of it," Garth told Maggie. "Can you do that?"

"I . . . I don't know." She looked down at the man whose head rested in her lap. "I . . . I guess I can try, but I'm worried about Ike . . ."

Garth drew his bowie knife. In a low, dangerous voice, he said, "I can promise you one thing, lady. If you don't help us, that husband o' yours won't live out the night."

Of course, Winslow probably wouldn't be alive come sunup anyway, but his wife didn't have to know that.

"All right," Maggie said. "I'll do it. Are you going to give me a horse?"

"That's right. And don't even think about tryin' to double-cross us, ma'am. We'll have your husband and

your baby, and you won't never see either one of 'em
alive again if you try anything funny."

"Don't worry, Mr. Garth. I'll find out what you need
to know." She stroked back a few strands of hair that
had fallen over Winslow's closed eyes. "And maybe by
the time I get back, Ike will be awake again."

"I reckon there's a good chance of it," Garth lied.
The longer Winslow remained unconscious, the
greater the chances that he would never wake up.

It was a good thing Garth didn't give a damn
whether the pilgrim lived or died.

Pancake Flats was considerably smaller than Arrowhead, with only one real street that stretched for a
couple of blocks north and south. It had something the
larger settlement didn't, though——an adobe railroad
station that fronted the tracks of the Southern Pacific.

Matt glanced eastward along those tracks and
thought that if you kept following them far enough,
you'd wind up right back in Sweet Apple, Texas, which
he and Sam had left weeks earlier. He wondered how
their friend Marshal Seymour Standish was doing these
days. To tell the truth, Matt wouldn't have minded if
Seymour was here in Pancake Flats right about now.
For a skinny Easterner, Seymour was pretty tough.

And things weren't looking too promising at the
moment.

"What do you mean a bridge is out?" Marshal Asa
Thorpe demanded angrily of the eyeshade-wearing
gent on the other side of the ticket window. "I have a
prisoner I've got to get to Yuma!"

"I understand that, Marshal," the railroad clerk said
nervously, "but I can't do anything about it. That flash

flood last week washed out the trestle over Bowtie Canyon, and it'll be another couple of days before it's repaired enough to get a train over it. There's nothing we can do except wait."

The wagon with Joshua Shade locked up inside it was parked next to the station. Matt, Sam, and the remaining deputy, a man named Everett, stood around the vehicle with rifles in their hands. Thorpe had stomped up onto the platform and gone over to the window to find out when the next westbound was due.

Now it had become crystal clear that there wouldn't be a train rolling into Pancake Flats for a couple of days at the very least, maybe longer. Thorpe's face was dark with anger in the lamplight that spilled through the ticket window onto the platform. He looked like he wanted to reach through the window, grab the unfortunate clerk by the throat, and squeeze a solution to the problem out of him.

But there was no solution to be had, so Thorpe turned away from the window with a disgusted curse. He stopped and looked back.

"You got any law around here?"

"Just a town marshal," the clerk said. "His office is back up the street, half a block on your left."

Thorpe grunted. "Obliged," he said in a surly voice, then stalked along the platform to the steps at the end.

As Thorpe came down the steps, Sam said, "It sounds like we're stuck here for a while."

"Stuck is right," Thorpe snapped. "Sitting ducks, that's what we are."

"I reckon we could follow the railroad tracks and keep goin' in the wagon," Matt suggested.

Thorpe shook his head. "That'd be even worse. There's only four of us now. We've already beaten the odds in fighting off those outlaws twice. I don't reckon we could do it again."

Matt didn't think they could either, but he would have been willing to give it a try. Still, maybe there was a better way.

"We'll hole up and wait for the train," he said. "Find some nice sturdy place with walls thick enough to stop bullets."

"Shouldn't be too hard," Sam added. "Most of the buildings around here are made of adobe. Their walls are probably pretty thick."

"I saw a livery barn back up the street that looked like it'd stand up to anything short of a cannonball," Matt said.

Thorpe said, "Let's talk to the local law first. Maybe he's got a good jail we can use."

Sam climbed onto the wagon seat again and untied the reins from the brake lever. He got the mules moving, and followed Thorpe up the street toward the marshal's office. They hadn't noticed it as they went past earlier because there was no sign, but one of the citizens now pointed it out to Thorpe.

"You won't find Marshal Lopez there right now, though," the man added. "He'll be havin' his supper."

"Whereabouts?" Thorpe asked.

"Over at the cantina." The man pointed to a building on the other side of the street.

"Stay here and keep your eyes open," Thorpe growled at Matt, Sam, and Everett. He walked across the road and vanished into the cantina.

Matt licked his lips and said, "My whistle could sure use wettin'."

"I seem to recall you saying the same thing when we got to Arrowhead," Sam commented.

"Well, it was true then and it's true now. Nothin' works up a man's thirst like trail dust and gettin' shot at."

Thorpe emerged from the cantina a minute later, followed by a short, round man in a shabby black suit and with a high-crowned sombrero. Judging by the federal lawman's long, angry strides that forced the smaller man to trot in order to keep up, Thorpe wasn't happy.

"This is Marshal Lopez," he said as he came up to the wagon, jerking a thumb over his shoulder at the other man. "He says we're welcome to use his office, but he doesn't have an actual jail."

Matt looked at Lopez. "Where do you lock up prisoners then?"

The man shrugged and spread his hands. "I try not to have to lock up anybody, Señor. Pancake Flats is a peaceful place. About the worst trouble we get is a cowboy who's had too much to drink now and then. When that happens, I clout 'em over the head, toss 'em in the barn, and let them sleep it off."

"That barn?" Sam asked, pointing to the livery stable. It was a low, rambling adobe building with a slate roof.

Lopez bobbed his head. *"Sí, señor."*

"We can bar the doors," Matt said. "Looks like there are only a couple of windows, so we can trade off standin' watch. As much as we've whittled down Shade's gang, maybe they won't want to come right into town to try to take him back."

"It seems to be our best bet, Marshal," Sam added.

Thorpe nodded. "I realize that. The livery stable it is then." He looked at Lopez. "If there's trouble, can we count on you and the townspeople to lend us a hand?"

Lopez grimaced uncomfortably. "Most of the folks

around here are peace-lovin' hombres, you know what I mean?"

"I know what you mean," Thorpe said disgustedly. He studied Matt, Sam, and Everett. "It appears that we're on our own until that train comes through."

"Why should this be any different?" Matt asked.

Chapter 27

Maggie Winslow couldn't breathe because her heart had crept right up into her throat and lodged there, choking her.

That was what it felt like anyway as she rode into Pancake Flats not long after dark.

Her face burned with shame because she had to ride astride, with her skirt pulled up over her calves. It had been bad enough when she was forced to ride like that in front of the leering outlaw called Jeffries, whom she hated because of the way his arm had pressed up against the underside of her breasts, and because of the vile things he had whispered in her ear when no one else could hear.

This was worse, though, because now decent people would witness her shame, instead of just a bunch of terrible outlaws. And of course she was worried about Ike and Caleb. Having to ride away and leave her husband and son in the clutches of those beasts was like having part of her soul ripped away.

But the only possible way to save them was to do what Garth told her, no matter how ashamed or frightened she was. She had been prepared to give her body to the outlaws if she had to. Surely she could act as a spy for them.

She spotted the closed-in wagon Garth had told her to look for. It was being pulled into what appeared to be a large livery barn. Two men shoved the doors shut behind it as Maggie reined the horse to a halt. She heard the solid *thunk!* of a bar being dropped into place on the other side of those doors.

Maggie nudged her horse forward again. She headed for the railroad station at the far end of the street. Garth wanted to know when the next westbound train was due to arrive. Maggie figured that information would be chalked onto the board next to the ticket window. If not, she could ask the clerk.

Before she could reach the station, however, four men emerged from a building with a sign fastened to it that read simply SALOON, and began to cross the street in front of her. She pulled the horse to a stop to let them go by, but to her dismay, one of the men stopped, looked at her, and said with a big grin, "Hey, fellas, look what we got here."

The other three men stopped as well to leer up at Maggie. From the way they swayed slightly, she knew they were all drunk, or at least had been drinking quite a bit. They wore big hats and range clothes, and each man had a holstered gun on his hip.

Cowboys from one of the nearby ranches, in town to blow off steam. That's what they had to be. Maggie wished she hadn't encountered them, but now that she had, all she could do was try to avoid trouble.

"Please let me pass," she said. The way they were standing in the street, she couldn't get around them very easily, and she wasn't that good a rider. She was afraid that if she tried to rein the horse to the side, she might hit one of the cowboys.

"Aw, you don't want to ride off just yet, sweetie," the first cowboy said. "We just met."

"We haven't been introduced," Maggie said in a brittle voice.

"That's right, we haven't. My name's Dub. What's yours?"

Maggie didn't answer the question. Instead, she said, "Please, I have business to attend to."

"You're a workin' girl, are you?" one of the other men asked with a leer.

"No, I—" Maggie began before she realized what he meant. When she did, she gasped and felt her face turning hot. "Of course not! I just need to go down to the railroad station—"

"You can't be leavin' already," Dub said. "You just got here. I seen you ridin' down the street." He reached for the horse's harness. "Why don't you come on back into the saloon and have a drink with us? We'd sure admire to spend some time in your company, wouldn't we, boys?"

"We sure would, Dub," one of the other men said. Ugly grins were plastered on their faces.

"No!" Maggie said, pulling back on the reins. "Let me go!"

Dub's face turned uglier. "You don't want to be standoffish like that. Just be friendly to us, and we'll let you go in a little while—"

"You'll let her go now," a new voice said.

They would need supplies if they were going to stay holed up in the livery barn until the trestle was repaired and the train could reach Pancake Flats. They still had some jerky left from the trip, but it wouldn't last long. There was the matter of fresh water, too.

Matt had volunteered to slip out the back and fetch everything they needed while the other three stayed there to guard Joshua Shade. Thorpe had already unlocked the wagon to check on the prisoner, found him as loco and filled with hate as ever, and locked it up again.

"Are you sure you'll be all right?" Sam asked before Matt left the barn. "I could come with you."

Matt shook his head. "That would leave just the marshal and Everett here. I'll be fine."

Earlier, he had noticed a general store that appeared to be open despite the hour. Hoping that it still was, Matt circled the barn and came out onto the street. He glanced one way toward the general store, and was pleased to see that its windows were still lit up.

Then, hearing loud, raucous voices, he looked the other way . . .

And saw four cowboys blocking the path of a young woman on horseback. She seemed scared as she tried to pull her mount away from the men, but one of the cowboys had hold of the horse's harness. "Let me go!" she cried, and she sounded scared, too.

The cowboy holding the horse leered up at her and made some rude comment about letting her go in a little while.

By that time, Matt was already striding toward them. He didn't think about what he was doing. He just acted according to his instincts, which just weren't about to allow him to let those hombres bother the woman any longer.

She was young and pretty, Matt couldn't help

noticing, with pale blond hair hanging loose around her shoulders, but that didn't matter. He would have done the same if she had been old and gray and wrinkled. Where Matt came from, men didn't mistreat women.

If they did, they risked dying for it.

"You'll let her go now," he said.

He hadn't sneaked up on them; they would have been able to see him coming if they hadn't been so busy ogling the young woman. He didn't raise his voice all that much, but it carried clearly and made the cowboys turn sharply toward him. The woman glanced over her shoulder at him, and Matt saw that her eyes were wide with fear.

"Don't worry, ma'am," he told her. "These gents won't bother you anymore."

"You're talkin' mighty big considerin' that there's one o' you and four of us," the man holding the horse shot back.

"The way I see it, I've got you outnumbered," Matt drawled.

"How the hell do you figure that?"

Matt shrugged. "One man counts for more than four polecats, at least where I come from."

"Why, you son of a—"

Matt held up his left hand to stop the cowboy, while keeping his right close to the butt of the Colt on that side.

"Watch your language, amigo," he said softly. "There's a lady present."

A voice in the back of his head warned him that he shouldn't be getting in more trouble while he and Sam and Thorpe and Everett still had the problem of Joshua Shade to deal with. But there were some things in life that a man just couldn't walk away from, and as far as Matt Bodine was concerned, this was one of them.

The cowboy let go of the horse's harness at last. He took a couple of steps to the side, his face contorted with anger and his right hand held out in a clawlike shape above the butt of his gun, ready to hook and draw. He said, "All right, mister, you wanted trouble, you got it. You don't know who you're messin' with here."

"A drunk, from the looks of it." Matt nodded toward the other cowboys. "Why don't you just go with your friends and find someplace to sleep it off? That way, nobody has to get hurt."

"It's too late for that," the cowboy insisted. "My name's Dub Branch, and I'm the slickest draw in these parts. What do they call you?" He sneered. "I like to know who I'm about to kill."

One of his friends said, "Uh, Dub, maybe you better think twice about this. That fella don't look like he's got much back-up in him."

"That's right," Matt said. "The Good Lord plumb left it out of me. And by the way, the name's Bodine. Matt Bodine."

The eyes of all four cowboys widened in surprise, as did the eyes of the young woman, who still hadn't moved on. Matt didn't want any gunplay to start while she was still close by, so this was one time he was hoping that his reputation would be enough to make a potential opponent decide not to fight after all.

Dub Branch didn't want to give up that easy, though. He said, "Hell, anybody can call himself Matt Bodine! We don't know that you're really him."

"Dub, I've heard about Bodine," one of the others

said. "This fella matches the description. And look at those two irons he packs. He's a gunslinger, all right."

"Aw, it's all for show!" Branch insisted. "And I'm gonna prove it right now! Any o' you boys with me?"

One of the cowboys said, "I'll back your play, Dub."

Matt glanced at him, saw that he wasn't as drunk as the others. And the man had a certain cool fatalism in his eyes that marked him as a dangerous hombre. If Matt had to take both of them, he'd go for the other man first, then Branch.

"Thanks, Court." Branch moved to one side while Court went the other way, spreading out so that Matt would have a harder time getting lead in both of them before one of them dropped him.

That was their plan anyway.

But that wasn't now it worked out, because as Branch cried, "Get him!" and both men slapped leather, Matt palmed out both guns and fired so fast that it seemed the Colts had appeared in his hands by magic.

The right-hand gun roared, sending a bullet into Court's chest just as he cleared leather. The impact rocked him back and then sent him reeling.

Matt held his fire with the left-hand gun, which was lined up on Branch's shirt pocket. Branch's Colt was only halfway out of the holster.

"Let it slide, Dub," Matt said while keeping watch on Court out of the corner of his eye. "Let it slide, and you won't have to die tonight."

Instead, Branch screamed, "You bastard!" and hauled his iron out the rest of the way. Matt waited until it was coming up before firing a single shot that ripped through Branch's throat, severed his spine, and dropped him in the dirt of the street like a puppet with its strings cut.

"Look out!" the woman cried.

Matt had already seen Court regain his balance and swing up the gun he still held. Matt fired before the man could squeeze the trigger. This slug went into Court's forehead, leaving a black hole over his right eye. Court went over backward, arms and legs flinging out to the side as he died.

From the size of the pool of blood forming around Branch's head, Matt knew the reckless cowboy wasn't a threat anymore. He looked at the remaining two punchers, who seemed cold sober now, shocked out of their drunken haze by the deaths of Branch and Court.

"You fellas want to take a hand in this game?" Matt asked them.

Both men practically broke their necks shaking their heads so hard as they backed away. They held up empty hands and one of them stammered, "N-no, sir, Mr. B-Bodine!"

"When the marshal asks you about this, you'll tell him the truth about what happened, won't you?"

"Y-yes, sir! You don't have to worry about that. Dub and Court were damn fools, that's what happened!"

"Damn fools," the other puncher repeated, "to go up against Matt Bodine!"

Matt nodded. "Best go fetch the undertaker then, if this burg's got one." The two surviving cowboys hustled away up the street as he pouched the left-hand iron and began reloading the two chambers he had emptied in the other Colt. When that was done, he replaced the expended round in the second gun.

Then he looked up and saw that the young woman was still sitting there on her horse. She wore a long gingham dress, not the sort of outfit that was suitable for riding. She stared at Matt and said, "You're Matt Bodine."

He smiled as he holstered the left-hand gun, then touched the brim of his Stetson and gave her a polite nod.

"Yes, ma'am. You've got the advantage of me."

"My name is . . . Jessica Devlin."

He noted the slight hesitation, and wondered briefly if the name she had just given him was the right one. It didn't really matter, though, so he didn't press her on it. He just said, "I wish we'd met under better circumstances, Miss Devlin."

"Yes. So do I. But I . . . I thank you for your help." She looked nervous, a little like a wild animal that's realized it's being stalked. "I . . . have to go now."

Matt tugged on his hat brim. "Ma'am."

She turned her horse and kicked it into a trot that carried her toward the railroad station. Matt watched until she got there safely and dismounted, then turned toward the general store again.

He still had to pick up those supplies and get back to the barn. Sam was probably wondering what those shots had been about.

And knowing Sam, he'd just assume that Matt had been mixed up in the fracas . . .

Chapter 28

Maggie's heart wasn't choking her anymore, but it still pounded a mile a minute in her chest. She had heard the outlaws talking about Matt Bodine, about what a deadly gunman he was, and now she had seen the proof of that with her own eyes.

If she hadn't witnessed it, she wouldn't have believed that a man could draw and fire even one pistol that fast and with such accuracy, let alone two. And Bodine's companion, the half-breed called Two Wolves, was supposed to be almost as good with a gun, according to the outlaws.

No wonder they'd been able to fight off the two attempts to rescue Joshua Shade. Bodine and Two Wolves were alone now, though, except for the marshal and one deputy. They couldn't outfight what was left of the gang. Their only real hope of getting their prisoner out of here lay in catching the train.

Maggie understood that was why Garth wanted to know when the next train was due. They had to free Shade before the train arrived.

She glanced up the street as she dismounted by the

train station. Matt Bodine still stood there, obviously keeping an eye on her to make sure no one else bothered her.

She started to lift a hand and wave to him to let him know that she was all right, but she didn't do it. She didn't want to be friendly toward him. It was bad enough that she was helping Shade's gang, after he had risked his life to keep those cowboys from molesting her. What she was doing now might allow the outlaws to kill him later on.

She had no choice, though. Not as long as they had Ike and Caleb in their power.

Maggie almost wished Matt Bodine hadn't stepped in when those men accosted her. She certainly wished he hadn't asked her what her name was. For some reason, she hadn't wanted to admit the truth. So she had given him the name of her best friend back in Ohio instead. Jessica would never know the difference.

Pausing at the top of the steps leading to the station platform, Maggie glanced up the street again. Bodine was gone. She felt oddly relieved.

The ticket window was still open, but as Maggie hurried toward it, she saw the clerk reach up to pull down the shutter that would close it off for the night. She looked at the board next to the window, saw that nothing was written on it, and hurried forward to catch the clerk's attention before he could pull down the shutter.

"Sir! Please, wait a minute!"

The clerk hesitated, and for a second Maggie thought he was going to ignore her plea and close up anyway. But then he let go of the shutter, sighed, and asked, "What can I do for you, ma'am?"

"I need to know when the next westbound train will arrive, please."

The clerk laughed. "I don't have any passengers headin' west for a week at a time, or sometimes even more, and now tonight there's all sorts of folks wantin' to catch a train goin' in that die-rection."

Maggie tried to look only idly curious as she said, "Someone else wanted to know about the westbound?"

"That's right. A deputy United States marshal, of all things. He didn't give me any details, but I reckon he must have a prisoner he's got to deliver, from the looks o' the wagon he had with him."

"What about the train?" Maggie asked, trying to curb her impatience.

"I'll tell you the same thing I told that lawman, missy. There won't be no westbound train through here, nor eastbound neither, until the work crews get through repairin' the trestle over Bowtie Canyon. That's gonna be another couple o' days at least."

"No train?" Maggie didn't know whether to be relieved or even more worried. If the marshal and his companions were stuck here in Pancake Flats with their prisoner for several days, would Garth attack the town in an attempt to free Joshua Shade? She wouldn't put anything past the outlaws, but she didn't think there were enough of them left to risk a raid such as that.

"That's right, no train," the clerk said, talking to her now like she was a not-very-bright child. "When I hear any different, I'll put the news on the chalkboard. Now, would you like to buy a ticket for when the train *does* run?"

"What? Oh." Maggie shook her head. "No, thank you."

The clerk rolled his eyes, as if wondering why she had bothered him about it if she didn't want a ticket. He reached for the shutter and said, "Good night, then," rolling it down with a solid thump before Maggie could change her mind and ask him anything else.

She didn't know how Garth, Jeffries, and the other outlaws would take this news, but there was no doubt in her mind that she would go back and pass it along to them, as Garth had instructed her to do. For a second while she was talking to Matt Bodine, she had considered telling him everything and throwing herself on his mercy, begging him to rescue Ike and Caleb somehow.

If anyone could do such a thing, it would be Matt Bodine and Sam Two Wolves, she sensed.

But it was too big a risk. She couldn't disobey Garth's orders, because she knew he wouldn't hesitate to cut Caleb's throat, and he might do the same to Ike. Or he might just leave Ike somewhere in the wilderness to die slowly and painfully from his head injury. Maggie couldn't take a chance on either of those things happening.

So she went back to her horse, swung up into the saddle without worrying now about riding astride so that her calves were exposed, and sent the horse back up the street at a fast trot. She was thankful she had learned how to ride a horse as a girl, back on her family's farm.

As she passed the general store, Matt Bodine was stepping out of the establishment. He raised a hand to wave at her, but she didn't acknowledge him. She didn't have time to stop and chat, and anyway, as long as her husband and son were prisoners, Bodine was one of the enemy.

She didn't look back as she rode out of town, heading north.

* * *

Now that was mighty funny, Matt thought as he watched Jessica Devlin—if that was her real name—leaving Pancake Flats. She had ridden into the settlement—not wearing riding clothes—gone to the train station, spent a few minutes there, then mounted up and ridden right back out of town.

From the looks of it, she had come to find out the train schedule. Matt couldn't think of any other reason why she would have stopped at the depot. The clerk must have told her about the trestle being out.

Well, it was none of his business, Matt told himself. Carrying the bag of supplies he had picked up at the store in his left arm so that his right hand was free in case he needed to slap leather, he headed back to the livery barn.

He went around back and kicked the door. "It's me, Sam," he called through it. A moment later, he heard the bar being lifted; then the door swung open.

Matt stepped inside quickly. In the dim light of the lantern that had been lit earlier, he saw Sam and Everett flanking the door, each of them holding a Winchester. Marshal Thorpe was beside the wagon, the shotgun in his hands.

"Any trouble?" Sam asked as he closed the door behind Matt.

"Not a bit." Matt hesitated. "Oh, wait a minute. I had to shoot a couple of hombres who were botherin' a woman."

Sam sighed. "I heard those shots and wondered if they had anything to do with you. I figured that chances were they did."

"I knew that's what you'd think," Matt said as he set the supplies down on the wagon seat. "But you'd have done the same thing, Sam. They'd been drinkin', and they would have molested the gal if I hadn't come along."

"What gal?"

Matt shrugged. "I don't know. Somebody from around here, I guess. She told me her name—Jessica Devlin. But it didn't mean anything to me."

"Me either," Everett put in. "I don't know everybody in these parts, but I don't recollect any Devlins hereabouts."

Sam said, "I'll bet she was young and pretty, wasn't she?"

Matt smiled. "Well, now that you mention it . . ."

Thorpe said, "You shouldn't have gotten mixed up in a shooting, Bodine. Lopez is liable to try to throw you in jail for killing a couple of locals."

Matt shook his head. "No, there were a couple of other punchers there, and they said they'd tell the marshal what happened. I gave those fellas every chance not to turn it into a corpse-and-cartridge session."

Thorpe grunted and said, "You walk a fine line, Bodine. All you gunslingers do. If it was up to me, I'd disarm the lot of you so you couldn't go around killing each other."

"Not in our lifetime, Marshal," Matt said with a shake of his head. "And if something like that ever happened, I might just have to hunt me a new place to live, because this sure wouldn't be the same country I grew up in."

"Just try to stay out of trouble the rest of the time we're here," Thorpe said.

"Sure, Marshal. I always do."

Sam just rolled his eyes at that.

* * *

A mile north of town, Maggie Winslow was riding along when several dark shapes suddenly appeared out of the shadows around her. She hadn't seen them coming, and she gasped as she instinctively jerked back on the reins.

"Take it easy, girl," Garth's harsh voice said. Maggie recognized it instantly, and even though she knew the man was a cold-blooded killer, she relaxed a little.

Better the devil you know, as the old saying went, than one you didn't know.

"What did you find out?" Garth asked. "Is there a train comin' in tonight?"

"First, tell me about Ike and Caleb," Maggie said with more than a hint of stubbornness in her voice. "Are they all right?"

"Sure they are. The tyke's sound asleep."

"What about Ike? Is he awake?"

"Not yet," Garth admitted grudgingly. "I'm sure he's gonna be fine, though. Like I told you, when a fella gets walloped on the head like that, he needs some time to sleep it off."

Deep down, Maggie didn't believe him, no matter how much she wanted to. She had a terrible feeling that Ike would never wake up, that she would never hear her husband's laugh or feel his arms around her again.

But there was nothing she could do for him other than what she was already doing, so when Garth asked again about the train, she said, "There won't be a train. Not tonight, and probably not tomorrow either. A flash flood washed out a trestle east of here, at a place called Bowtie Canyon. The trains aren't running in either direction until it gets repaired."

One of the other men who had met her was Gonzalez, who seemed to be at Garth's side most of the time. Maggie suspected that was because the Mexican was ambitious and was watching for a chance to take over the gang. Jeffries was the same way.

Gonzalez said, "That's lucky for us, no? Gives us more time to figure out a way to get the rev'rend away from them."

Garth didn't answer Gonzalez. Instead, he asked Maggie, "Where are they holdin' Joshua? The local jail?"

She shook her head. "No, I saw the wagon they have him in. They were taking it into a barn, probably the local livery stable."

"Are you sure they weren't just puttin' it away after lockin' up Joshua somewheres else?"

"I don't think so. The door on the back was still locked. I saw the padlock, and it was fastened. And the way the marshal and the other men were watching, they were still on guard. To tell you the truth, I didn't see a jail, and I looked up and down both sides of the only street."

"So the place is too small to have a jail," Garth mused. "They're fortin' up inside the livery instead. That ain't a bad idea. What's the buildin' made of?"

"Adobe."

"What about the roof?"

"I'm not sure. Some sort of tile."

Gonzalez made a disgusted sound. "So we can't burn 'em out very easy."

"How many windows does the place have?" Garth asked.

Maggie took a deep breath. She hadn't even realized that she'd been noticing such things, but she was certain she was right as she replied, "I don't know, but not many. I didn't see any on the front, and maybe one or two on the sides."

"So they can cover 'em all," Garth said. He scratched his jaw in thought. "If we rush the place, we're gonna lose a lot of men, especially with Bodine and Two Wolves in there."

Maggie caught her bottom lip between her teeth. She hadn't said anything so far about meeting Matt Bodine, and she decided it would be better not to. She didn't want Garth and the others suspecting her of some sort of double cross, even though her encounter with Matt Bodine hadn't had anything to do with Joshua Shade.

"We'll have to think of some other way to flush 'em out into the open," Garth went on. "At least we've got a little bit of time."

He reached toward her. Maggie flinched, but Garth just took hold of her wrist, pulled her hand toward him, and pressed something into her palm. She felt the crinkle of money.

"Ride on back to town," he told her. "Find a hotel or a boardin'house or some such place to stay. Keep your eyes and ears open, and if you hear anything about a train comin', you hightail it out here and let us know."

"How . . . how will I find you?"

"Don't worry about that. We'll be keepin' an eye on you, and if you start in this direction, we'll know it."

"What about Ike and Caleb?"

"We'll look after them."

Maggie took a deep breath and then shook her head. "No. Not unless you let me take Caleb with me."

"I said—" Garth began.

"I want my son with me."

Gonzalez spoke up, saying, "The *niño*'s kind of a handful, Garth. We still got the husband to make sure she don't try to trick us."

Garth bristled. "I reckon you've forgot who's givin' the orders here."

"I'm just saying that if you want me to cooperate and help you," Maggie told him, "you have to give me what I want, too."

Garth put a hand on the butt of his gun. "I could just shoot all three of you and be done with it."

"And then you wouldn't have anyone to spy for you," Maggie pointed out. "I suppose one of you could ride into town and handle that chore, but you can't be sure that Bodine or one of the others won't spot you. They don't know me, though."

That wasn't strictly true. She had met Matt Bodine— but he didn't know her real name or that she had any connection to the outlaws who had been trying to free Joshua Shade.

"How about if I go ahead and kill your husband right now," Garth said. "Gonzalez, go kill him if the lady doesn't get on her horse and ride."

"No, please," Maggie cried. "I'll go, just please don't hurt Ike or my son."

"Don't worry."

She did worry, though. That sense of fatalism still gripped her. They were all doomed, she thought. They had been ever since the outlaws had ridden up to the wagon. No one could change that.

But if anyone could, a tiny voice insisted in the back of her head, it was a man like Matt Bodine . . .

Chapter 29

The rest of the night passed quietly in the livery barn. After they gave Shade his supper, he ranted and raved some inside the wagon, but eventually he dozed off. Matt, Sam, Thorpe, and Everett took turns sleeping, with at least two of them always awake and alert.

After breakfast the next morning, Thorpe told Matt, "Go down to the train station and find out if that clerk's heard any more about when the trestle will be repaired. If he hasn't, tell him to come up here and let us know as soon as he does hear anything."

Matt nodded and tucked his Winchester under his arm. Sam and Everett followed him to the back door to guard it as they let him out.

Pancake Flats wasn't any more exciting this morning than it had been the night before, Matt noted as he walked toward the depot. Probably the only time the place really woke up was when a train came through.

"Bodine!" a voice called from behind him.

Matt swung around, instinctively bringing up the rifle and dropping into a crouch. His finger eased on the trigger when he saw the portly figure of the local lawman. Marshal Lopez had come to an abrupt halt as Matt's Winchester pointed at him, and now he backed off, hands up.

"Don't shoot, Bodine," Lopez said. "I didn't mean to spook you!"

Matt relaxed. "What do you want, Marshal?"

"I heard about what happened last night, with Dub Branch and Court Wesley, I mean. Those hombres were good with their guns."

"Not good enough," Matt said. "You're not thinkin' about tryin' to arrest me, are you, Marshal?"

"No, no," Lopez said quickly. "Their amigos told me what happened, how Dub and Court were drunk and Dub tried to molest some woman. They said you gave 'em a chance to go on with nobody gettin' hurt, but they slapped leather first."

Matt nodded. "That's the way it happened, all right."

"I just thought I should warn you, even though you're in the clear with the law, those boys had some hotheaded friends around here who might not see it that way. I ain't sayin' they'll come after you, but, ah . . . just when were you plannin' on leavin'?"

Lopez didn't care what happened, as long as it didn't happen in his town and he didn't have to deal with the aftermath, Matt thought. He said, "That all depends on when the train comes through. I was on my way to the station to check on that now."

Lopez took off his hat and scratched his head. "The sooner the better, I'm thinkin'."

"Sooner will be fine with us, too, but it's sort of out of our hands. We have to wait for that railroad repair crew to do its part."

"I'll walk with you, if that's all right."

Matt shrugged. "Suit yourself, Marshal." As they fell

in step alongside each other, he took the opportunity to ask, "You know a young woman named Jessica Devlin?"

"Devlin?" Lopez repeated with a frown. "I don't think so. No Devlins around here as far as I know."

That agreed with what Everett had told him the night before.

"She's blond, early twenties, easy to look at," Matt described her.

Lopez shook his head. "Still don't ring no bells. Sorry, Bodine. Was she the woman Dub and Court were botherin'?"

"That's right."

"Must be new in town . . . although why a young, pretty woman would choose to come to a dusty, no-account place like this, I don't know."

Matt recalled how nervous Jessica Devlin had been, even after the gunfight. Something had driven her to Pancake Flats, he thought, and whatever it was, she was scared and unhappy about it.

Of course, it could be anything . . . man trouble, family problems, what have you. None of his business, he told himself. Just the sort of idle curiosity he would feel about any good-looking young woman, and now that he and Lopez had reached the train station, he put the matter out of his mind.

The same clerk was on duty at the ticket window, and when he saw Matt coming, he started shaking his head.

"Sorry, there hasn't been any word this morning about the trestle," he said before Matt could even ask.

"If you hear anything, the marshal wants you to come up to the livery stable and let us know."

The clerk looked at Lopez. "Is that true, Marshal?"

"He means the other marshal," Lopez explained.

"The U.S. one. But I reckon it'd be a good idea if you do like he says, Harry."

The clerk nodded. "All right, as long as it doesn't interfere with my duties here. I work for the Southern Pacific Railroad, you know, not the U.S. marshal's office."

With that chore taken care of, Matt headed back to the livery stable. Sam let him in the back door, and he reported the bad news, or rather, the lack of news—which was pretty much the same thing.

"So we're still stuck here," Thorpe said. He glanced at the wagon, where Shade was quiet this morning. "If I wasn't a lawman, I'd open that door and put a bullet in that monster's head. That would settle things. The longer it takes us to get him to Yuma, the greater the chances of him escaping justice somehow."

"It'll catch up to him sooner or later, no matter what happens here," Sam said.

"In the next world, you mean?" Thorpe asked with a suggestion of a sneer in his voice. "I don't know what happens there, Two Wolves. All I know for sure is what happens here and now, and the law says Shade's got to hang."

"Sometimes prisoners get shot tryin' to escape," Matt said.

"You wouldn't solve the problem that way, though, would you, Bodine?"

Matt grunted and shook his head. "I reckon not. Not unless Shade was really gettin' away. Then I wouldn't hesitate to ventilate him."

"Maybe it won't come to that," Sam said. "Maybe the trestle will be repaired and the train will be here later today."

They all hoped that was true . . . but the worried

looks on their faces said that they would believe it when they saw it with their own eyes.

Late that afternoon, a knock sounded on one of the big double doors at the front of the stable.

Instantly, the four men inside the barn were fully alert and ready for trouble. Holding the shotgun poised in his hands, Marshal Thorpe went to the doors and called, "Who's there?"

As soon as the words were out of his mouth, he stepped quickly aside, just in case somebody tried to blast a rifle slug through the doors. They were made of thick, heavy wood, but they might not stop a bullet from a Winchester like the adobe walls would.

"It's Lopez," came the reply. "Open up. I got to talk to you."

The voice of the local lawman sounded strained. Thorpe turned his head and exchanged glances with Matt and Sam. It was possible that Lopez had been captured by the gang and was being forced to cooperate with them at gunpoint.

Thorpe said to Everett in a low voice, "Get over there by the wagon. If anybody busts in here, stick a six-gun through the window and empty it. I'd rather see Shade hang, but they're not taking him out of here."

Everett didn't look like he relished being given the job of executioner, but he drew his pistol and held it ready. Matt and Sam spread out, one on each side of the doorway, and leveled their rifles.

"Are you alone, Lopez?" Thorpe asked.

"*Sí*, Marshal. You have my word."

Matt didn't see why they should accept Lopez's word about anything, since they hadn't know the man for even twenty-four hours yet and he hadn't shown any signs of wanting to help them. But sooner or later, you had to trust *somebody*, he supposed.

Or maybe not, because Thorpe stepped closer to the door and said, "Anything you want to tell us, you can do it through the door. Is the train coming?"

"Not yet. Tomorrow maybe, Harry says. But this is about something else. More trouble."

"Just want we needed," Matt said under his breath.

"Go on," Thorpe urged.

"The word's gotten around town that you got Joshua Shade locked up in there. Some folks are gettin' worked up about the reward."

"Reward?" Thorpe repeated with a puzzled frown. "There's no more reward. Shade's already been convicted and sentenced to hang."

"That's what I mean," Lopez said. "Somebody started a rumor that Shade's gang will pay a thousand dollars to anybody who kills you four and sets him free."

Thorpe didn't seem to be the sort of man who surprised easily, but his eyes widened at that news. Matt and Sam glanced at each other, and the faces of the blood brothers were grim. This bounty on their scalps was an added complication they sure as hell didn't need.

"Someone from the gang must have slipped into town unnoticed and started spreading that rumor," Sam said quietly.

"They're tired of gettin' shot up, so they're tryin' to bribe somebody else into doin' their dirty work for them," Matt said.

Thorpe nodded in agreement with the theory. He called to Lopez, "What are you going to do about this?"

"Me?" The word came from Lopez in a plaintive yelp. "I can't do anything. Some of the cowboys in the saloon were already gettin' likkered up because they were mad about Bodine shootin' Dub and Court. I told you that was maybe gonna happen, Bodine."

"It's your job to put a stop to it," Matt called.

"I can't stop a whole mob of loco cowboys," Lopez protested. "And now it's just gonna be worse because of that bounty the gang put on your heads. I'm sorry, amigos, but the town don't pay me enough to get my ass shot off. I'm ridin' out."

"You're just going to leave and let all hell break loose?" Thorpe demanded, sounding as if he couldn't believe that any lawman would do such a thing.

"I got no choice," Lopez whined. "I got a family, a wife, and a bunch of kids. If I'm dead, who's gonna take care of them?"

"Let him go, Marshal," Sam advised. "I don't think he'd be much help anyway, even if he stayed and tried to stop the mob."

"Yeah, I guess you're right." Thorpe raised his voice. "All right, Lopez! Run out on us if that's what you want to do! Keep running long enough and far enough and maybe you can forget what you did here."

"You can shame me all you want, mister. At least, I'll still be alive to feel ashamed."

And with that, Lopez left. They all heard his boots scuffing away in the street.

"Every time we think things can't get any worse, they find a way, don't they?" Matt said. "Now probably half the town wants to kill us, and the other half will be too scared to do anything about it."

Thorpe grimaced and took off his hat. He scrubbed a hand over his face wearily. As he replaced his hat, he said, "If we stay here, they'll bust down the door and get in. We can't hold off that many men forever . . .

or even for as long as it takes that damned train to get here."

"Well, it seems like there's only one solution," Sam said.

The others all looked at him and waited for him to go on.

"We don't stay here," Sam said.

Chapter 30

Garth thought it was a good idea, and for once Jeffries and Gonzalez seemed to agree with him. Not that he really cared what they thought, but they had wormed their way into being his lieutenants, sort of, and he knew things would go better if they supported what he wanted to do.

Maggie Winslow had ridden out in the middle of the day, bringing the news that the trestle still wasn't repaired, but might be by the next morning.

"The clerk at the depot said the train might be here by nine or ten o'clock," she reported. Her voice was strained as she went on. "Now, can I see my husband and son?"

Ike Winslow had surprised Garth by living through the night. In fact, even though he still hadn't woken up, he seemed to be breathing easier and some of the color had come back into his face. The hombre might actually live, Garth thought.

Whether he would recover fully and ever be the same man he'd been before the injury was another question entirely. Garth didn't care one way or the other about that, but as long as Winslow was alive, that meant the hold they had over Winslow's wife was even stronger.

Since they might have only a day, maybe even less, before the train arrived to take Joshua on to Yuma, they had to act fast. But an open attack on the livery stable where the prisoner was being held would just result in more men lost, and the numbers had already shrunk a lot more than Garth liked.

Also, if they came riding into town with guns blazing, there was no telling how the citizens would react. Chances were, most of them would hunt for cover and lie low until the shooting was over. But some of them might get brave and join the fight. That could result in disaster, too.

Garth knew one thing he could always count on, though.

Greed.

So when he'd told Jeffries and Gonzalez what he wanted to do, they had thought it over and nodded. "Who are you going to send into town?" Jeffries had asked. "You can't use the girl for that."

"No, I reckon it'll have to be one of us." Garth looked at Gonzalez. "I'm thinkin' about sendin' you. We're close enough to the border that nobody's gonna notice one more greaser in town."

Gonzalez didn't take offense. He had been called much worse in his time. He nodded and said, "I can go to the saloon and tell the hombres there that somebody offered me a bounty if I helped bust into the livery stable. I can pretend that I turned it down."

Jeffries rubbed at his chin. "You really think that folks will be willing to help free Joshua when just about everybody in the territory is afraid of him?"

"Make the money high enough and they will,"

Garth declared. "I was thinkin' about offerin' a thousand dollars."

Gonzalez let out a whistle. "That's a lot of *dinero*, all right."

"Of course, we won't actually pay it," Garth went on. "And when Joshua's free, we'll loot the town like always." He looked around at the others. "Sound like a good plan?"

"It does," Jeffries admitted.

"Head on into town," Garth told Gonzalez. "Remember, though, you're not an owlhoot. You're just a driftin' vaquero."

Gonzalez nodded. "*Sí*, I can do that."

He rode off, and Garth turned to the place in the shade of a cutbank where Winslow was stretched out with his wife and baby now beside him. Maggie held the little one like she never intended to let him go.

"All right, you've seen 'em," Garth said to her. "You'd better get on back to town so's you can keep an eye on things for us."

"Please, just a little while longer," she said as her arms tightened around the kid. "I've done everything you told me to do, haven't I?"

"Yeah, you been pretty good about it," Garth admitted. "But somethin' could happen this afternoon that we need to know about."

Maggie had used some of the money Garth had given her to buy a riding outfit. She was cute as she could be, he thought. Cute as a speckled pup, folks used to say. It fit her.

Garth ignored the pang of sympathy that went through him when he looked at her, though. He couldn't afford feelings like that. He had to keep his attention fixed on the goal of freeing Joshua.

Like everybody else in the gang, Garth had been an owlhoot before joining up with Joshua Shade, but he'd never been a very successful one. That had all changed because of Joshua's audacity and planning and leadership. Most folks probably thought Joshua was crazy, but Garth knew better. Joshua Shade was actually the smartest man Garth had ever known.

That was why they couldn't take a chance on losing him. Garth motioned to Maggie Winslow and said, "Come on now. You got to go."

She sighed, leaned over to kiss her unconscious husband on the forehead, and gave the young'un another hug. Then she stood up and handed him to Garth, taking the outlaw by surprise. Garth hung on to the kid, frowning.

"Take care of both of them," Maggie said. "If you don't . . ."

By Godfrey, was she *threatening* him? The gal had a lot of brass, Garth thought. More backbone than her husband, more than likely, which meant Ike Winslow was a lucky man . . . or at least, he would be if he survived.

Maggie mounted up and rode off, dust trailing from the hooves of her horse. Gonzalez was already gone on his errand. Now all Garth and the others could do was wait to see what happened.

"There's bound to be a flag stop somewhere west of here," Sam went on. "If we can get Shade out of here tonight without anybody knowing about it, we can flag down the train when it comes through there tomorrow and board it there."

"We can't move him in that wagon without folks seeing it," Thorpe pointed out.

Sam shrugged. "We won't use the wagon, unless it's as part of a distraction so folks won't know what we're doing."

"We can put him on horseback," Matt said, eagerness showing in his voice as he grasped what his blood brother was talking about. "Stage some sort of ruckus to keep the town occupied and slip Shade out of here while that's goin' on."

Thorpe looked back and forth between them. "Do you know how loco this sounds?" he demanded.

Matt and Sam both grinned. "We've been accused of bein' a mite touched in the head before," Matt admitted.

"But we're still here when a lot of hombres have tried to put us in the ground," Sam added.

"All right, I'll listen," Thorpe said with a sigh. "But I'm not making any promises about whether or not we'll actually do it."

"First of all," Sam said, "we need to find out more about the railroad. We have to make sure the train will really be coming through tomorrow, and we'd better find out exactly where the next flag stop is."

"I can do that," Matt volunteered. He glanced at the gap between the shutters that were closed over the nearest window. The light that had been there earlier was fading. "It's startin' to get dark outside. I'll head down to the depot and try to make sure not too many people see me."

"All right, but don't be gone long," Sam said. "And be thinking about what we can to do throw everybody off the trail."

Matt slipped out the back door, hearing Sam bar it securely behind him as soon as he was outside in the gathering twilight. From what Lopez had said, the cowboys who had a grudge against him for shooting Dub and Court were drinking in the saloon, stocking up on liquid courage. Their grudge against him, plus the bounty that had been placed on his head and the heads of those with him, would be enough to make the mob storm the livery stable, Matt knew, but it would probably take them at least a couple of hours to work themselves up to actually doing it.

That gave them a little time, Matt thought, to figure out what they were going to do—but they couldn't afford to waste any time either.

As he swung around the corner of the depot and headed for the platform steps, he came to a sudden stop as he almost ran into someone leaving. A grin creased Matt's face as he recognized Jessica Devlin.

"Well, good evening again, Miss Devlin," he said. "Checking to see when the trains are gonna be runnin' again?"

"That . . . that's right," she replied with a nod. "Is that why you're here, Mr. Bodine?"

"Yep. You probably heard around town that some fellas and I are waitin' to catch the westbound. We're helpin' out a federal marshal who's got a prisoner to deliver to Yuma Prison."

Matt didn't see any harm in telling her the truth. It was common knowledge around Pancake Flats anyway.

"Yes, I've heard," Jessica said. "Some sort of outlaw, isn't he?"

"The worst sort," Matt said, his expression growing solemn. "He's a loco killer, a pure-dee hydrophobia skunk. And his gang is just as bad."

"I . . . I wouldn't want to cross paths with them then."

"No, ma'am, you sure wouldn't."

Matt tugged on the brim of his hat and stepped

around her. "I'll be seeing you," he said as he started toward the steps again. He had to get on with the errand that had brought him here.

He couldn't help but glance at Jessica Devlin again, though. She definitely had a troubled look about her, and he wanted to do something to give her a hand if he could.

Unfortunately, he and Sam already had too much on their plates to be taking on any more problems. Matt hoped that whatever was bothering Jessica Devlin, she could figure it out for herself.

"Good news, Mr. Bodine," Harry, the clerk, said before Matt could even ask. "I just got a wire saying that the repair work on the trestle is finished. The trains will be running again first thing in the morning. I expect the westbound to come through here at eight thirty. That's even earlier than I'd hoped for."

"Thanks," Matt said with a nod. Harry didn't know it, but eight thirty in the morning was going to be too late. "I've got another question."

"Of course."

"How far is it to the nearest flag stop west of here?"

Harry frowned. "Why do you want to know that?"

Matt hesitated. Harry seemed like a law-abiding gent, but evidently he hadn't heard about the price the outlaws had put on the heads of the men holding Joshua Shade prisoner.

"Marshal Thorpe wanted to know. In fact, he wants a map of all the stops between here and Yuma, if you've got one."

Harry's frown deepened. "I do, but it's the property of the Southern Pacific Railroad."

"I'll see that you get it back," Matt promised. He

didn't know if he'd be able to keep that promise or not, but at least he'd try.

After a moment, the clerk shrugged. "All right, here." He reached under the ticket counter and brought out a folded map. "You can let the marshal look at it. I'll need it back before you leave town, though."

"Sure," Matt said as he took the map. This was working out even better than he had hoped.

He said so long to Harry and hurried back toward the livery stable. As he glanced up the street, he saw light spilling out of the saloon and heard loud voices drifting through the evening air from that direction. The mob was forming inside, and soon would spill out into the street like the light from the saloon's lamps. Their goal would be the livery stable, where they hoped to collect that thousand-dollar bounty and Matt Bodine's blood to boot.

Matt hoped that Sam had come up with something that would work, because he was sure as hell drawing a blank.

Chapter 31

By the time Matt got back to the stable with the good news about the trestle and the railroad map, Sam had had an idea. Matt spread out the map first, though, and the rest of them gathered around to look.

"There's a water stop twenty miles west of here," Matt said, pointing to it on the map. "That's even better than a flag stop, because there's no chance the engineer will miss it."

"I'm starting to think this might work," Thorpe said. "But how do we get Shade out of here?"

"He'll go on horseback—" Sam began.

"He'll have to be tied up mighty damn tight," Thorpe said, breaking in.

Sam nodded. "That goes without saying, Marshal. And he'll have you and Everett guarding him."

"What about us?" Matt asked. "And what about that distraction you were talkin' about?"

Sam smiled. "That's going to be our job."

"Let me guess," Matt said. "It means we'll be the ones gettin' shot at, right?"

"If all goes according to plan. We're going to take the

wagon and make the mob think that we're headed for Bowtie Canyon so we can stop the train and get on there."

"But the wagon will be empty," Thorpe guessed.

Sam nodded. "That's right. Matt and I will bust out of here with guns blazing and head east, drawing the mob after us. That's when you and Everett will take Shade the other way on horseback. We'll rendezvous with you later at that water stop west of here."

"If you don't get shot full of holes," Thorpe said.

"Well, yeah, there's that chance," Sam admitted with a shrug. "But there are no guarantees in life, are there?"

"Just that we'll wind up gettin' shot at too damn often," Matt said, but the reckless grin on his face belied the words.

Thorpe thought it over for a few moments and then nodded. "All right. We'll give it a try. For the life of me, I don't see anything else we can do. When will we get started?"

Matt looked toward the front doors as the murmur of loud, angry, excited voices in the distance began to grow. "Like the saloon girl said to the padre," he noted, "it won't be long now."

Maggie Winslow had heard Garth plotting with Jeffries and Gonzalez earlier in the day when she visited the outlaw camp, so she knew what was going on now as she watched from the lobby of the hotel, peering anxiously past the curtain she had pulled back from the window.

Men walked out of the saloon and began to congregate in the street, talking loudly among themselves.

They looked toward the livery stable as their discussion grew more animated.

Maggie thought about Matt Bodine, his friend Sam Two Wolves, and the two lawmen who were in there along with their prisoner, Joshua Shade. They had to know what was going on, because the talk was all over town about how the outlaws had placed a bounty on their heads.

They were probably aware as well that the local lawman, Marshal Lopez, had ridden out of town earlier, leaving Bodine and the others on their own like a craven coward.

Lopez had claimed that he was just trying to do what was best for his family. Maggie could certainly understand that. She had been spying for the gang for the past twenty-four hours now. It made her feel dirty, as if she were an outlaw herself. But she had no choice except to cooperate if she wanted to protect Ike and Caleb.

Maggie suspected that Garth and the others were somewhere close by now, waiting in the darkness just outside town for the roar of gunshots that would tell them the attack on the barn had started. Would they wait until the shooting stopped to rush in and set Shade free?

The proprietor of the hotel stood behind the desk. He said nervously, "I'd get away from that window if I was you, ma'am. It might not be safe in a few more minutes."

She knew what he meant. It might not be safe to stand by the window once the bullets started flying.

Her fingers clutched the curtain tighter. She was thinking about what would happen once the mob attacked the jail. The wild young cowboys who had spent the past few hours drinking thought that they would be earning themselves a reward as well as getting their revenge on Matt Bodine.

But it wouldn't work that way, Maggie suddenly realized. They were fools to trust anybody in Shade's gang. The outlaws wouldn't pay off on the bounty Garth had promised.

Instead, it was much more likely they would turn on the town, looting and killing wantonly, as they had done in so many other places. A lot of people would die here tonight, Maggie thought as her heart began to pound harder in her chest. Innocent men, women, and even children . . .

And weighed against that was the safety of Ike and Caleb, one innocent man and one innocent—oh, so innocent!—child. To save her own family, could she allow the people of Pancake Flats to be duped into participating in their own massacre?

It was the most horrible question she had ever been forced to ask herself.

But she didn't have to answer it, because at that moment someone yelled, and guns began to roar.

With no time to waste, Matt and Sam had gone over to the wagon as soon as they decided on the plan with Thorpe and Everett. They stood behind the wagon with their rifles trained on the door as the marshal unlocked it.

"Come out of there, Shade," Thorpe ordered harshly as he swung the door open.

Shade came out, all right. Like a mountain lion springing on an unsuspecting deer, the outlaw burst from the wagon like a shot. Mouthing obscenities,

Shade slammed into Thorpe and knocked him over backward. He landed on top of Thorpe and clawed at the lawman's throat.

Shade got his fingers fastened around Thorpe's windpipe, but he didn't have time to tighten them into a choke hold. Matt stepped up and brought the butt of his Winchester crashing down on Shade's head. Shade went limp, collapsing on top of Thorpe.

"Get this crazy, foul-smelling bastard off me!" Thorpe yelled.

Shade smelled bad, all right. They had stopped often to let him relieve himself, and he had a bucket inside the wagon for that purpose, too. Evidently, though, he had stopped using it.

Matt and Sam both wrinkled their noses in disgust as they grasped Shade's arms and hauled him off Thorpe. They dumped the unconscious man on the hard-packed dirt floor of the stable, and didn't worry about being gentle in how they did it.

"He's like a wild animal that's been caged," Thorpe said as he got up and brushed himself off. "I'd almost feel sorry for him if he wasn't responsible for the deaths of probably a hundred innocent people, maybe more." Thorpe shook his head. "Get him on a horse."

Matt and Sam lifted Shade into the saddle of one of the extra horses they had gotten ready to ride earlier. Then Everett held the unconscious man in place while Matt and Sam tied him.

Matt lashed Shade's feet together under the horse's belly. Sam tied the outlaw's wrists to the saddle horn, then cinched another rope tight between Shade's elbows and tied that to the saddle horn as well. Shade couldn't possibly fall off the horse now, even while he was out cold. He was forced to lean forward over the horse's neck, too, so that he would make a smaller target if bullets started to fly.

The racket in the street was louder now as Matt and Sam stepped back from their work. "He's not goin' anywhere," Matt said. "At least, not without that horse."

A shout came from outside. "Bodine! Matt Bodine! You hear me?"

Matt didn't answer. He hurried to the horses and tied Sam's mount, along with a couple of others, to the back of the wagon while Sam was climbing onto the driver's seat. The mules were already hitched up, so all he had to do was turn the team and the wagon around. He did that while Thorpe and Everett blew out the lanterns and hurried to their own horses.

"Bodine, if you and your friends let the prisoner go, we won't kill you!" the man who had shouted before called from the street. "We don't want any bloodshed!"

"That's a damn lie," Matt said quietly to Sam as he brought his horse alongside the wagon. "The way they're likkered up, somebody's bound to let off a shot, and that's all it'll take."

Sam nodded. "Yes, it would be quite a bloodbath— if it went the way they think it's going to."

Everett held the reins of Shade's horse while Thorpe went over to the double doors. "This is Deputy U.S. Marshal Asa Thorpe!" he yelled. "Hold your fire! We're coming out!"

There was a moment of surprised silence from the mob, and then the spokesman called, "All right, Marshal, come on out! There won't be no shootin'!"

Barely visible in the gloom, Thorpe nodded to Matt and Sam. Then he flung the bar up, unfastening the doors. Sam cried out and slashed the mules across their rumps, driving them forward. Thorpe whirled his horse and dashed back along the barn's center aisle, joining Everett and Shade in the deep shadows at the rear.

Matt crashed out first, Winchester in hand. Yelling, he fired over the heads of the startled crowd. Men shouted in alarm and leaped aside to keep from being run down as the mules burst out of the barn with the wagon right behind them.

Sam swung the wagon in a sharp turn toward the railroad station. The horses tied on at the back had to gallop along with the vehicle, and they caused members of the mob to scramble out of the way to avoid being trampled, too.

Matt was still firing as he crouched in his saddle and broke a path through the crowd for the wagon. He aimed high, though. As far as he was concerned, the men who had been about to storm the livery barn were sorry sons of bitches for trying to free Shade, but maybe they didn't deserve to die for it.

If any of them got in the way of a stray bullet or a charging horse or mule, though, he wasn't going to lose any sleep over it. Most of them would get off luckier than they deserved.

"Stop them!" somebody yelled. "Stop that wagon!"

More guns began to roar. Powder smoke spurted from gun muzzles, stinging noses and blinding eyes.

Matt and Sam were counting on that, along with the darkness and confusion, to keep the mob from noticing that Thorpe and Everett weren't with them. If everything went according to plan, the drunken, greedy cowboys would think that all four of them were getting away, along with Shade. The extra horses tied to the wagon would contribute to that illusion, too.

As Matt pounded down the street at a hard gallop, he glanced to his left and saw the town's lone hotel looming there. Someone stood at the front window, peering out with a wide-eyed, worried expression, and Matt felt a second of recognition as he realized the watcher was Jessica Devlin.

There was no time to acknowledge her, though. Matt flashed on past the hotel with the wagon careening behind him. He glanced over his shoulder, saw that Sam was staying low on the driver's seat.

Colt flame bloomed from the scattered mob, until a man yelled, "Stop shootin'! Stop shootin'! Shade's worth a thousand dollars *alive*!"

Someone else shouted, "Get your horses! Let's get after 'em!"

Matt wasn't too worried about pursuit, though. All he and Sam had to do was stay in front of anyone who came after them for a couple of miles. Then they could abandon the empty wagon and ride off into the night. Thorpe and Everett would have a big enough lead then that they could reach the water stop west of town before anyone figured out what was going on. Even when the cowboys found the empty wagon, if they did, they wouldn't know where Shade had gone.

Of course, somebody might figure it out if they talked to the railroad clerk and found out that Matt had been asking about stops west of Pancake Flats . . . but again, by that time, Matt hoped they would be on the train rolling toward Yuma.

It was a shame, though, he thought as they raced on into the darkness, that he would never see Jessica Devlin again.

He would have liked to find out just what it was that was troubling that pretty young woman.

At the moment, of course, he had his hands full just staying alive . . .

Chapter 32

Guns were still going off behind them as they left Pancake Flats behind. Matt figured several of the cowboys had been able to grab their horses and give chase fairly quickly.

To discourage them, he reined in and wheeled his horse around while Sam kept the mules racing eastward. He lifted his Winchester and sprayed an arc of bullets across their back trail, still aiming high. He hoped the muzzle flashes from the rifle would be enough to make the pursuers think twice about chasing them.

Then he whirled his mount and pounded after the wagon. He caught up to it a few moments later, and gave Sam a reckless grin as he drew even. Sam returned the grin, and kept slashing at the mules' rumps with the reins.

Guns kept flashing and banging behind them, but none of the bullets came close as far as Matt could tell. More than likely, the cowboys chasing them were blazing away with six-guns, and they weren't going to hit anything at that range unless it was by pure luck.

Every so often, Matt stopped and threw a few shots behind them with his Winchester as Sam continued to follow the railroad tracks toward Bowtie Canyon. The pursuit fell farther and farther back.

Finally, Sam hauled on the reins and called, "Whoa! Whoa!" to the mules. Matt reined in as well and swung down from the saddle to untie Sam's horse from the back of the wagon while Sam was climbing down from the driver's seat. He untied the spare horses as well.

Matt pressed the reins into Sam's hand and said, "Let's get out of here."

It went against the grain for them to ride away from trouble, rather than charging straight into it, but it was more important tonight that they rejoin Thorpe and Everett and make sure that they'd reached the water stop safely with Joshua Shade.

Leading the extra horses, Matt and Sam rode carefully across the railroad tracks, then headed south toward the border. They didn't intend to go as far as Mexico, however. After a mile or so, they turned west, paralleling the Southern Pacific right-of-way.

There were no more shots. The blood brothers figured that the cowboys who had chased them from Pancake Flats would find the wagon and realize they'd been tricked when they discovered the vehicle was empty. By then, it would be too late. They wouldn't be able to track Matt and Sam by starlight, and they'd have no idea where Joshua Shade really was.

All Matt and Sam had to do now was reach the water stop, rendezvous with Thorpe and Everett, and hope that nobody figured out where they were before the train came through in the morning. It was pretty simple . . . but there was still a lot that could wrong between now and then.

* * *

Garth knew something was wrong when he saw the muzzle flashes streaming out of Pancake Flats to the east. He and the rest of the gang were less than half a mile north of the settlement.

They had left Winslow and the kid alone back at the place where they had been camped. It was a risk, not leaving a guard behind, but with the way the gang's numbers had shrunk since that damned Bodine and Two Wolves had poked their noses in, Garth wanted every man with him. Winslow was still out cold, and the kid was asleep. They weren't going anywhere.

Now, as he listened to the shots and saw the orange spurts of flame trailing off to the east, Garth cursed bitterly under his breath.

"Those lawdogs must've made a break for it with Joshua," he said. "Mount up! We'll try to cut 'em off!"

"Wait a minute," Jeffries said.

Garth whirled on him. He didn't like having his orders contradicted, and he'd had just about enough of the dapper gunman anyway.

"What the hell's the idea?" Garth demanded.

"We can't get ahead of them," Jeffries said. "Not from this angle. They've got too big a lead on us."

"What do you reckon we ought to do then?" Garth didn't bother trying to keep the anger out of his voice.

"The only reason for them to go east, away from Yuma, is if that they're trying to catch the train before it ever gets to Pancake Flats. Marshal Thorpe must plan to commandeer the locomotive and highball it right through town instead of stopping."

Garth frowned and chewed his mustache. What Jeffries said made sense, even though Garth didn't want to admit it. As he thought about it, the glimmerings of another idea came to life in his brain.

"The train's still got to go through Pancake Flats before it can get to Yuma," he said.

"Exactly," Jeffries agreed.

Gonzalez, who had returned earlier from spreading the rumor in the settlement concerning the reward or bounty or whatever you wanted to call it, said, "What are you two talkin' about?"

Garth turned toward him and raised his voice so that the rest of the men could hear, too. "We're gonna ride in and take over that two-bit town," he declared. "Then, when the train comes through, we'll stop it and take Joshua off of it."

Murmurs of agreement came from the other outlaws. Garth nodded, confident again in his decision, even though so far his quarry had seemed able to stay one jump ahead of him.

"Those men who went chasing off after the wagon might actually catch it," Jeffries suggested.

"All the more reason to get into town and take over," Garth snapped. "If they come back with Joshua, we'll be ready for 'em. If they don't, we know what we'll have to do."

With that, the outlaws mounted up and headed toward Pancake Flats.

Maggie had recognized Matt Bodine as he galloped past the hotel, leading the way for the wagon, and she thought he had recognized her, too, in that brief instant. He hadn't slowed down, though, even for a second, which came as no surprise. Bodine and his companions were making a break for it with their prisoner before the mob had a chance to storm the livery stable.

Or were they? Maggie saw the riderless horses tied onto the back of the wagon, and asked herself where Marshal Thorpe and the other deputy were. They wouldn't be *inside* the locked wagon with Joshua Shade.

That meant they were still in the barn—or maybe they had gone out the back with the prisoner while Bodine and Two Wolves were going out the front and capturing the attention of everyone in the mob.

Like a flash of lightning, the whole thing was crystal clear in Maggie's mind. She knew what they had done, and as she watched the angry cowboys stream out of town after the wagon, she realized that the trick had worked. Like hounds baying after a false scent, the mob had taken the bait.

Maggie felt a wave of dismay go through her. It wasn't that she trusted Garth and the other outlaws or anything like that. But as long as Joshua Shade was a prisoner, they still had a reason to keep holding the safety of Ike and Caleb over her head and forcing her to help them.

Was she never going to be free of those awful men? Would her husband and son ever be free? Those questions went through her head as she closed her eyes for a moment and sighed.

The hotel proprietor came up beside her. "What's wrong, Miss Devlin?"

Since Maggie had given Matt Bodine that name, she had used it here at the hotel, too, after slipping off her wedding ring so that she wouldn't appear to be married. She wasn't sure at the time why she had done that; it had been an instinctive move.

But later, when she'd had a chance to think about it, she had realized that by pretending to be unmarried, she stood a better chance of getting closer to Matt Bodine if she needed to in the future. She had seen the way he looked at her. He thought she was pretty, and it wouldn't take much encouragement on her part to get him interested in her.

She could carry off that masquerade if she had to, she decided, in order to save her family.

Now, of course, it looked like that wouldn't be necessary, because Bodine and Two Wolves were gone, and Maggie would have been willing to bet that Joshua Shade was, too. The other two men must have tied the prisoner on a horse and escaped with him that way, while Bodine and Two Wolves distracted everyone with the wagon.

Maggie realized that the hotel keeper was standing beside her, waiting for an answer to the question he had asked her. She said, "I just don't like all this shooting. I wish those men had never come here."

"You and me both, miss," the man agreed. "All this trouble is bad for business and bad for the town's reputation. I'm glad those men are gone."

Maggie wasn't, but she kept that to herself. She had hoped that things would end here, one way or the other, but unless she was completely wrong in her guess about what had happened, it wouldn't.

Ike and Caleb would still be in danger, and of course, so would she, although she didn't really care anymore about what happened to her.

She wished she could see her husband and son right now, and know that they were all right.

* * *

The night wind stirred the sand on top of the tiny ridge against which Ike Winslow lay with his son, Caleb. In this dry, semiarid land, the temperature dropped rapidly once the sun went down, and as the air cooled, the sleeping little boy had instinctively nudged closer to his father for warmth.

Neither of them was aware of the lean, gray shape gliding through the shadows toward them. The coyote was hungry, as coyotes nearly always were. He sensed prey, but he approached carefully, his natural caution outweighing his hunger.

The bigger shape wasn't moving, but it didn't smell dead yet. The smaller one shifted around from time to time, but didn't seem to represent any threat. The coyote slunk closer, figuring he would grab the little creature by the leg and drag it off away from the bigger one, so he could make a leisurely meal on it.

The wind picked up again, blowing their scent to the coyote. His tongue lolled from his mouth, saliva dripping from it. His muscles tensed.

One quick dash in, and he could clamp his jaws around the little one's leg. He wouldn't go hungry tonight.

Grains of sand from the top of the ridge trickled over Ike Winslow's face. Some of it fell in his left eye. The eye twitched in irritation. Ike grimaced.

His eyes opened, and without thinking about what he was doing, he reached up to rub at the irritated one. That made thunderous peals of pain go through his head.

But even over that horrible racket, he heard the growling somewhere close by.

His eye watered as he blinked rapidly, trying to get the sand out of it. He put a hand on the ground and pushed himself up. Darkness surrounded him, but it was relieved somewhat by the light from millions of stars.

That starlight was bright enough for Ike to see the ugly shape crouched only a few feet away. He recognized it as a coyote and yelled hoarsely. The coyote whirled and dashed off into the darkness, unwilling to do battle against such a larger foe.

Only then did Ike become aware of the warm little body nestled against him. He looked down in amazement at his son. His shout had woken Caleb, who was now stirring. A thin cry came from him.

Ike struggled to sit up, lifting Caleb and holding the boy against his chest. His head hurt like hell, but all his muscles seemed to be working and he was grateful for that.

But where were they? he wondered as he looked around at the empty landscape. The last thing he remembered, he had regained consciousness after falling off the runaway wagon and stumbled north, until he ran into the outlaws who had Maggie and Caleb.

Caleb was still here, but the outlaws were gone.

And so was Maggie.

Ike's brain wasn't working at its full capacity yet, but one thought was crystal clear in it.

He had to find his wife. He had to find Maggie.

Cradling Caleb against him, he fought his way to his feet. He tipped his head back, which caused a moment of excruciating dizziness before things settled down again, and studied the stars. He knew how to steer by them, so he knew which way was south.

That was the way Marshal Thorpe had been taking the prisoner. Ike knew that if Joshua Shade hadn't been freed yet, the gang would have continued in that direction, hoping to rescue their leader.

So Ike started that way, too, none too steady on his feet, not at all sure what he would do if he caught up to the gang . . . but he was certain of one thing.

If those bastards had hurt Maggie, he would kill them, each and every one of them, no matter what it took. A part of his mind was aware that it was ludicrous for an injured man with a baby on his hands to make such a vow, but he didn't care.

If Maggie was hurt, they would pay. He would see to it.

Chapter 33

Maggie went up to her room in the hotel, struggling with the decision of what to do next. She had a pretty good idea what the outlaws would do. Any time now they would show up in Pancake Flats to find out what had happened. She knew she ought to warn the towns-people.

But if she did, if the citizens were ready and fought back, then Garth and the others would know who had alerted them to the impending raid. The outlaws were vicious and brutal, but they weren't stupid.

They would regard her warning the town as a double cross, Maggie knew, and they could easily take out their anger at her on Ike and Caleb. She couldn't risk that.

All she could do was hope that when they rode in and found out that Joshua Shade wasn't here, they would ride out again in search of him.

If they did, she hoped they would take her with them. She never would have dreamed she would hope such a thing, but she wanted to be with her husband and son, wherever they were.

Maggie had been up in her room for only a short

time when loud, angry voices in the street drew her to the window. She opened the curtain and peered out.

She wasn't surprised to see the wagon that Sam Two Wolves had driven out of town at such a breakneck pace earlier in the evening. The vehicle was stopped in the middle of the street, with one of the cowboys who had pursued it now on the seat. He must have driven it back into town.

A large group of men was gathered around the wagon, some on foot and others on horseback. The riders were the ones who had given chase to the wagon, Maggie decided.

One of the other men shouted, "Are you sure there was no sign of Shade?"

"The wagon's empty, I tell you!" the man on the seat replied. "Those bastards Bodine and Two Wolves fooled us."

"Then where *is* Shade?"

No one seemed to know the answer to that question. Maggie wanted to lean out the window and tell them that they were fools, that Joshua Shade was probably miles from town by now, heading west toward Yuma along with Marshal Thorpe and the other lawman.

She didn't do it, though. They could figure that out for themselves if they wanted to. If they had enough sense.

They didn't have enough time to figure out anything, though, because at that moment the swift rataplan of hoofbeats sounded loudly from both ends of the street, and suddenly more riders poured into town, bristling with guns.

"What the hell!" one of the cowboys yelled. He tried to claw the Colt on his hip out of its holster.

With a roar and a spurt of muzzle flame, one of the newcomers fired. The cowboy who had slapped leather doubled over in the saddle as the bullet tore through his guts. Slowly, groaning in pain, he toppled off his horse.

An ominous silence settled over the street following the shot.

Maggie recognized the man who had just gunned down that cowboy. He was Willard Garth, the leader of the outlaw gang while Joshua Shade was still a prisoner.

She saw Jeffries and Gonzalez as well, along with the other members of the gang. They had split up as they entered the settlement so they could catch the men in the street in a cross fire if need be.

This was exactly what Maggie had been expecting. The outlaws had ridden in to find out what had happened.

The ones she *didn't* see were Ike and Caleb. Her heart began to pound harder as she realized that they weren't with the gang. The outlaws must have left them somewhere outside of town.

Some instinct made Maggie clutch the windowsill as she looked out. Her eyes widened with shock and horror as she made a quick count of the outlaws. She gasped as she reached fifteen.

That was all of them. Wherever Ike and Caleb had been left, they were alone.

Maggie covered her mouth as the implications of that discovery soaked in on her. The outlaws had either abandoned an injured, unconscious man and a baby—or killed them before riding into Pancake Flats. Maggie shuddered at the thought of that awful Gonzalez and his knife . . .

All that passed through Maggie's mind in a matter

of seconds. Down below in the street, the outlaws still menaced the citizens with drawn guns as Garth demanded, "What happened? Where's the prisoner who was in that wagon?"

"Your guess is as good as ours, mister," the cowboy on the driver's seat replied. "We would've sworn he was in here when we chased the blasted thing out of town, but when we caught up to it, it was sittin' there empty, with nobody around."

"Was the door still locked when you found it?" Jeffries asked.

"What?" The cowboy seemed confused.

"The door, damn it! The door on the back of the wagon. Was it locked?"

"Yeah . . . Yeah, I reckon it was."

Garth asked Jeffries, "What difference does that make?"

"If Bodine and Two Wolves had taken Joshua out of the wagon where they abandoned it, they wouldn't have taken the time to put the lock back on the door." Jeffries shook his head. "My guess is that Joshua wasn't in there when they left town."

"Wasn't in there! But that'd mean—"

"Yeah," Jeffries agreed grimly. "They put one over on these folks." He looked at the man on the driver's seat. "Exactly who did you see with the wagon when it left town?"

"Why, they were all with it! That U.S. marshal and his deputy and those two gunfighters who were sidin' 'em."

"No, that's not right," another man said. "I got a pretty good look, and Bodine and Two Wolves are the only ones I actually saw."

Garth put it together. Maggie knew that Jeffries already had.

"Blast it," Garth said. "Bodine and Two Wolves tricked you, all right. While they went out the front, Thorpe and the deputy went out the back with Joshua. That's got to be it."

"Bodine and Two Wolves are probably circling around to meet up with them right now," Jeffries said.

"They can't make it all the way to Yuma on horseback," Garth argued. "They have to know that we'd catch up to 'em before they got there."

"They can still catch the train once it goes through here," Jeffries pointed out.

"Yeah, if we let it go through," Garth said. Without lowering his gun, he used his other hand to scratch at his jaw in thought. "Maybe that's just what we ought to do."

A grin appeared on Jeffries's face. "If you're thinking what I think you're thinking . . . that's a good idea, Garth."

Gonzalez spoke up. "The train won't be through here until mornin'. What are we supposed to do until then?"

An evil leer spread across Garth's craggy face. "I reckon we can have a little fun," he said.

Some of the citizens of Pancake Flats realized who these men were and what Garth meant by that sinister statement. Faced with almost certain doom no matter what they did, they grabbed for their guns.

Maggie's horror deepened, sickening her, as shots roared out. Garth and the other owlhoots opened fire, cutting down the townspeople in an almost casual manner. Maggie had to turn away from the muzzle flashes and the bits of flesh and blood flying in the air as outlaw lead tore through the crowd in the street.

But even though she clapped her hands over her

ears, she couldn't completely shut out the gunfire and the screams and the outraged, futile curses.

The massacre went on for what seemed like an eternity but was probably less than a minute. When it was over, Garth bellowed to his men, "Spread out! I want everybody in town rounded up! But don't set fire to the buildings. Everything's got to look normal when that train gets here in the mornin'!"

Something drew Maggie back to the window, even though she didn't want to look. She cringed as she saw the evidence of the bloodbath that had taken place in the street. Gore-splattered bodies lay everywhere. Moans came from men who had been wounded instead of killed outright. Garth dismounted and stalked among them, dispatching them with a single shot each to the head.

Instinct must have made him glance up. Maggie saw the killer's eyes boring into hers.

"Stay there!" Garth shouted, and then he stalked out of her sight, into the hotel.

Another shot blasted downstairs. Maggie moaned. She knew that Garth had just killed the proprietor.

A moment later, she heard Garth's footsteps stomping up the stairs. Fear froze her, although for an instant she considered throwing herself out the window rather than letting Garth get his hands on her again.

She couldn't do that, though, not as long as she didn't know what had happened to Ike and Caleb. So she stood her ground, summoning up what little courage remained inside her, and faced the door of the hotel room as Garth slammed it open and stalked in.

"Did you know anything about what Bodine and Two Wolves were plannin'?" he roared at her.

"If I had known, don't you think I would have found a way to let you know?"

The coolness in her voice surprised her. She was glad for it, because she didn't want Garth to know what she was really feeling.

"Where are my husband and son?" she went on. "I know they're not with you, and the rest of the gang is here."

His eyes narrowed. "Mighty smart, ain't you?"

"I know how to count, if that's what you mean. What about Ike and Caleb?"

"You're like a damn bulldog when you get your teeth in somethin'. Don't you worry about your husband and the young'un. They're in a safe place."

She didn't believe him, but yet there was just enough of a sliver of a chance he could be telling the truth that she couldn't afford to ignore the possibility.

"Listen, I've done everything you asked me to do. I've done everything I can to help you. Why don't you bring them to me and let us go? Or just tell me where they are and I'll go to them."

Ponderously, Garth shook his head. "Nope. We ain't done with you yet, missy."

Maggie's self-control, which she had been holding on to so tightly, finally slipped a little. "My God!" she cried. "What more do you want from me? Just give me back my family!"

"Not until Joshua Shade is free," Garth said with the inevitability of a landslide. "And you're wrong . . . there *is* somethin' else you can do to help us." He lowered his gun at last. "Just hush up and listen if you ever want to see that husband and boy o' yours again . . ."

Chapter 34

Time had no meaning to Ike Winslow now. Only two things existed for him—the incredible ache in his head and the will to keep putting one foot in front of the other.

And Caleb, too. His son was still real to him. He clutched Caleb to his chest, being careful not to drop him.

The boy had been fussy for a while after being awakened, but then he dozed off again with his head resting on Ike's shoulder. Ike could feel him breathing. He drew strength from that. Caleb was all right, and to keep him that way, Ike had to keep going.

The pain in his head thudded with each step he took, but gradually it began to lessen. He started thinking more clearly, and he asked himself where the outlaws had gone.

More importantly, where was Maggie?

He knew her well enough to know that she would never desert them unless she was forced to. The outlaws must have taken her with them. But for what purpose? She couldn't help them rescue Joshua Shade, could she?

Another possible answer lurked in the back of Ike's head, but he refused to even think about it. If those bastards were going to molest her, they would have done it before now, he told himself.

Besides, the one called Garth seemed single-minded in his determination to free Shade from the law. If he had taken Maggie when the gang left, it would be because Garth thought she could help accomplish that goal, even though Ike couldn't see how.

Once he thought that through, he felt a little better. Maggie had to be with the outlaws, which was bad, but it could have been worse. She was still alive and all right, he told himself, and after a while he began to believe it.

That helped him keep going, too.

His concentration on that goal kept him from hearing the hoofbeats at first. Then, suddenly, he became aware of them. A lot of horses were coming up behind him.

The gang? Why would they be behind him? They would have gone south when they abandoned him and Caleb, wouldn't they?

Ike couldn't figure it out, but after everything that had happened, he didn't believe that whoever it was meant him any good. Before this terrible business with Joshua Shade's gang, in a situation like this, he would have sought help from whoever he ran into.

Now, though, he tightened his grip on Caleb and launched himself into a stumbling run, trying to stay ahead of whoever was behind him. *Get away*, a voice said inside his head. *Just get away.*

If he had been able to think a little more logically at the moment, he would have known that he couldn't outrun the riders who were closing in on him. Right now, though, he was just a creature of raw instinct, an animal in flight.

"Hey, LaFollette, there's somebody up there! Somebody on foot!"

"Well, don't just sit there. Go get him."

Ike heard the voices and understood the words well enough to know that he and Caleb were in danger. He started to run faster, but he hadn't gone very far before he heard the thud of hoofbeats right behind him. He twisted his head around to gaze behind him in terror, and that caused him to stumble as he saw the dark, looming figure of a man on horseback towering over him.

Ike cried out as he fell to his knees. He cradled Caleb against him, trying to protect the boy. Caleb woke up and cried, a thin wail that grated on Ike's ears.

"Son of a bitch! It's an hombre with a baby!"

More hoofbeats came up. Ike hunched over as he knelt there on the ground. Somebody said, "A baby?"

"Yeah. What do we do about this, LaFollette?"

"Get him on his feet," a voice growled in command. "I don't know what he's doin' out here, and I don't like things I don't know."

Strong hands grasped Ike's arms and hauled him upright. He yelled, "Let me go! Leave us alone!"

"Get the baby," the man called LaFollette said, but when the others tried to pry Caleb out of Ike's arms, Ike howled and thrashed around, bouncing off the men as they surrounded him.

Disgustedly, LaFollette said, "All right, all right, let him keep the kid." He stepped up in front of Ike and went on in a loud voice. "Damn it, mister, listen to me. Settle down. We don't mean you any harm."

Gradually, Ike stopped fighting. Breathing heavily, he said, "Who . . . who are you men?"

"Never you mind about that," LaFollette snapped. He had dismounted like the others. There was enough starlight for Ike to be able to see that he was a compactly built man in range clothes and with a dark, closely trimmed beard. LaFollette went on. "Who are you, and what are you doin' wanderin' around out here with a kid?"

"He . . . he's my son. My name is Winslow . . . Ike Winslow."

"That tells us who you are, but not what you're doin' here."

The whole thing was almost too complicated to explain, Ike suddenly realized. Joshua Shade, the gang of outlaws, the way he had been forced to act as a spy for them, the attack on the wagon in which he had been injured . . . and after that, he didn't even know what had happened. He didn't know where Shade was now, or the rest of the gang, or Maggie . . .

"I was attacked . . . by owlhoots," he said, struggling to find the words. "They took my wife . . . my wagon . . . I don't know where they are."

All that was true, as far as it went.

"Outlaws," one of the men repeated. "You reckon it was Shade's bunch, LaFollette?"

Instead of answering the question directly, LaFollette asked Ike, "How many were there?"

"I'm not sure. Fifteen or twenty . . . maybe more."

LaFollette grunted. "Shade's gang is the only one that big in the territory, as far as I know," he said. "I reckon this fella was unlucky enough to run into them."

Ike was surprised at first that these men knew about Shade, but as he thought about it, he realized that the gang's notoriety must have spread all over Arizona.

LaFollette went on. "It just so happens that we're on the trail of that bunch, mister. You have any idea which way they headed?"

"I know . . . exactly where they're going. I heard them . . . talking. They're headed for a place called . . . Pancake Flats."

"The Southern Pacific goes through there," one of the other men said.

LaFollette nodded. "Yeah, Thorpe must be plannin' on catchin' the train there. I happen to know that the bridge over Bowtie Canyon washed out a while back, though, and the railroad's just now gettin' it repaired. Thorpe may be stuck up there with his prisoner."

They knew a *lot* about what was going on, Ike realized. He still wondered who they were, what their part in this bloody affair was. Maybe they were bounty hunters of some sort.

It didn't matter, though, as long as they agreed to what he said next.

"Take me with you," he said, his voice stronger now that hope was flooding through him again.

"No offense, mister," LaFollette said, "but why would we want to saddle ourselves with a wounded man and a baby?"

"Those bastards have my wife. I'll help you stop them."

LaFollette chuckled. It wasn't a friendly sound.

"You don't look to be in any shape to help anybody do anything, Winslow. You might just slow us down."

"I won't," Ike said. "I swear it. If I do, you can leave me behind. Just leave me some food . . . for the boy."

"We're a long way from nowhere, LaFollette," one of the men said. "I wouldn't feel right about leavin' a kid out here."

LaFollette rubbed his bearded jaw for a moment, then shrugged. "I reckon you're right. This hombre can ride double with the lightest man. That's you, Sinclair."

"All right," the man called Sinclair agreed.

"I warn you, though," LaFollette went on to Ike, "we aren't gonna slow down for you. If you can't handle the pace, you *will* get left behind."

"I can handle it," Ike promised. "As long as I know you're going after Shade's bunch, I can do whatever I need to."

"You know, I believe maybe you can." LaFollette turned to his men. "Mount up! We've got ground to cover!"

Chapter 35

Matt and Sam estimated that it was well after midnight when they spotted the elevated water tank ahead of them, next to the railroad tracks. They had circled back north once they were sure they were well clear of Pancake Flats, finally intersecting the steel rails and then following them westward.

"I hope Thorpe and Everett made it here with Shade," Matt said as they rode along, leading the extra horses. "If they didn't, I'm not sure where we ought to look for them."

"We could backtrack toward the settlement," Sam said, "but we'd be taking a chance on running into Shade's gang."

Matt grunted. "I almost wish we would. I'd like another crack at those varmints. They'd look mighty good over the sights of my guns."

"I know what you mean, but right now we need to concentrate on getting Shade to Yuma so he can hang."

"You know, you got a mighty highly developed sense of responsibility for a carefree redskin who's supposed to be livin' in harmony with nature and the land and your fellow man."

"You've been reading those Eastern newspapers and illustrated weeklies again," Sam said with a disgusted snort. "You start going on about the noble redman or *lo, the poor Indian,* I'll bust you in the nose. Sure, the Cheyenne are a noble people overall, but some of 'em are pure-dee jackasses . . . just like every other breed of folks."

They had almost reached the water tank by now, and before they could continue the conversation, someone shouted, "Hold it! Who's out there?"

The blood brothers both heaved sighs of relief as they recognized Marshal Asa Thorpe's voice. Matt called, "It's us, Marshal—Bodine and Two Wolves."

"Just the two of you?"

"That's right."

"Come ahead then!"

Holding a rifle, Thorpe stepped out from behind the shed the railroad used to store tools and a handcar.

"Where's Shade?" Sam asked.

Thorpe lowered the rifle and jerked a thumb over his shoulder toward the shed.

"Tied up around behind that tool shack," the marshal said. "Gagged, too. Everett and I got tired of listening to his line of bull. Everett's standing guard over him."

"You run into any problems gettin' out of town?" Matt asked.

Thorpe shook his head and said, "No. You fellas did a good job of drawing all the attention to yourselves. We made it out the back of the barn with nobody seeing us and rode straight here. How about you? Are either of you hurt?"

"Nope," Matt replied as he and Sam swung down from their saddles. "Plenty of lead got tossed around, but none of it landed on us."

"We led the pursuit a good two miles east of the settlement," Sam added. "Then we abandoned the wagon just like we planned and circled around to get back here."

"No one followed us either," Sam said. "We made sure of that."

Thorpe nodded. "It's nice to have a plan work out for a change. Now all we have to do is wait for the train to show up in the morning."

Even though it was dark, Matt and Sam exchanged a glance. Thorpe sounded optimistic, and the blood brothers wanted to feel that way, too . . .

But they had seen too much trouble in their young lives to believe it was going to be that simple.

Sam pulled his Winchester from the saddle boot and nodded toward the water tank.

"I believe I'll climb up there and stretch out on that little platform," he said. "Should be able to see a long way from there."

Matt gathered up the reins and asked, "Where are the horses?"

Thorpe pointed to the north. "There's a little wash about fifty yards in that direction. It's just deep enough to hide them, and there's a little grass in the bottom for them to graze on. Still handy enough to get to in a hurry, though, if we need to."

Matt nodded. "I'll take these over there and picket them, too."

Sam was already climbing the rungs that were nailed to one of the thick posts holding up the water tank. He reached the platform next to the long spout that could be lowered when a train stopped to take on water in its boiler. He lay down on his belly, facing back toward Pancake Flats. From there, he had a good view of the tracks as they dwindled into the distance.

The night was cool, which was good because it would help keep him awake, Sam thought. He was tired, but there would be time enough to rest when Joshua Shade was safely behind the walls of Yuma Prison, awaiting his fate. That ought to be by sundown of the next day, Sam figured.

Whenever it was, it couldn't be too soon to suit him and Matt. Once again, they had landed up to their necks in danger, despite all their good intentions.

But as long as that kept happening, Sam thought with a wry grin in the darkness, at least life wouldn't get boring.

The town of Pancake Flats looked normal in the morning as the sun rose, scattering its widespread golden light over the Arizona landscape. All the bodies had been hauled into the livery stable and stacked like cordwood, and frightened citizens working at gunpoint had shoveled dirt over the pools of blood in the street.

Everybody in town had been disarmed and rounded up, just as Garth had ordered, and herded into the hotel. There were enough of them that they outnumbered their captors by quite a bit. They could have overwhelmed the outlaws if they had all attacked at once.

But nobody wanted to be among the ones who would die if they tried such a thing. That fear and indecision kept anybody from even making the attempt until it was too late. Once they were all gathered together, unarmed, under the guns of the lawless men, the only thing that would happen if they tried to fight back was a massacre.

That was what the townspeople told themselves anyway. It was easier than dying.

Once all the signs of the previous night's violence had been covered up, the men who had done the work were marched back into the hotel. If anyone wondered what had happened to the woman who had registered as Jessica Devlin, nobody said anything about it.

She was nowhere to be seen, though.

Garth singled out the ticket clerk who worked at the Southern Pacific depot. Gesturing with the gun in his hand, he said, "Come along with me, hombre."

The clerk hung back like he wanted to melt into the crowd of prisoners in the hotel lobby. "Wha . . . what do you want with me?" he asked.

"I'll explain that when we get where we're goin'," Garth snapped.

The clerk had no choice but to go with him. They walked down the street in the light of the rising sun, toward the train station. As they went inside, Garth heard the telegraph key clicking.

"Go see what they're sayin'," he said, punctuating the order by prodding the gun barrel into the clerk's back.

The man hurried over to the door that led into the little cubicle behind the ticket window where the telegraph apparatus was located. He sat down, picked up the pencil and pad that rested on the table beside the key, and began listening intently, writing down the tapped-out words that came over the wire.

Garth crowded into the room behind him. "What're they sayin'?"

The clerk looked around at him. The man's face was pale with fear as he glanced at the gun in Garth's hand. It was clear that he wouldn't even consider lying to the outlaw.

"It's the district office in El Paso. They're advising everyone along the line that the repairs to the trestle at Bowtie Canyon are finished and that a westbound train is on its way." The clerk looked at the clock on the wall. "It should be here in less than an hour."

Garth grunted in acknowledgment of the news. "*Bueno.*"

The clerk summoned up his courage and asked, "What are you going to do? Are you going to rob the train when it gets here?"

"Now, that's a thought," Garth said with a grim smile. "Since traffic along the line's been backed up, there might be a pretty good pile o' loot in the express car. But we got bigger fish to fry today. The train's gonna stop and pick up a few passengers, and then it'll be on its way just like normal."

The clerk frowned. "I don't understand."

Garth felt like walloping the nosy son of a bitch across the head with his pistol, but he decided against it. Everything had to look normal when the train rolled into the station, and that included the clerk.

"Me and some of the other fellas are gettin' on the train," Garth explained. "Nobody on there will know who we are—and you ain't gonna tell 'em."

The clerk shook his head emphatically. "No, sir. No indeed."

"We figure Marshal Thorpe will be waitin' somewheres west o' here to board the train with Joshua. Once they're aboard, we'll take it over and set our boss free."

After a moment's thought, the clerk said, "You know, I'll bet you're right. Matt Bodine was in here yesterday asking about flag stops to the west. I gave him a map." Somewhat peevishly, the man added, "That map belongs to the railroad, too, and you know, I didn't get it back."

The fella picked strange things to worry about, Garth thought.

"Once we're gone, you won't be tryin' to send any wires to warn folks about what's goin' on, now will you?" he asked as he moved the gun barrel closer to the clerk's face.

Beads of sweat popped out on the man's forehead. "N-no, sir, of course not. I wouldn't do that. You have my word."

"Your word ain't good enough, amigo. I'm gonna make sure."

The clerk paled even more. He licked his lips nervously and said, "Please, I swear—"

"We're gonna pull down the telegraph wires both ways," Garth went on after savoring the man's fear for a second, "and smash that apparatus to boot. The rest of the gang will drive off every horse in town as they're leavin', too. You folks'll have a long walk if you want to go anywhere."

The clerk swallowed. "I . . . I was afraid you were going to—"

"Gonzalez wanted to just kill you all and burn the town down, to make sure," Garth went on, interrupting. "I don't figure that's necessary, though. And the smoke could be seen for a hell of a long way. Somebody on that train might spot it behind 'em and wonder what was goin' on. Don't want to spook anybody before we have to."

"Thank you. We . . . we appreciate you not killing us."

"Just remember that and play your part. No funny business while the train's here."

"No funny business," the terrified clerk swore.

The door opened and Jeffries came in, along with the Winslow woman. Maggie wore a nice traveling outfit now, complete with a hat with a couple of feathers on it perched on her fair hair.

The clothes had come from one of the stores in town, all of which had been looted of everything the outlaws thought they might need, along with all the cash on hand, of course. Not a great haul, Garth reflected, but they might as well get *something* for their trouble.

"You ready to do your part, missy?" Garth asked the young woman.

Maggie nodded. She looked about as pale and scared as the clerk, but Garth had seen the steel core inside her and knew it was still there.

"I don't understand why you need me, though," she said. "I can't really do anything."

"Except keep Matt Bodine distracted and off his guard," Garth said. "Do a good job of that, and you'll be back with your husband and kid by the time this day is over."

"You swear?"

"Sure. You got my word."

Of course, that wasn't worth much, he thought . . . but she didn't have to know that.

Garth glanced at the clock on the wall. "We've still got a while to wait," he told Maggie. "You might as well go sit down on that bench over yonder."

"I'll keep you company," Jeffries said to her. He had been guarding her most of the night. Garth wondered idly if Jeffries had taken any liberties with her. She didn't seem any more upset than usual, so he supposed not.

If Jeffries wanted the woman, he could have her as far as Garth was concerned . . . but only when this was over and Joshua was free again. Until that goal had been accomplished, nothing else mattered.

Garth looked at the clock again. Time sure passed slow when you were waiting to kill people.

Chapter 36

Maggie couldn't get Ike and Caleb out of her mind. Images of her husband and son filled her brain, threatening to crowd out everything else. She imagined them both dead, lying on the barren sand. Or else savaged by scavengers . . .

She knew she couldn't afford to give in to despair, so she forced those thoughts out of her head as she stood there in the train station, waiting. In addition to Garth and Jeffries, three more of the outlaws had joined them on the platform, leaving nine men to guard the prisoners in the hotel. The remaining outlaw was sitting in the clerk's cubicle, out of sight, with a gun in his hand to make sure the man didn't try any tricks.

Garth had picked three men who didn't look quite as hard-bitten as the others. In their worn range clothes, they could have been cowboys catching a ride on the train in hopes of finding jobs somewhere else. In his dusty black suit, Jeffries looked like a businessman, or possibly a gambler.

Garth himself had the most sinister appearance of those who would be boarding the train. It might have been smarter for him to trust that job to someone else, but he wasn't going to do that. He was too worried about something else going wrong, Maggie knew.

It did seem that every time Garth and the other outlaws tried to free Joshua Shade, Matt Bodine and Sam Two Wolves ruined those plans, along with Marshal Thorpe and the other deputy, of course. Having seen Bodine in action, Maggie knew just how dangerous he was, and from what she had heard the outlaws saying, Sam Two Wolves was almost as fast and deadly with a gun.

Eventually, though, the odds had to catch up to them. They couldn't keep on defeating a much larger force again and again. Maggie wasn't even sure she wanted them to. It was only a slender hope that the gang would reunite her with Ike and Caleb and then let them all go if they rescued Joshua Shade, but it was better than no hope at all.

"Train's comin'," Garth said from the edge of the platform where he was peering eastward.

Maggie moved forward and looked in that direction herself. She saw smoke rising from the locomotive's stack as the wheels churned along the rails. She couldn't make out the train itself very well at first, but as it came closer, she could see it better.

In less than five minutes, the train rolled into the station, the huge, noisy locomotive pulling on past it so that the passenger and freight cars lined up with the platform. As the cars jolted and clattered to a stop, the conductor, in his blue suit and black cap, swung down from the steps attached to one of the passenger cars.

"Howdy, Harry!" he called to the clerk behind the ticket window. "Any freight goin' out?"

"Not today, Brett," the clerk replied. "Just a few passengers."

The conductor looked surprised. "With the trestle being down and no trains rolling for a while, I figured the freight would've backed up."

"I guess nobody's shipping anything right now," the clerk said. He looked and sounded nervous to Maggie, but the conductor didn't seem to notice. She supposed she might be imagining it.

"All right, folks, everybody on board," the conductor called to Maggie, Garth, Jeffries, and the other men. "If there's no freight to load, we won't be stopped long."

Maggie carried a carpetbag that had some clothes stuffed in it just to give it some weight. The outlaws had their saddles, rifles, and warbags. A porter slid back the door of the baggage car and loaded the bags while the passengers climbed on board. The clerk had prepared authentic tickets for all of them, so the conductor had nothing to be suspicious about there.

He punched the tickets and ushered the passengers into the car. As Maggie passed him, he touched the brim of his cap and said, "I hope you're comfortable traveling with us, ma'am. If you'd like a pillow or a blanket, just let me know."

"Thank you, sir," Maggie forced herself to say. She hoped her voice sounded normal. She thought it did.

"Next stop where you can stretch your limbs will be Tucson. We stop once between here and there, but only to take on water."

She wasn't sure why he was telling her this, maybe just to make conversation, but she managed to smile and nod and say, "That will be fine."

She sat down on an empty bench. There were quite a few of them, because the train wasn't crowded.

Garth lowered himself onto the bench across the aisle from her, evidently wanting to keep an eye on her.

From the things she had heard Garth and Jeffries talking about, and the things that Garth had admitted openly, she had a pretty clear idea of the outlaws' plan. After isolating the town by cutting the telegraph wires and hazing off all the horses in the settlement, the rest of the gang would follow the train. Garth and the other outlaws on board would take over the train as it approached the water stop where Thorpe, Bodine, and Two Wolves had to be waiting with Joshua Shade. They wouldn't know anything was wrong until it was too late. Once they were on board and settled in for the trip, the outlaws would stop the train again and the rest of the gang would swoop in to reinforce Garth and his men. The marshal and his companions would be taken by surprise and trapped.

Maggie thought this plan stood a good chance of working, more so than the other attempts the gang had made to free Shade. They would probably rob the train while they were at it, just as they had looted Pancake Flats when the opportunity presented itself.

Once Shade was in charge again, the gang would rebuild itself in no time, replacing the men who had been lost in the fighting so far, and before you knew it, they would be terrorizing the territory again under the leadership of the crazed preacher turned bloodthirsty killer.

And she was going to help that happen, Maggie thought as she closed her eyes in dismay for a moment. She struggled to control her emotions.

When she opened her eyes, she saw Garth glaring at her warningly. She knew the message he was trying to communicate.

Any chance Ike and Caleb still had depended

completely on her. She couldn't let them down, no matter what sort of evil she would be helping to unleash on the rest of the territory. The citizens of Arizona would just have to look out for themselves.

Garth nodded, evidently satisfied that Maggie was under control again. No one else in the railroad car seemed to notice the fleeting byplay.

The locomotive's whistle shrilled, and the cars lurched into motion. The station platform seemed to move past and then suddenly was gone. Pancake Flats fell behind the train.

They were on their way to the final act in this bloody drama, Maggie thought.

At least, she prayed that it would soon be over, one way or the other.

Sam dozed off every now and then as he lay on the water tank platform, but those few catnaps were the only sleep he got that night. He was young and resilient, though, so he actually felt fairly well rested the next morning.

Because of that, he was alert enough to spot the approaching locomotive while it was still quite a distance away. He watched the smoke rising from its stack for a minute or so, then cupped his hands around his mouth and shouted down to the others, "Train's coming!"

Matt stepped out from behind the shed and nodded. "I'll go fetch the horses," he called in return. He turned and trotted off toward the arroyo.

Sam tucked his Winchester under his arm and started climbing down the ladder. By the time he reached the ground, Thorpe and Everett had come out from behind the shed as well, prodding Joshua Shade in front of them with their rifles.

Shade's wrists were tied together, and several turns in the rope had been taken around his body, pinning his arms at his sides. A short length of rope bound his ankles so that he could walk, but would fall on his face if he tried to run.

The gag was still in place, but Shade was as wild-eyed as ever and made grunting noises through it. Sam had no doubt that the loco outlaw would be cussing and ranting up a storm if not for the gag. Probably foaming at the mouth, too. Shade had the look of a rabid animal about him.

Matt came back from the arroyo leading all the horses. He looked at Shade, grinned, and said, "He doesn't look so dangerous now, does he?"

"Don't you believe it," Thorpe said. "I won't believe that Shade is past the point of hurting anybody else until he's swinging from a hangrope."

"That shouldn't be too much longer now," Sam said. "The train will be here in a few minutes, and by tonight he'll be safely locked up at Yuma. How long do you think it'll take for the sentence to be carried out, Marshal?"

Thorpe shook his head. "I don't know, but it can't be soon enough to suit me. If not for my orders, I'd throw a rope over one of the beams on that water tank and haul him up right here and now."

"That sounds like a good idea to me, too," Matt said.

"I didn't say we were actually going to do it," Thorpe replied with a frown. "Shade's going to hang, but it'll be legal. If you wanted a lynching, you should have let that mob have him the first time back in Arrowhead."

Sam said, "Take it easy, Marshal. Nobody wants a lynching."

The train had drawn closer as they were talking. Its whistle blew, and steam billowed as the drivers reversed and the locomotive began to slow down. The screech of metal against metal rose into the hot morning air.

Thorpe and Everett forced Shade forward, each of them gripping one of the outlaw's shoulders. Matt and Sam flanked them and held their Winchesters ready.

Suddenly, the blood brothers glanced at each other. Sam felt instinct prickling the hairs on the back of his neck, and he could tell from Matt's expression that he was experiencing the same thing.

Something was wrong here, even though everything about the train looked completely normal.

Garth had been keeping an eye on the passing landscape and estimating how far the train had come from Pancake Flats. He knew from what the ticket clerk had told him that the water stop was twenty miles west of the settlement, and he knew about how long it should take them to reach it.

When he figured there were only a few miles to go, he stood up and started toward the front of the car, giving minuscule nods to Jeffries and his other men as he passed them. Jeffries waited a moment and then followed him.

The other three outlaws remained behind. They wouldn't reveal their presence until the rest of the gang arrived. As far as anybody other than the conductor, the engineer, and the fireman were concerned, everything about this water stop would be perfectly normal.

Garth hadn't decided how far to let things go before he forced the engineer to stop the train again. Before it got to Tucson, that was for damned sure. He wanted Bodine, Two Wolves, and Thorpe good and relaxed before he made his move, though. He wanted those sons of bitches to think all their troubles were behind them.

It would be that much sweeter when they realized that they were all doomed.

Garth had seen the conductor pass through the car a few minutes earlier, headed toward the front of the train. He and Jeffries caught up to the man at the front of the first passenger car, with only the coal tender between them and the engine. As they stepped out onto the platform where the conductor was standing, the blue-uniformed man nodded to them and asked, "Something I can do for you gents?"

Garth drew his gun as Jeffries closed the door behind them so no one in the car could see what was going on. Before the conductor had time to realize what was going on, Garth jammed the Colt's muzzle in the man's belly. He said, "You can do what you're told, or I'll blow your guts right through your backbone."

A sharply indrawn breath of surprise hissed between the conductor's teeth as he stiffened in alarm. "Is this a holdup?" he asked.

"Nope. You're gonna take my pard and me up to the engine, you understand? You cooperate with us, and nobody'll get hurt."

Nobody but Thorpe, Bodine, Two Wolves, and anybody else who got in their way, Garth thought.

For a moment, the conductor looked like he might

be stubborn, but then he sighed and nodded. "All right," he said. "Just leave the passengers alone."

Garth jabbed harder with the pistol, making the man gasp in pain. "Don't go givin' orders," Garth snapped. "Now move."

The conductor turned and started making his way along the narrow walkway built onto the side of the coal tender. Garth held the gun in his right hand, and used the left to hold the grab-irons along the way. The train swayed slightly, and if a man wasn't careful, he could get pitched off. Jeffries came along behind him, also with a drawn gun.

They reached the end of the walkway. The conductor stepped around onto the platform at the front of the tender, which was closely coupled to the locomotive. The engineer sat on his stool, leaning over slightly to peer out the window along the tracks as he held his hand loosely on the throttle. The fireman was on the other side of the cab, leaning on his shovel at the moment.

The fireman spotted Garth and Jeffries first, and started to lift his shovel as if he intended to use it as a weapon. Jeffries stepped around Garth and the conductor and leveled his gun at the man.

"Don't do it, friend," he warned.

The engineer bolted up off his stool. "What the hell!"

"Careful, Fred," the conductor warned. "This bastard's got a gun in my back!"

Garth said, "And since we don't need you anymore, I don't cotton to bein' called a bastard!"

His gun rose and fell suddenly, crunching down on the conductor's head. The man groaned in pain and fell to his knees, driven down by the blow, then pitched forward on his face.

His face mottled with rage, the engineer started toward Garth, but the outlaw stepped back quickly and leveled his Colt again. "Might as well tell you now," Garth said, "I can run one of these contraptions if I have to. So don't think I won't plug you if I have to."

The engineer stopped and struggled to control his anger with a visible effort. Finally, he asked, "What do you want? Is this a robbery?"

"Nope," Garth said again. "Just keep this locomotive rollin' all the way to that water stop up ahead. When we get there, you can take on water just like you always do. Nobody has to know anything's goin' on except us." He paused. "There's one more thing. I think some fellas are gonna be waitin' there to get on the train. You'll let 'em do it, understand?"

"Friends of yours?" the engineer grated.

"One of 'em is. The others . . . not hardly."

Garth moved so that he could cover both the engineer and the fireman, then nodded toward the unconscious conductor. "Get that uniform on, Jeffries. I don't reckon any of those lawdogs ever got a good enough look at you to recognize you."

Jeffries nodded and holstered his revolver. He bent and began pulling the blue coat off the conductor.

By the time the water tank had come into view up ahead, Jeffries had the uniform on and was tugging the black cap down on his head. "How do I look?" he asked with a grin.

"Good enough to fool those varmints. Just stay out of the passenger cars and away from the brakes. We don't want any of 'em to realize you ain't the real conductor."

Jeffries nodded in understanding. He had taken off

his gunbelt, but he had the Colt tucked behind his belt. The conductor's coat concealed the gun butt.

"Slow and easy, just like normal," Garth told the engineer. The man blew the whistle and then worked the control levers, slowing the train. Garth risked a glance toward the water tank, and felt a surge of excitement and anticipation as he spotted the small group of men standing near the tracks.

The wind blew the long hair of the man in the center. That would be Joshua. He was flanked by Thorpe and some nameless deputy, who were hanging on to him. Bodine and Two Wolves were on either side of them.

All nice and neat, Garth thought, and he and Jeffries could have just gunned them all down, if not for the fact that Joshua would be in the line of fire, too. After this much time and trouble, Garth didn't want to take any more chances on harming his leader and friend.

Steam shot out in clouds as the train slowed more. The locomotive was almost even with the water tank now. With practiced ease, the engineer brought it to a smooth halt. With a giant hiss, more steam billowed out, obscuring Garth's view of the waiting men. He crouched, not wanting any of them to spot him.

Then, as the steam blew away, Jeffries let out a startled, bitter curse and exclaimed, "Bodine and Two Wolves—they're gone!"

Chapter 37

As the train eased to a stop next to the water tank, Matt said to Thorpe, "Something's wrong, Marshal. Better get Shade back under cover while Sam and I check it out."

"What—" Thorpe started to ask, but he was too late. The blood brothers were already moving.

Matt and Sam went in different directions. Sam ran around the front of the engine, leaping across the tracks in front of the cowcatcher, while Matt raced alongside the train. When he came to the first passenger car, he bounded up the steps to the platform at the front of it.

Sam reached the engine cab, which was partially open on the sides. Through that opening he saw the men crowded into the cab, including an hombre dressed only in long underwear who lay on the floor of the cab, either unconscious or dead.

The engineer and the fireman were easy to spot. So was the conductor. That left one man who had a gun in his hand, a craggy-faced, mustached gent who obviously had no business being up there.

As soon as Sam saw that man, everything clicked together in his mind. The outlaws had figured out the plan Matt and Sam had come up with to get Joshua Shade to Yuma, and they had taken over the train to stop that from happening.

The gunman in the cab must have seen Sam from the corner of his eye. He whirled, bringing up his gun as he did so. "Two Wolves!" he exclaimed as his face contorted in anger and hate.

Sam snapped the Winchester to his shoulder and fired just as flame spouted from the muzzle of the outlaw's revolver. The Colt's roar blended together with the whipcrack of the rifle. Sam felt the wind-rip of the bullet next to his ear.

His shot didn't miss. The rifle bullet drilled into the outlaw's chest, flinging him back against the engineer. Reacting swiftly, the engineer brought his hand down in a slashing blow against the gunman's wrist, knocking the revolver loose. Then, as the outlaw began to sag, the engineer clouted him with a big fist to the jaw, knocking him the rest of the way to the floor of the cab.

Sam lowered the Winchester and looked toward the conductor, intending to ask the man if he knew how many outlaws were on the train. A shock went through him as he saw the gun in the conductor's hand, and he realized too late that the unconscious gent who'd been stripped was the *real* conductor. The man now wearing the blue suit was one of the outlaws.

Sam tried to bring the rifle to bear on the phony conductor, but before he could, the glare of a muzzle flash filled his eyes. He felt the heavy slam of a bullet's impact against his body, rocking him backward. His feet slipped on the gravel roadbed. He heard another shot, but didn't feel that bullet. He had already fallen to the ground and barely clung to a shred of consciousness.

Meanwhile, Matt had plunged headlong into the first passenger car, and the sight of a man running in with a rifle in his hands spooked the passengers into thinking the train was being held up. A couple of women screamed, and men started to their feet as they yelled questions and curses.

"I'm a lawman!" Matt shouted over the hubbub. That was stretching the truth more than a little, but it might quiet them down quicker than anything else he could say. "Take it easy!"

His eyes scanned the passengers and didn't see anybody who looked like an outlaw. Just then, he heard shots from the engine and knew that his instincts, as well as Sam's, had been right. If the gang had taken over the train, there had to be more of them somewhere in the cars. He ran toward the rear of the train.

As he came into the next car, somebody yelled, "Bodine!" and a gun cracked. A bullet smacked into the wall near the door after whipping past Matt. Screams filled the air.

"Everybody down!" Matt shouted. The passengers dived for the floor, leaving three hard-bitten-looking hombres who had stood up to blaze away at him.

A Winchester was no good in a fight like this. He dropped the rifle as he went into a crouch and palmed both Colts from the thonged-down holsters attached to the crossed gunbelts.

It would have been a sight to see if anybody had been looking. The innocent passengers were all bellied down on the floor, though, with their arms over their heads even though that wouldn't offer any protection from flying lead. Matt stood at the front of the car with his guns roaring and flashing as the three outlaws blazed away at him from the other end of the car.

The man on Matt's far left stumbled back with a couple of .45 slugs in his chest and then collapsed. The man on the far right twisted around, dropped his gun, and clawed at his throat as blood spouted from the place where a bullet had ripped it open. The third and last man got off a final shot that came close enough to knock Matt's hat off his head, but that was the last chance the outlaw got. A bullet slammed him back against the rear door of the coach. He hung there for a second and then slid down it, leaving a crimson smear on the wood.

With his pulse pounding heavily in his head, Matt slowly lowered his smoking guns. All three of the outlaws were down, their bloody forms motionless in death. Out of habit, Matt holstered his left-hand gun and used that hand to reach to the loops on his shell belt so he could start reloading.

"Drop it," a voice said.

A woman's voice.

Shocked, Matt looked down to see the blonde who had introduced herself to him as Jessica Devlin back in Pancake Flats. She knelt in the aisle holding the rifle he had dropped. Her pretty face was lined with strain. She was pale, but looked determined.

"Miss Devlin——" he began.

"Drop your gun, Mr. Bodine," she repeated. "I don't want to shoot you, but I . . . I will if I have to."

Matt didn't really believe her, but you sort of had to give somebody the benefit of the doubt when they were pointing a .44-40 repeater at you. He didn't drop the Colt, but he slid it back into leather.

He didn't need the gun anyway. He wasn't going to shoot Jessica.

"Look, I'm not an outlaw," he said, thinking maybe that was what she believed. "In fact, I'm working with the law—"

Jessica came to her feet, keeping the rifle leveled at him. The barrel shook a little. The Winchester was heavy, and she probably wasn't used to handling a rifle.

"Where is Joshua Shade?" she demanded, shocking him again.

"Shade?" Matt repeated. "You don't mean—"

"Just tell me where he is."

Obviously, there was a lot more to this young woman than there appeared to be. A bitter, sour taste welled up under Matt's tongue as he realized that she must be working with the gang. He didn't know how she had gotten mixed up with Shade's bunch, but that didn't really matter now.

He didn't answer Jessica's question, though, because suddenly there was a lot more shooting outside.

Maggie couldn't believe what she was doing. She had never pointed a gun at anybody in her life. She had never even shot a bird or a squirrel or anything like that.

And yet here she was, threatening to kill a man.

She had no choice, though. She didn't know what had gone wrong with Garth's plan, but if the outlaws succeeded in freeing Joshua Shade, there was still a chance, slim though it might be, that they would take her back to wherever they had left Ike and Caleb. All she could do was try to put them in her debt.

So for that reason, she had picked up the rifle and

pointed it at Matt Bodine, taking him by surprise. She would force him to take her to Shade, she thought, and then Garth and Jeffries and the others would come and see what she had done . . .

Shots roared somewhere close by, outside the train. A window in the car shattered, and a woman shrieked in terror. Maggie couldn't stop her head from jerking around toward the sounds.

From the corner of her eye she saw a flicker of movement, and instinctively squeezed the trigger. The roar of the shot slammed against her ears like a thunderclap.

Matt leaped forward, reaching for the Winchester's barrel. He got his fingers around it and wrenched it upward just as the rifle blasted. The slug punched harmlessly into the train car's ceiling, showering down some splinters.

Jessica Devlin cried out as Matt jerked the rifle from her hands. He leaped to one of the windows and saw the riders galloping past, firing into the cars. Matt recognized several of them from trading shots with them on previous occasions, and knew they were the rest of Shade's gang.

He didn't know exactly what the plan had been, but obviously the outlaws had split up, some of them boarding the train as passengers while the others waited for the shooting to start before rushing in to take a hand in the fight.

Matt broke out the window with the Winchester's barrel, poked it through, and started firing. He picked off a couple of the outlaws, his bullets knocking them out of their saddles. But then he was forced to duck as a hail of bullets stormed back at him.

With a sudden lurch, the train jolted into motion.

Now what the hell . . .

Willard Garth struggled up out of the pit of pain into which he had been dropped. That damn half-breed Two Wolves had shot him, he remembered.

But he wasn't dead yet, which meant he might still succeed in freeing Joshua.

Garth started struggling to his feet, but was only halfway there when a hand grasped his arm and helped him up. He blinked blearily at Jeffries, who still wore the conductor's outfit and was covering the engineer and the fireman, who had been forced at gunpoint to the other side of the cab.

As Garth spotted Sam Two Wolves lying on the ground beside the engine with a dark bloodstain on his buckskin shirt, he felt a surge of satisfaction. The pain deep inside told Garth that he probably wouldn't live to see the sun set again, but at least that damn 'breed was dead.

"Gimme . . . gimme my gun," he rasped to Jeffries.

"You're hurt, Garth—" Jeffries began.

"Hell, I know that! Just gimme my gun."

Jeffries picked up the fallen revolver and pressed it into Garth's hand. "I'll watch these two," Garth went on as he leaned against the side of the cab. "You go get Joshua."

"Thorpe and that deputy hustled him around behind that shed."

"You can take 'em by surprise," Garth said. "They'll think you're the conductor."

Jeffries's eyes lit up. Garth was right. The lawmen wouldn't recognize him.

"You'll be all right here?"

"Sure. Just—" A wracking, agonized cough shook Garth for a second. He used his free hand to wipe bloody foam from his lips. "Just go get Joshua."

Jeffries nodded, then leaped down from the cab and dashed toward the shed.

Garth's head was swimming, and he knew he couldn't count on staying conscious for any length of time. His lips drew back from his teeth in a grimace as he swung his gun up.

"Won't need you two anymore," he told the shocked engineer and fireman, then pulled the trigger twice.

The engineer doubled over as a bullet tore into his guts. The fireman went over backward under the impact, falling out of the cab and landing a few feet away from Sam Two Wolves.

Satisfied that neither of them was a threat anymore, Garth turned to the locomotive's controls. As he had mentioned earlier, he had driven a train before, back in the days before he became an outlaw, and not much had changed since then. The throttle, the brake, the gauges were all the same. He was confident he could get the train moving again.

He heard shots from behind the shed, as well as from somewhere back along the train. *Bodine*, he thought. Bodine was in the passenger cars, shooting it out with the men who had been left there.

But the shots from the shed meant that Jeffries had found Joshua. Garth gritted his teeth against the pain, and leaned against the window in the side of the cab as he waited to see who would come out from behind the little building.

Jeffries appeared a moment later, leading an obviously unsteady Joshua Shade. Joshua's feet were free, and he was unwinding some cut ropes from around his wrists. The gag in his mouth was gone.

"Praise the Lord!" Shade cried as he climbed into the cab, helped up by Jeffries. "You've freed me from the heathens, Brother Willard!"

"Good to see you . . . Boss," Garth managed to get out. "What about Thorpe . . . and the deputy?"

"I plugged both of them," Jeffries said as he climbed into the cab behind Shade. "You were right, Garth. They thought I was the conductor and didn't know any different until I had lead in them." He laughed curtly. "I never saw anybody look so surprised as that damned marshal."

Garth heard more shooting, and looked back to see the rest of the gang slamming bullets at the passenger cars as they galloped past. That was a good distraction, but not necessary now.

"Let's get . . . outta here," he said as he shoved the throttle forward. "Jeffries . . . go back behind the tender and uncouple the rest o' the cars . . . No need in haulin' them with us."

Jeffries nodded, and started along the walkway on the side of the coal tender as the train began to pick up speed.

Shade looked at Garth and said, "You're hurt, Brother Willard."

"It don't matter," Garth said. "All that matters is . . . we finally got you away from those damn lawmen, Joshua."

"Yes, and again, praise the Lord for that. We're going back to Arrowhead and Pancake Flats and wipe those dens of iniquity off the face of the earth. They deserve to be punished by holy fire for how they treated a humble servant of the Lord."

"Gonna have to . . . build the gang back up first," Garth suggested. "We lost a bunch o' men . . . tryin' to get you loose."

"Very well. The Lord's work takes time."

Garth hunched over against the pain as another coughing fit seized him. As it faded away, he realized that Joshua hadn't thanked *him* yet. Joshua was quick to give the Lord credit, but it was Garth with a bullet through his lungs who was slowly drowning in his own blood.

But it didn't matter, Garth told himself. He'd been willing to do whatever it took to save his friend from the hangman, even if it cost his own life.

Still, a simple *gracias* would have been nice . . .

Garth's head slumped onto his chest and he died then with his hand on the throttle. The weight of his hand slowly shoved the control forward, and the train began to pick up even more speed.

Chapter 38

A few minutes earlier, the eyes of Sam Two Wolves had flickered open as he sprawled there on the ground next to the locomotive. He hadn't been unconscious long, only a minute or so, and the memory of being shot by the man in the conductor's uniform came back to him instantly.

His vision was blurred at first, but as he heard more shots, his sight began to clear, and as he looked up at the cab through slitted eyelids, he saw the craggy-faced outlaw leaning against the side of the cab by the controls, and Joshua Shade being helped up into it by the phony conductor.

Sam wanted to find his gun and start shooting at them, but his muscles flatly refused to work. The shock of being wounded had paralyzed them momentarily.

He realized a second later that that shock had probably just saved his life. If he'd tried to struggle upright, the outlaws would have filled him full of lead. As it was, they were ignoring him, as if they were convinced he was dead.

Having no real choice in the matter, Sam lay there

gathering his strength. He heard shooting all up and down the other side of the train, and wondered where his blood brother was. Knowing Matt Bodine, he was right in the thick of the fighting.

Steam hissed, and the train began to move.

As the cab pulled away from him, Sam rolled onto his side and then over on his belly. His hands and feet pushed against the ground, lifting him into a crouch. He would have liked to rest a while longer before having to move again, but the outlaws were getting away with Shade—and stealing a whole blasted train to boot!

Sam stumbled toward the coal tender. It had a walkway with a short railing on each side. Sam lunged toward it and reached out. He caught hold of the railing and pushed off hard with his feet, throwing a leg up onto the walkway.

Then he hung there, his other leg dragging on the gravel roadbed next to the rails, unable to pull himself up any farther. If he let go, he might fall under the wheels and be chopped to pieces. With his head thrown back, his teeth bared in an agonized grimace, and cords of muscle standing out in his neck, he struggled to save himself from that grisly fate.

Matt left Jessica Devlin where she was and ran forward through the first passenger car. He flung the door open and hurried out onto the platform, carrying the Winchester at a slant across his chest.

The first thing he saw was the conductor kneeling on the narrow platform at the rear of the coal tender. Matt realized with a shock that the man was struggling to uncouple the rest of the train from the locomotive and the tender. There was no good reason for him to be doing that . . .

Unless he wasn't really the conductor.

That thought flashed through Matt's brain in the same instant that the man in the blue uniform glanced up, saw him standing there, and started clawing a pistol from behind his belt.

"Bodine!" the man exclaimed involuntarily.

Knowing now that the "conductor" had to be one of the outlaws, Matt snapped the rifle down and fired from the hip. The man dropped into an even lower crouch, though, and the .44-40 round spanked off the tender's rear wall. The phony conductor fired, spraying slugs across the passenger car platform and forcing Matt to dive back through the open door behind him.

Lying in the aisle, Matt tried to draw a bead with the rifle again, but before he could do so, the outlaw finally succeeded in yanking loose the pin that coupled the cars together. He darted back around onto the walkway that led to the engine as a gap suddenly opened up between the tender and the first passenger car.

Matt knew he had only seconds to act. Abandoning the Winchester because a rifle really wasn't much good in a close-quarters fight, he scrambled to his feet and lunged out onto the platform. Without hesitating, he leaped into the air, throwing himself toward the tender with all the strength at his command.

If he failed in this desperate move, he would fall onto the roadbed, where the rest of the cars would run over him as their momentum kept them rolling forward.

One foot smacked down on the tender's tiny rear platform. Matt grabbed for one of the iron handholds fastened to the wall of the car. His fingers slipped a little and he started to go backward, but then his grip tightened and he was able to pull himself upright. He leaned against the back of the tender, breathing heavily.

After a moment, he turned around, pressed his back against the rear of the tender, and pulled his right-hand gun so he could reload it. He looked back along the tracks and saw the rest of the cars beginning to slow down even more as their momentum wore off.

Unfortunately, he also saw the rest of Shade's gang, half a dozen men, galloping after the locomotive and tender.

And now he was their target, he realized as powder smoke spurted from gun muzzles and bullets began to splatter against the metal wall behind him.

Maggie realized that the train was slowing down. She didn't know what else was going on, but she knew they had left the water stop behind them. Where was Shade? Had his men freed him?

Shame burned inside her. She had tried to kill Matt Bodine. She never would have believed that she could take a human life, especially the life of someone who had never done her any harm. The thought sickened her, and she was glad Bodine had knocked the rifle upward as she pulled the trigger.

Now she ignored the chaos and confusion inside the car and ran toward the exit, intending to see if she could tell what was going on. She stepped out onto the platform as the train slowed even more.

But not *all* the train, she realized. She clung to the railing, leaned out, and saw the locomotive and the coal tender pulling away. They had been uncoupled from the rest of the cars.

The outlaws on horseback were giving chase and firing at a man who crouched on the narrow platform at the back of the tender. She recognized him as Matt Bodine.

She watched in horror, figuring that Bodine would be riddled with bullets at any moment. He ducked around the rear corner of the car onto the walkway that led up the right side of the tender toward the locomotive. That didn't offer him any protection, though.

But then he began climbing, using the grab irons bolted to the side of the car as ladder rungs. As Maggie watched, Bodine reached the top and flung himself over, dropping onto the coal in the tender.

She didn't see what happened after that, because the cars that had been cut loose ground to a halt and Maggie heard the pounding of more hoofbeats. She looked frantically toward the rear of the train, wondering what awful thing was going to happen next.

Instead she saw a miracle.

She saw her husband and son.

More men were galloping alongside the tracks, and riding double with one of them was Ike. He had Caleb clutched tightly to him with one arm while he hung on with the other. He yelled, "Maggie! Maggie!"

A bearded man who seemed to be leading the newcomers reined to a halt beside the platform where Maggie stood and called, "Ma'am, do you know where Joshua Shade is?"

Maggie waved toward the locomotive and tender. "I think he must be up there in the engine!" That was just a guess on her part, but she didn't see any other reason why the outlaws would have cut those cars loose from the rest of the train.

The man nodded and spurred his horse into a run

again. The men with him had halted for a moment, too, and Ike seized that opportunity to slide down from the horse he had been riding. Now he came toward the platform in a stumbling run, still crying, "Maggie! Maggie!"

Heedless of her own safety, she leaped to the ground and ran to meet him. They flung their arms around each other and held on for dear life, as if they would never let go.

"Are . . . are you all right?" she sobbed.

"I am now," Ike insisted.

"And Caleb?"

"He's fine."

"Oh, thank God! Thank God!" It was all Maggie could say as she stood there hugging her husband and son and shook with the sobs of relief that went through her. Finally, she was able to ask, "Who . . . who were those men with you?"

He shook his head, which now had a crude bandage wrapped around it. "I don't know, but they've been looking for Shade and his gang. I think they must be lawmen of some sort."

A sudden chill went through Maggie. Would she be arrested for trying to help the outlaws? She had been forced to do it, but the authorities might not see it that way.

She didn't care what happened to her, she decided. She knew now that her husband and son were safe, and that was all that really mattered.

She found herself hoping, though, that after all this, Joshua Shade wouldn't get away.

Kneeling on the pile of coal, Matt stuck his head over the tender's side wall and leveled his Colt at the outlaws as they charged after the locomotive. He squeezed off two shots and emptied a saddle. Bullets whining around his head forced him to duck back down.

Suddenly, he heard shots coming from somewhere close by. It was hard to tell because of the noise of the engine, but he thought the shots came from the other side of the tender, at the back.

Matt scrambled over the coal and looked over the wall. A shock went through him as he saw Sam crouched on the walkway on this side of the tender, leaning around the rear corner to fire at the pursuing outlaws.

"Sam!" Matt yelled.

On reflection, that probably wasn't a very smart thing to do, because Sam started in surprise and almost lost his balance on the precarious perch. He caught hold of a grab iron, though, and steadied himself as he looked up.

"Matt?"

"Yeah!" Matt saw blood on Sam's shirt. "You all right?"

Sam waved his six-gun. "Just a scratch! Nothing to worry about! You?"

"I'm fine!" Matt ducked again as a bullet whipped past his ear.

This one came from behind him, though.

The bastards had him in a cross fire.

"He's in the tender!" Joshua Shade told Jeffries as the wind in the cab whipped the crazed outlaw's long hair around his head. "Get up there and kill him!"

Shade was at the controls of the locomotive now, but he wasn't slowing it down any. Jeffries wasn't sure that Shade even knew what he was doing. The engine continued to rocket along the tracks.

"Kill Bodine!" Shade screamed again.

Jeffries took off the conductor's cap and flung it away. He stepped over Garth's body and started climbing the rungs fastened to the outside of the tender's front wall.

When he reached the top, he saw Bodine at the back of the coal car. Jeffries threw a leg over the wall and perched there atop it as he swung up his gun. As it came in line, he squeezed the trigger.

The train jolted a little at that moment, just enough to throw off Jeffries's aim. His bullet pulverized a lump of coal instead of blowing Bodine's brains out.

Then Bodine was turning and his gun came up with blinding speed and Jeffries saw the orange flash of powder inside the barrel. In that shaved fraction of a heartbeat, he could have almost sworn that he saw the bullet itself flying out of the barrel on a straight line at him.

Then the chunk of lead smashed into his forehead like a hammer blow, shattering bone and boring deep into his brain. Jeffries felt a burst of pain and then nothing as he went over backward, toppling into the cab to crash down next to Garth.

He was just as dead as Garth when he landed, too.

Matt saw the black-rimmed hole appear in the phony conductor's forehead; then the man fell out of sight. He turned his attention back to the rest of Shade's gang, but as he rested his gun barrel on the tender's wall, he saw that the outlaws had their hands full with a new battle.

Men on horseback, men Matt had never seen before, had overtaken the desperadoes and attacked them from the rear. Shade's men had no choice but to turn and fight back. Clouds of powder smoke rolled, bullets buzzed through the air like giant insects, men on both sides yelled, threw up their hands, and toppled from their saddles.

The fight was fierce, but lasted only moments. As the locomotive and tender continued to pull away, the smoke cleared enough for Matt to see that all the outlaws were done. A handful of the men who had attacked them were still mounted, but their losses had been heavy, too. The survivors spurred after the locomotive and tender.

Matt turned and began climbing over the coal toward the front. He didn't know who was left up there. Maybe nobody. The locomotive could be running away on its own, with its throttle locked in place. Somebody needed to slow it down and stop it.

He reached the front end of the tender and looked over the wall, then ducked as Joshua Shade fired a pistol at him. The loco, longhaired outlaw chief stood at the controls, twisting around to shoot at Matt. A crazed laugh came from the man's mouth as he pushed the throttle even harder, opening it up all the way.

The son of a bitch must be trying to wreck them, Matt thought. He sprang up and fired, sending a bullet ricocheting off the controls. Another shot sounded, this time from down below and to his left, and when he glanced in that direction he saw Sam thrusting a Colt around the front corner of the tender. Sam fired again, and glass shattered as the bullet smashed one of the gauges.

It was the steam pressure gauge, Matt realized as a

narrow stream of the white, scalding stuff suddenly shot out. It washed right over Shade's gun hand, and Shade screamed as the burning pain made him drop the gun.

Matt vaulted over the top of the tender and landed lithely in the cab, neatly avoiding the bodies of the dead men that lay there. He swung his pistol in a backhanded blow that slashed across Joshua Shade's face and drove the outlaw away from the controls. Matt lunged for the throttle and pulled it back, then grabbed the brake and hauled on it as hard as he could. With jolting shudders that rattled his bones and threatened to shake his teeth out of his head, the locomotive began to slow.

Sam swung around into the cab and kicked away the gun Shade had dropped, just to make sure the lunatic didn't get his hands on the weapon again. Then both of the blood brothers stood there covering Shade as the train gradually stopped.

"Looks like you'll live to hang after all, Shade," Matt said as the four strangers who had survived the battle with the outlaws galloped up alongside the cab.

"That's where you're wrong, mister," the bearded leader said as he and the others suddenly trained their guns on Matt and Sam. "You're all dyin', right here and now."

Chapter 39

Matt and Sam reacted instinctively. Sam kicked Shade's feet out from under him and dropped into a crouch next to the outlaw as the strangers opened fire and sent bullets screaming through the air over his head. Matt filled both hands with his irons and backed against the tender as he blazed away at the would-be killers.

Neither of them knew who these men were or why they wanted them dead. Neither of them cared.

It was a fight to the finish.

Sam drilled one of the men and knocked him out of the saddle. Matt ventilated another, then staggered as a bullet creased his thigh. His guns had each held only a few rounds when he slapped leather, but those bullets would have to be enough.

Matt's last round blasted a hole in the middle of a gunman's forehead, but that left the bearded man still alive, and Sam's Colt had just clicked on an empty chamber, too. The bearded man chopped down with his gun, ready to fire again, but before he could pull the trigger, the whipcrack of a rifle sounded.

The man jerked in the saddle, arching his back. He grimaced as his grip on the gun butt slipped. The barrel dropped as the weapon pivoted on the man's trigger finger. Then it slipped off entirely and thudded to the ground.

The man followed it a second later, falling off his horse to land beside the locomotive's cab.

Matt leaned out to look back along the tracks. A man on horseback sat about a hundred yards behind the locomotive. Matt recognized him as Marshal Asa Thorpe. Smoke trickled from the barrel of the rifle Thorpe had pressed to his shoulder.

Slowly, Thorpe lowered the rifle and then rode forward. As he came closer, Matt saw the dark stain on the lawman's shirt and knew that Thorpe was wounded.

Matt turned and saw that Sam was checking on Shade. "Was he hit?"

Sam shook his head. "No, he's fine, just out cold from hitting his head on the floor when I knocked him down. Matt . . . what just happened here?"

"Beats the hell out of me," Matt said.

He thumbed fresh shells into his gun, and then climbed down from the cab as Thorpe rode up and reined to a halt. "How bad are you hurt, Marshal?" Matt asked.

Thorpe grunted. "I'll live. Some son of a bitch pretending to be the conductor creased me and knocked me out. I reckon he thought I was dead." The lawman shook his head. "He killed Everett, though, I'm sorry to say, then got away with Shade."

"Shade's up here in the cab," Sam called down. "He's all right. But who are these hombres?"

"This one's still alive," Thorpe said as he knelt beside the man he had shot. "Let's ask him."

Matt hunkered on the other side of the bearded man and lifted his head. The man's eyes flickered open. Thorpe said, "Who are you, mister, and why did you just try to kill Joshua Shade?"

The wounded man struggled to speak. Finally, he got out, "Wasn't Shade . . . we were really after. We were paid to kill . . . Thomas Jeffries."

"Who in blazes is Thomas Jeffries?" Matt asked.

The man lifted a shaky hand. "I saw him . . . up there . . . in the cab . . . dressed like . . . a conductor."

"He was one of Shade's men, all right," Thorpe said.

"He had . . . a fifty-thousand-dollar . . . price on his head," the dying man gasped.

"Who would put a bounty that big on some owlhoot?" Matt wanted to know. "He wasn't even the leader of the gang!"

"It was . . . his father."

"His father!" The exclamation came from Matt, Sam, and Thorpe all at the same time.

"Yeah." The bearded man grimaced. "Senator . . . Jeffries. Bastard got me and all my men . . . killed . . . don't figure we owe him . . . any loyalty anymore."

Thorpe leaned over the man and said urgently, "Don't die, you son of a bitch! You've got some more explaining to do!"

But it was too late. Thorpe was talking to a dead man.

Two days later, at dawn, Joshua Shade was led out of his cell at Yuma Prison and taken under heavy guard to the courtyard where a gallows awaited him. Under an arched door at the edge of that courtyard stood Matt Bodine, Sam Two Wolves, and Marshal Asa Thorpe.

"As best we've been able to piece it together,"

Thorpe said, "Senator Jeffries knew his son had turned outlaw and had been trying to find him. He got word that the boy was riding with Shade's gang just about the same time the news reached Washington that Shade had been captured and was going to be put on trial. The senator figured that Shade's gang would try to rescue him, so he hired that killer, LaFollette, to put together a group of gunmen and follow Shade's gang."

"So they could get Jeffries away from the gang?" Matt asked.

Thorpe shook his head. Out in the courtyard, Shade and his guards had almost reached the thirteen steps that led up to the gallows.

"No, that fella Winslow overheard enough while he was with LaFollette's bunch to put it together with the other things we know and figure that they were supposed to kill Thomas Jeffries, Shade, the rest of the gang, and anybody who knew anything about Jeffries riding with them."

"That explains the bounty," Sam said. "My God, to think that a man would pay to have his own son assassinated just to spare himself some political trouble."

"The senator didn't want it known that his son was an owlhoot," Thorpe agreed. "He was willing to go to any length to cover that up, including putting pressure on the Justice Department to set me up as a Judas goat."

Matt shook his head in awe at the brutal plan. "So you weren't ever supposed to get Shade here. The senator figured Shade's gang would kill you and free Shade, and then LaFollette and the rest of those hired guns could wipe out the gang."

"That's about the size of it," Thorpe agreed. "They had to wait until Shade was back with the gang before they made their move, though. Senator Jeffries couldn't risk leaving Shade alive to maybe reveal the truth."

"Did Shade even *know* that Jeffries was related to a senator?" Matt asked.

"I couldn't tell you," Thorpe said with disgust in his voice. "Shade won't—or can't—answer any questions. He's completely lost his mind now."

They heard the outlaw's ranting as he was led struggling up the steps to the platform. It was a mixture of Scripture, obscenity, and pure gibberish.

"That hombre's crazy as a hydrophobia skunk," Matt said. "Something must be rottin' his brain."

"It won't have a chance to rot much longer," Thorpe said. "Or, in one way, I guess it will. It'll rot along with the rest of him."

The grim-faced hangman lowered a black shroud over Shade's head, muffling the incoherent shouts.

"What about the Winslows?" Sam asked. "Will they be facing any charges for helping Shade's gang try to rescue him?"

"The federal government's not going to prosecute them." Thorpe looked at Matt. "You want to press charges against the lady for trying to take a shot at you?"

"After what she went through? Hell, no."

"What's going to happen to the senator now?" Sam asked.

Thorpe gave a grunt of grim laughter. "I suppose they'll bury him. According to a telegram I got just a little while ago, he put a bullet in his head last night when he realized the whole thing was coming out in the open."

Sam shook his head. "All that killing over politics."

"It wasn't *all* about politics," Matt said. "Some of it

was because Shade and his men were a bunch of low-down skunks."

"Well, yeah, that, too."

They looked out into the courtyard. The hangman had the noose around Shade's neck now. A preacher—a *real* preacher, not a loco outlaw—finished whatever he was saying and stepped back, closing the Bible in his hands.

"Do you really want to watch this?" Sam asked.

"You know," Matt said, "I don't reckon I do. So long, Marshal."

"Where are you two headed?" Thorpe asked.

"Someplace a long way from here," Matt said.

He and Sam turned and walked away along a passage that led to the prison's front gate. They heard the clatter of the trapdoor dropping open in the courtyard, followed an instant later by the sharp snap of a broken neck, but neither of the blood brothers looked back.

They were thinking about how good it would be to leave this behind, to find someplace where the air was clean and eagles soared through blue skies high overhead.

THE FIRST MOUNTAIN MAN SERIES BY
WILLIAM W. JOHNSTONE

Available Wherever Books Are Sold!

Visit our website at **www.kensingtonbooks.com**

THE MOUNTAIN MAN SERIES BY
WILLIAM W. JOHNSTONE

__The Last Mountain Man	0-8217-6856-5	**$5.99**US/**$7.99**CAN
__Return of the Mountain Man	0-7860-1296-X	**$5.99**US/**$7.99**CAN
__Trail of the Mountain Man	0-7860-1297-8	**$5.99**US/**$7.99**CAN
__Revenge of the Mountain Man	0-7860-1133-1	**$5.99**US/**$7.99**CAN
__Law of the Mountain Man	0-7860-1301-X	**$5.99**US/**$7.99**CAN
__Journey of the Mountain Man	0-7860-1302-8	**$5.99**US/**$7.99**CAN
__War of the Mountain Man	0-7860-1303-6	**$5.99**US/**$7.99**CAN
__Code of the Mountain Man	0-7860-1304-4	**$5.99**US/**$7.99**CAN
__Pursuit of the Mountain Man	0-7860-1305-2	**$5.99**US/**$7.99**CAN
__Courage of the Mountain Man	0-7860-1306-0	**$5.99**US/**$7.99**CAN
__Blood of the Mountain Man	0-7860-1307-9	**$5.99**US/**$7.99**CAN
__Fury of the Mountain Man	0-7860-1308-7	**$5.99**US/**$7.99**CAN
__Rage of the Mountain Man	0-7860-1555-1	**$5.99**US/**$7.99**CAN
__Cunning of the Mountain Man	0-7860-1512-8	**$5.99**US/**$7.99**CAN
__Power of the Mountain Man	0-7860-1530-6	**$5.99**US/**$7.99**CAN
__Spirit of the Mountain Man	0-7860-1450-4	**$5.99**US/**$7.99**CAN
__Ordeal of the Mountain Man	0-7860-1533-0	**$5.99**US/**$7.99**CAN
__Triumph of the Mountain Man	0-7860-1532-2	**$5.99**US/**$7.99**CAN
__Vengeance of the Mountain Man	0-7860-1529-2	**$5.99**US/**$7.99**CAN
__Honor of the Mountain Man	0-8217-5820-9	**$5.99**US/**$7.99**CAN
__Battle of the Mountain Man	0-8217-5925-6	**$5.99**US/**$7.99**CAN
__Pride of the Mountain Man	0-8217-6057-2	**$4.99**US/**$6.50**CAN
__Creed of the Mountain Man	0-7860-1531-4	**$5.99**US/**$7.99**CAN
__Guns of the Mountain Man	0-8217-6407-1	**$5.99**US/**$7.99**CAN
__Heart of the Mountain Man	0-8217-6618-X	**$5.99**US/**$7.99**CAN
__Justice of the Mountain Man	0-7860-1298-6	**$5.99**US/**$7.99**CAN
__Valor of the Mountain Man	0-7860-1299-4	**$5.99**US/**$7.99**CAN
__Warpath of the Mountain Man	0-7860-1330-3	**$5.99**US/**$7.99**CAN
__Trek of the Mountain Man	0-7860-1331-1	**$5.99**US/**$7.99**CAN

Available Wherever Books Are Sold!

Visit our website at **www.kensingtonbooks.com**